AF211551

OPTIX

Written from January 2022 to August 2024
© 2024 Kevin James Richards - Yunikew Books

Verlag: BoD · Books on Demand GmbH, In de Tarpen 42,
22848 Norderstedt
Druck: Libri Plureos GmbH, Friedensallee 273,
22763 Hamburg
ISBN: 978-3-7693-2268-2

CONTENTS

1 - THE OFFICE

On a cloudy Thursday Lamorna felt like her birthday couldn't get much worse. She had hardly slept the night before and watched her alarm clock tick minute for minute until it showed 6.30 a.m. Her back felt like she had been contorted, her neck ached as if she had been lightly choked and her head throbbed. As she tossed the covers aside and looked back at the bed she took a long look at the clock. Its long white hand crept towards the next minute, 6.31 a.m., then another, 6.32 a.m. Lamorna wished that it would already fast forward to 1.30 a.m. so that she could collapse into unconsciousness once more and the day would be over.

The pervasive desire to stay there all day wouldn't fade from her mind and she wondered if anyone would notice if she followed through with it. Lamorna's world was a closed loop, a fishbowl of an existence. Either she was at Optix, or cooped up safely in the functional pen of her small flat in the city. The lonesome bed was surrounded with worn and crumpled clothes, almost empty crisp packets and sticky shot glasses. The blatant necessity to clean her room was just one of the many things she was a master of avoiding. And it wasn't as if anybody was going to notice. The steady hum of passing traffic punctuated by car horns reminder her that there were other people around.

Many a time she had used the covers as a kind of time machine to move the clock forward a few hours. And it wasn't the first birthday where she could have used the trick. But today was a working day and she resolved to take baby steps and slowly get up. As usual she started by checking Platform:

her phone lit up with a couple of messages from people she had never met in real life. Pepper, a young photographer was one such friend. She wondered if Pepper was a bot, that might explain why she answered so quickly and always got in touch. At least one person knew it was my birthday, she smiled and then opened her meditation app, downloaded on a whim and rarely used. The yellow glow of the screen reminded our protagonist of the garish morning television of her childhood. Half expecting a lycra-donned man of middle age to try to motivate her to do some improbable stretches, she swiftly closed the app and put on some music, something repetitive without lyrics. It was too early for words.

Lamorna begrudgingly heaved herself out of bed and made her way to the bathroom, where a bright neon explosion assaulted her senses. The penetrating hum and shrill brightness made her feel like she was being held in a black ops military facility, being interrogated at gunpoint. Her knees felt weak, creaky even, and she held her hand up to shelter her eyes, pained by the ocular onslaught. The birthday girl took a quick shower, focussing on cleanliness and efficiency, rather than enjoying any particular self-care routine. Her long brown hair didn't require much attention, she half-dried it with a towel and put it up in a bun. On her bedroom floor she looked around for clothes clean enough to wear once more, found a red t-shirt as well as some faded black jeans and made her way towards her living room.

Lamorna's flat was spacious enough, but she had crammed it full of nostalgia, hobbies and art. Not necessarily things she was nostalgic of, more like things which popular culture had agreed on being nostalgic for. Film memorabilia from cult films, science fiction and fantasy genres. Expressionist art prints, framed in black. Reissue modernist lamps, ironic placemats and a few medium sized cacti. Here she could be surrounded by popular culture without the need to go out too much. Her work at Optix and the demands of her boss, Jason Chamberlain placed certain restrictions on her. Nevertheless, it suited her just fine. She was doing important, necessary work and had everything else she needed at home.

Lamorna made herself a bowl of porridge with soya milk and honey, switched on her phone and scanned the news for any tech updates. She ignored some ads for a fortune-teller, blue robed and dark hair, "such a cliché", she muttered to herself. Checked the news and wolfed down her breakfast. She read some rumours of a supposed Optix update, but knew it wasn't worth reading, she was probably the best informed person in the company. Working closely with the CEO and company guru, Jason Chamberlain for over five years now, Lamorna knew all of the inner workings of the company. He was not easy to work for, being very exacting and expecting nothing more than great sacrifice from his most trusted employees. To which Lamorna duly obliged, *'with great power comes great responsibility'*, she often told herself. Lamorna knew the lingo, understood the importance of maintaining an impregnable facade. Talking of which, she gave her pristine white teeth a proper scrub, flung on a jacket, checked herself in the mirror for fidelity, being sure to check the deepest blue of her eyes for any sign of spasm, and made her way out the door.

Lamorna's short ride to the Optix head quarters took her down the main road into the city. On that particular dull and drab day she was loath to hang around and get wet. Lamorna's wont was to tread as hard as possible on the pedals and fly past the buildings, avoiding gaping potholes and ominously parked delivery vans, having learnt her lessons in the past. Her precious little brain needed protecting and one's legs were principally there to transport the central nervous system to the place it was needed.

Having arrived, she locked her bike in the underground car park, not leaving it unlocked outside. The city was not a safe place to leave such things just standing around. The Optix office building was the only well looked after building in that part of town, despite initial appearances. And that had nothing to do with the particular architecture of the Optix building itself. It was a relatively modern eight storey tower, no more than six or seven years old. Covered in glass and zinc, it imbued any observer with the feeling of seeing a ginormous mobile phone stood upright and inflated to improbable dimensions. The periphery of the building contained a blue hued light system tracing a line around the seventh story, where the Alpha team's offices were located. The company's purpose was to make sure the office building did indeed fit in with the run down and dilapidated surroundings. The entire company's purpose was built around this. Urban decay had heavily set in and most of the other premises were either already empty and ridden with squatters, or on the way out. Many companies to struggled to find customers, most goods were bought elsewhere nowadays and had little need to go into the city to shop. Most people would rather do their purchasing at their own leisure in the living quarters, or at their desks at work. The shells of old buildings, the run-down facades and decrepit veneers of dead domiciles were no longer visible anymore to the naked eye. Optix saw to that.

Founded on a desire to improve quality of life and raise levels of happiness to unprecedented levels Jason Chamberlain, a bright spark and charismatic nerd, had introduced the Optix technology seven years ago to an astounded tech congress in Munich. There, hundreds of tech heads held a great conference and developed new ideas for the future, be it in the realms of food, entertainment or commerce. Yet, Chamberlain surpassed them all when he revealed the eye implant technology he had developed, *'Optix'*. Instead of seeing old surfaces, a new pristine texture and colour would be overlaid in real time. Street surfaces appeared newly laid, urban decay became a thing of the past, at least on the surface, and the implants brought people's lives back into a kind of new technicolour. The devices worked like a hearing aid for the retina, adapting the perceived image and manipulating the brain signal sent for processing in the visual cortex. Implantation of the devices was conducted at local Optix offices which had taken on the role of local opticians for the users. The procedure was minimally invasive and a closely guarded company secret. Each user was given a local anaesthetic and it was all over within mere minutes. A remote link-up via the ever-present wireless network meant that one was forever connected and always able to see what you wanted to see.

The new Optix implants provided a beautiful facade which hid the ugly truth and helped society to appreciate a more palatable aesthetic. Local redevelopment projects were put on the back-burner, gentrification was abound, regardless of the actual state of the buildings, local councils raised tax income, the poor were priced out of living in their family homes or of renting in newly flourishing neighbourhoods. Governments had little incentive to invest and at the same time they were raking in millions of tax income.

The architects were the main designers at Optix, working on new texture updates which users could subscribe to for a small monthly fee. By now Optix already had over two billion worldwide monthly users, on a par with the larger tech companies like Platform. You could never be certain if any two people were seeing exactly the same thing. Users just got used to seeing different coloured walls, customised textures and idealised veneers. The basic package included all necessary gentrification improvements; making sourdough bakeries out of ruins, coffee shops out of husks. The premium package had more luscious finishes and more detailed textures. The adaptive artificial intelligence involved also enabled the signs to be automatically translated to the user's preferred language, where desired. The Alpha package was looked after by Lamorna and her team, they were pushing the implant towards what wasn't yet possible and curating the entire user experience. They were given a great deal of creative licence to experiment and try new things in different environments. They applied Yves Klein's IKB 79 to an entire city block in New York at the behest of one client. The project was especially complex because all infrastructure was to appear in the exact shade of blue, in real time, in different light environments. With different textures and colours at the same time it was a lot easier. The premium clients were often well-paid lawyers and city investors, who would need an ever more intensive hit. They would also compete with each other over the newest updates and bragging rights were very important. Glass prism surfaces also proved to be quite a conundrum, as well as those in absolute black, denying any reflection of brightness from its surface.

Lamorna tried to push Alpha packages onto artistic types, but they were the most resistant and underrepresented demographic. Many even forwent having the implants in the first place, even though they cost nothing to have installed. Lamorna pondered their potential reasons, laziness or risk aversion seemed unlikely to her. *'Could they be waiting for a more extreme version? Was it generally a step too far? Did they want to just rebel and decry this exploitation of man's gift, the gift of vision? Were they planning an uprising?'* Lamorna didn't ponder these questions too often, she and the company had enough users to keep them busy.

Entering the building via the basement level Lamorna boarded the lift and took the glass elevator up to the seventh floor. Upon arrival she passed the coffee area and went past the long rows of cubicles which reached as far as the windows; the greyness of their walls matched only by the faces of their occupants. Thankfully the higher-ups each got their own private offices. Lamorna's name was emblazoned on the door: *'Lamorna Cruickshanks - Alpha'.* The dull environs of her office enabled her to concentrate on her twin screens. The uninspiring walls, patchy and badly painted, lacking any flair or flash of colour, made all else seem so much more fascinating. Lamorna's implants were always in use anyway and so the office wasn't too ugly for her. The patchy walls, like a faded monotone Mondrian, were just too much for any significant period of time.

Sat at her desk she could hear a soft voice on the other side of the thin walls. One of her closer colleagues, Felix, was already speaking with his team. Felix was one of the few people she would consider inviting to her flat for some beers, providing she still had the need to see people after work. Alas, that was rarely the case.

Demanding and draining, the latest developments of the beta testing had been met with unsatisfying results. Jason Chamberlain was on the war path and the Alpha team were on his hit list. The premium and basic package workers, constantly under pressure to deliver, suffered relentless deadlines. Their life was one of fear. Pressed for time, constantly being observed thanks to computer software monitoring their productivity and proficiency. The Alpha team members had the dual role of working on their own projects and man-managing the basic and premium package employees. Some of the aggression and stress the Alpha members received from Chamberlain inevitably bled down into the rest of the company. Lamorna felt that they were all working towards a future where things would become easier for everyone involved and it was worth giving everything now for the reward of making something truly life-changing. Unfortunately, it was more a case of out-of-their-depth Alpha members blindly leading the lower-downs, without any personnel training, without any proper resources and without enough time. Chamberlain promoted the members of the Alpha Team based on their coding and architecture prowess, not their soft-skills or interpersonal competences. He favoured a leading-by-example style of management over any cohesive, well thought out leadership strategy. In some teams this worked fine, in other cases there were high stress levels, sick leave aplenty, regular burnouts and even some cases of attempted suicide. Over the course of the entire enterprise this was just the kind of error rate Jason Chamberlain expected. There was always a work-around, a rewrite of a line of code or a new architect coming through the door. Optix had to look forward and remain focussed on the big picture, not to keep track of every individual passing through its doors.

Chamberlain came out of his office just as Lamorna was outside it, "Lamorna, good morning, come in for a sec, will you?", he asked.

"Sure thing, what's up?", she replied. He looked like he hadn't slept, with dark rings around his eyes and dishevelled light brown hair. His t-shirt looked even more wrinkled than hers. Lamorna remained standing while he told of his frustrations at some of her recent work. She had missed a few deadlines on Alpha package commissions. The complexity of the work was ridiculous, mirrored chrome and diamond surfaces interlaced with mother of pearl, just for a single villa. And the client had gone to Chamberlain and vented his own issues at her work. Her exacting nature, as well as her pride in her detailing didn't allow her to turn in sub-standard results. Despite what the client said, Lamorna felt that the time frame had simply not been enough time for the level of artistry to achieved.

"I am an architect, Jason. It takes a lot of work to get it right, you understand that right?", Lamorna looked up at Chamberlain looking for confirmation and support, receiving none of the sort. His face was set in stone. The elf-like appearance of a young twenty-year-old programmer, soon to turn forty, met with the grim contours of a Picasso. His face was oftentimes at a perpendicular to Lamorna, not deeming it necessary to look at her directly. She took in his sharp profile, his slim build, his slim fingers and impatient manner. This was not a person she wanted to anger, but neither could she hold her tongue much longer. Too many of her team had suffered at her own hand of late and she needed to pass on some of the pressure. Our heroine added: "The team needs a break, Jason. There are only so many times I can tell them I need them to pull another double-shift or to stay for the weekend. There are only so many times I can tell them the same thing over and over again".

Jason Chamberlain, slowly turned to face her, "You are one of the most important architects here Lamorna and I expect more from you. You have to understand that these deadlines are not arbitrary, they are reality. They govern what work you have to do and by when. For the reputation of this company, for my reputation. It reflects on us all. You have already spent enough time on your own projects for this month. It is time you realised what you are really here for. Here is a list of tasks I expect done by you and your team by this time next week and I will not be happy if you fail to complete it. You should know better, Lamorna. How many years have we been working together? Have you ever known me to risk our reputation? The Alpha team has been resting on their laurels as of late and I have decided to give some of your duties to Savia. She has shown me enough in her work in the premium team that she is ready for the step-up. Look sharp Lamorna, the Alpha team can't afford these kinds of failures, you can't afford it either".

"I know, I'm sorry Jason", immediately, Lamorna felt disappointed at herself for apologising. Why was this now her fault? But Chamberlain wasn't done yet, his chiseled chin continued to wag magnanimously. She resented Savia being given any more responsibility; her star had risen quickly enough already. She would do anything and everything Jason requested.

While dwelling on her anger, Chamberlain cut back in, "it's not your apology I need, it's results. Your ideas are important for us, but you are also a role-model to others. New people come into the company all of the time and some of them will fall by the wayside. You are here to guide those who stay, who have made the grade. But it is a high-water mark that you have set while you have been here Lamorna. You cannot afford to let your standards slip, there are others ready to take over your role here. And I don't think that is what you want, is it?".

"Of course not", her head now sunken, her will once again pliable.

"Good, then back to your office and get going!", Lamorna trundled back to her office, resigned to accepting Chamberlain's will once more. Picturing the ground tearing apart beneath her, a tightrope revealed itself upon which she was balanced. Either side there were flames ready to engulf her and ahead was only a never-ending rope. She knew that she had earned her place at the company and wasn't ready to relinquish it. The mere thought of being replaced surprised her. *'Had she really been slacking off recently?'* Despite the disorder she kept at home, her Optix workplace was mostly spotless, save a few old coffee mugs she hadn't yet cleared away. Lamorna was always so hard-working and eager to please. Her colleagues and clients always seemed happy with her contributions at least. Why couldn't they just voice their concerns directly with her, or was there not really anything to worry about? She ran the dressing-down from Chamberlain through her mind a few times and wished that she had stood up for herself more. Lamorna never knew what to say to criticism, apart from *'yes, okay'* and *'no problem, I'll get right on it'*. Clamming up inside her protective shell made a lot more sense to her.

In the end, however, she felt that Jason Chamberlain had to be right. Ultimately, he had to be. He knew what he was doing and had led the company to become a tech behemoth. In his more than capable hands they were sure to emerge in new markets with great new technological advancements and lead the way in shaping a better future. She wanted to be a part of that, now and for the next thirty years. Up till now she had deserved it. She surely had her best interests at heart; he trusted her judgement and valued her input, after all. He knew how to lead her and how to deal with her when she was angry. It felt like protection, security. He was a mentor to her, she had a lot to learn from him, now and also in the years to come.

Lamorna took a walk around her office, there wasn't much to look at, but retracing conversations made more sense to her if she paced around the room, talking to the walls. For a minute she even deactivated her implant, inspected the finer details of her office; the matt wallpaper and the mahogany wood grain of her desk. She rarely deactivated Optix, but it made little difference inside the pristine office building. A little break from her standard reality was necessary, so she opened the app and put it on a ten minute timer. Officially, this was also something that Optix advised in their instruction manuals, available online. But statistics showed that few people actually opened them, let alone read them. Optix was the new reality, the status quo; a way to ignore the lack of public investment, the corruption and the broken promises. A life of keeping your head in the sand.

2 - LAMORNA'S LAMENT

Lamorna spent the next few weeks working a great deal of overtime, powered by caffeine. She met her targets, accomplished great results and her team were rewarded with a spa day, Just what she needed: being damned to have to spend even more time with her colleagues. They had surely had enough of her by now already.

She stretched out on the sofa and picked up her phone. She had a few messages from friends on Platform; they were responding to some recently posted photographs from her latest photo tour. By taking photographs she hoped to be able to see nature for what it was. Her preference was macro photography, where she would get really close up and capture the detail of a leaf's veins, a tree's bark or a lake's shimmer. Looking back over her photographs she quickly realised that she had a clear modus operandi. Go out to the forest, get really close and take some macro shots, post a couple of pictures the following days, and wait for the praise. But really it was so much more for her. It was a chance to listen to electronica through her headphones and be alone, all the while ignoring the call of the ducks landing on the lake, the shivering of the trees and the water lapping on the edge of the lake. Whilst walking through the forest she ignored what made it so enjoyable. Even with the camera, she was just collecting information. Try as she might to do something artistic with it, she rarely felt she was adding any value to her captured image. If anything, she was cutting away and abstracting the image away from that which made it magical in the first place. As she persisted with this newest of hobbies she pushed through this phase and realised that the abstraction of nature was not in her best interest, that the natural light and changing seasons be best captured in colour and her black and white fascination best left for man-made constructions. Lamorna's love of black and white images was not a new thing: it was how she had spent most of her life, in hindsight. Either you were with her, or against. Things were either true or false. She held grudges, lost friends, forgotten shared stories because of it.

Now back at her flat a frustrated Lamorna opened a recently downloaded mindfulness app, it promised to bring her mind to a state of atonement and peace; the ratings were really good and she wanted to give it a try. She wanted to meditate and find her centre, wherever that may be. The app promised a lot: enabling her to eventually become one with herself and feel rejuvenated. At least, that's what the paid reviews seemed to have said. Lamorna lay on the floor listening to the first lesson, she found it very difficult to lie still, she felt hyper-aware of herself and thought only that if anyone was watching, they would believe her to be crazy. In her own flat, with headphones on, t-shirt and underpants, lying on her rug.

The instructions began, "Welcome to mindfulness. We want to help you relax after a busy day, to help you focus on your goals and to build a better future. Perhaps you feel stressed out by work, feel like you are losing control of your feelings or just need a bit of *'me'* time".

Lamorna let out a long punch of air out of her lungs. *'Oh boy'*, she thought to herself, talk about hitting the mark.

The soft male voice continued, "we all sometimes have that feeling that we need a little help with sorting our thoughts and other times it is necessary to let some things go".

Lamorna closed her eyes and concentrated on the guy's voice. He proceeded to describe a situation where a dog is stood at the side of the road and watching cars zoom past, some red, some grey, some large, others very small. Lamorna wanted to be all the dogs, all the time, catching all of the cars. She knew it was impossible, but her stubbornness and determination wouldn't allow her to stop. Choosing any particular car felt impossible, leaving all to their own devices felt like failure. Standing on the sidelines wasn't her style. Lamorna needed to find another solution. A roadblock, a car crash, a terrorist attack. Anything to slow them down. She needed to just let them be, just be the dog on the side of the road. Then she wondered what kind of dog she would be, a Rottweiler? A Collie? A Dachshund? The passing cars were of different marques, BMW, Ford, Tesla, but she wasn't interested in chasing them particularly. Unlike the thoughts racing around her brain, the cars were of little interest to her and an insufficient metaphor. She removed her headphones and simply lay in her quiet living room, cycling through her apps before getting bored and rolling into bed a couple of hours later.

***

Fitness was important to Lamorna and so was being a recluse. Unwilling to risk bumping into anyone she knew, Lamorna had developed a way of keeping fit at home. She plugged her bike into a turbo trainer to get that hamster-wheel-like burn in her legs, being careful to take a towel with her before covering her oak floor in sweat. Pedalling for a good hour, doing intervals, drinking fluids and watching an episode of her favourite fantasy series, gave her the rewarding feeling of exhilaration without needing to go outside. The series itself being an inevitable clash of warring parties, subterfuge, dragons, romance and magic. These other worlds, wrought in mystique and sorcery, unlike the sterile senility of her own, allowed her brain to run amok while imagining all possible endings to the story. Myriad conclusions coursed through her mind as she pedalled up the mountain, and rode into battle to defeat the army of the dead. As the series progressed and things reached its inevitable climax, where the good guys win, she clung to her hopes that one of her predicted endings would come true, before being disappointed. Before long another show would pop up and Lamorna could pin her hopes on the next tale of rogues, sorcerers, mercenaries, battles, dynasties and destiny. And so it continued for a long while, a hamster wheel of time, evening escapism from her drab routine. The main thing was that she kept fit. Fit enough to keep working.

3 - THE MESSAGE

On a bright spring morning Lamorna received a message from Pepper, a Platform friend telling her about a chill coffee shop which had been garnering some attention in recent days. There had been some amazing reviews on Platform and apparently you just had to give it a try. Lamorna wondered to herself whether she should bother, it would surely be overfilled with young professionals, like herself. She had enough of those types at work. But Pepper was rarely wrong, seemingly in possession of clairvoyant talents.

It had been a few days since she had been to work, it was a rare free weekend. Lamorna, who had kept herself to herself in the flat, was ready to brave the fresh air, she donned her favourite faded black jacket and high-tops and made her way down the road. She popped in her headphones, chose some darkwave to listen to and looked up at the sunshine, the sky was a bit bright for her that morning so she adapted her Optix implants accordingly. She preferred to keep herself in the dark.

In the city the store fronts had, in her opinion, the most garish fonts for their signs: Comic Sans here, Stencil Script there. And so she changed them to a crisp Gotham or Futura, much more suiting her palette. The colours seemed ill-suited to their purposes too. A deli with squiggly black signage seemed better attuned to a tattoo studio and pink equally ill-suited to a petrol station, so she simply switched them around and adjusted the RGB values on the fly. She was unable to leave her work alone; never holding herself back from commenting on how garish or dull something was, poorly designed or overly complicated. As she approached the cafe she saw that two other people were waiting outside, a short dark-haired man of about forty-five, the little hair left on his head stood up in the wind as if trying to flee, and a woman of about forty, with thin blonde hair and a green felt jacket on.

"Hi, have you been waiting long?", Lamorna asked, as she approached.

The short man turned to her and said: "We have been coming here for years and now we can't get a seat. We went to the school with the owner and now they are just eating up all the attention they can get. They just want to be popular".

He seemed particularly upset by the situation and Lamorna expressed her sympathy and had that problem with some of her former favourite bands, eventually they fit their style to the taste of their audience and lose the thing which made them unique in the first place. In reality selling out was something Lamorna understood in her own life too. She had also been more interested in nature than in computers, but that was just the way it was. Nature doesn't pay the bills, unless you chop down the trees to save on heating. As she stood there thinking about all of that the couple turned to her, said that they were tired of waiting and said: "So long". Lamorna had been too stuck in her own head to continue that basic human interaction and watched them walk away down the road, probably to the next greasy spoon.

She looked at the small signed stood at the entrance to the coffee shop, *'Please wait here'* stood on it. She waited a while and after a time a short grey-haired lady came out and beckoned her in and showed her to a formica table. The woman held a faded cream coloured coffee pot in her hand and asked her if she wanted a cup, she nodded and Lamorna watched the steam rise up to the yellowed ceiling. The place was grimy and simple, Lamorna ordered a pasty as she felt quite hungry, she had skipped breakfast, done an hour that morning on the bike, some simple weight exercises and felt pangs in her stomach. She got out her phone and checked her messages. She had a few new comments on her latest photos, *'awesome angle', 'cool'*, and a couple of invites from her Platform friends to concerts in towns over 300km away. She had no intention of going, but replied with a uncommitted level of enthusiasm. It had been about a decade since she last saw a band live.

She had a few other notifications to read, some new videos from her favourite Platform content creators, some program updates, as well as some work emails that she needed to work on over the weekend. This was how she usually spent her Sunday: first of all ignoring all thoughts of work and then reluctantly getting ready for Monday. She sat drinking her black coffee, slowly feeling its strength and then her Cornish pasty arrived. She smelt it closely on arrival and then eventually bit into its hot, crisp crust she was taken back to her childhood, to wet shopping trips into town with her parents and travelling back from town with a few pasties in the car to be eaten that evening at home. The smell was earthy, oniony and meaty. The moist beef steak was juicy, fatty and easy to chew, the potatoes moistened by the meat juices and the turnip just soaked everything else up. For the pasty alone Lamorna was happy to have visited the cafe, not so much for the coffee. It was overly bitter and quickly cooled. She opened up her phone again and looked at the online reviews for the coffee shop, averaged four and a half out of five, pretty skewed she thought, although maybe everyone else was also basing their review on the quality of their pasties as opposed to the cleanliness or coffee standard.

As she got stuck in another loop of her apps, cycling

through news, emails, Platform and photos she heard the bell ring for a new customer at the door. It was a tall, thin man of about sixty years and he was wearing a top hat. Lamorna's first instinct was to clandestinely angle her phone at him and take a snapshot to share later, but thought better of it as he, despite the clutter of pans and cups, might hear the shutter noise. He was guided to a table in the corner to Lamorna's left and sat down and received his own cup of diesel.

She watched him slowly raise the cup to his mouth and blow on the coffee's surface and she saw the man revel in seeing the spirals of steam fly up, just as she had enjoyed. The man turned to his right and noticed Lamorna grin, he gave her a nod in a nonchalant, almost disinterested manner. He took a sip of the black coffee, wincing as he placed it back down. Lamorna gave a chortle. This caught his attention and he looked over at her again, this time being looking distrustful and irritated. "Do they even know how to make coffee?", Lamorna let slip. She raised her own cup and gave it a try, mimicking his reaction in the process. The man now let out a huge belly laugh, which caught Lamorna off guard. The man had seemed so tense and reclusive and also not fully of this time, yet to see him laugh like that put her at a strange level of ease. If he had any sinister intentions, he surely would have maintained the mysterious facade.

"I think they forgot to add that special something", the man remarked. "A modicum of taste and good sense, that could be it." And with his words he let out another laugh. Lamorna was sure he was going to fall off his chair at that rate and she hunkered in for the show. She noticed now how his outfit resembled that of a circus master, only in black and white. His jacket had long tails down the back, he wore pointed shoes and his moustache was similar horned at each end.

"You know", he began, "there is quite a smashing place on the other end of town where one can really have their mind blown." This was taking an odd turn, Lamorna mused.

"Quite otherworldly; the most wonderful outer body experiences", the strange man continued.

Lamorna's smile now turning into a serious poker face replied, "Really? And how often have you been there?", she countered. Figuring it would be a good idea to be specific, rather than just trying to ignore the man.

"Oh, I've never been invited. Special invitation only, you see. It is a splendid establishment apparently and only the most promising and enlightened of individuals are even considered for invitation. The madam running the joint is a wise one indeed. She has what you would call protections in place to ensure verisimilitude and suitability for compatibility. Plainly put, she doesn't just open her doors for anybody."

"Sounds like quite the place", Lamorna tried to keep it polite, but in reality she was hankering for a look at her phone. She wanted to get back in touch with Pepper and check out the most recent black and white posts; the behatted man had inspired her in all of his Victorian glory: he would look amazing in black and white, astride a Dalmatian who is stood a chessboard. Or something of that ilk.

"You can't fathom how mysterious and elegant a creature she truly is", the kindly man continued, "truth be told, neither can I. She wouldn't allow me. We exchange letters, carried by pigeon, naturally. She is careful to phrase her thoughts as such that they are encoded, lest they fall into the hands of the enemy".

"The enemy?", Lamorna snapped out the trance she was in while swiping through black and white photos on her phone.

"Why, yes. The enemy. Haven't you heard? There are dark plans afoot and demons abroad. All fashions of mayhem are at hand and ahead."

Lamorna wondered whether he could at all be any more vague; she had read her fair share of the literature, be it biblical, fantastical or dystopian to know of the idea of the 'enemy, demons and mayhem'; it was always easier to depersonalise the common antagonist. She looked at the man, while taking another rank sip of the black tar coffee and thought back on her rhetoric classes at university: "How in the world do I reframe this conversation back to a realm where I am able to talk with this person on my level, on a topic I am comfortable with?" As she pondered the puzzle she lowered her cup, slipped her phone into her pocket and simply confronted the man. "Can I help you with anything specific, or are you just here to tell fantastical stories?"

The circus master smiled a wide, white grin and leaned closer, "you know, these demons are not like in the other stories, they have no wings, no red skin nor do they spout flames. The plans of the enemy have already been put into action and to some extent nobody can truly 'save the world', dear Lamorna".

"Who is Lamorna?", she countered; of course, her face told another story. She hadn't mentioned her own name to him yet. She was now feeling quite anxious. She looked towards the exit instinctively and crossed her foot over her opposite ankle with deepened tension, the pressure she applied with her own foot ever intensifying.

"My dear, don't look surprised, quite aside from the fact that your face is plastered all over Platform and that you work for Mr. Jason Chamberlain, our mutual friend knows almost everything. And it is she who sent me to you", he twisted one end of his moustache, as if running a victory lap and leaned in even closer to Lamorna. "Lamorna, Master Su has long wished to see you, face to face. Just the two of you."

"Now this is getting ridiculous. Now you tell me there is a mythical 'Master Tzu' character who has deemed me worthy? And she wishes to meet me in her castle and impart me with magical wisdom no doubt!", spat Lamorna.

"Master Su!", the man corrected.

"Whatever, I am sorry Mister, but I am far too busy to be going off on some adventure to save the world, or not, or anyway. I bid you good day kind sir, I wish you no ill. Your finesse and charm are quite beguiling and show no clear lack of skill. But our parting is upon us and yes, it is in rhyme, but I am afraid kind sir, that we are out of time."

The man let out a third great belly laugh. "Master Su was right, you really are the chosen one!"

"Don't get started on that too, you don't know how utterly ridiculous that sounds", Lamorna started laughing too, although she had some way to reach the tall man's volume. His guffaws had garnered considerable attention in the greasy spoon.

"Okay, you got me. Deeming you worthy of my own test, I was fit to let out that old chestnut. Some people just can't resist believing that they are some chosen one or of any particular importance; as if it were their destiny to fulfil some great purpose or save the world", the tall man added.

Lamorna, looked at his face closely, being careful to check for irony, "yeah, I guess I am way too jaded for that".

"Probably", the man said, "with a 95% chance, but we'll see. The more pressing point is that Master Su has indeed requested an audience with you, for she longs to speak to you. She has indeed been keeping an eye on you, seeks your council on some incredibly important matters and has already made arrangements for your travel".

"No doubt with some kind of flying pestle and mortar or a pumpkin carriage."

"Yes indeed, how wise you are Lamorna. And you can steer the mortar with a broom, being careful not to let the water turn your teeth to rusted iron. Honestly, do you really think we could let that happen in the city? Such conspicuous methods of transportation are much better served in the forest; most people wouldn't think to believe their eyes there and would keep such things to themselves. The absolute worst case would be that they tell everyone in the tavern once they have had a bellyful of beer and nobody believes them anyway. No, in the city we utilise standardised transportation, I have a bicycle waiting for you outside." The man made an elegant seated bow and rotated his eyes looking up to meet Lamorna's.

"Let us suppose that I agree to meet this Master Su. First of all, why should it be worth my time? And secondly, I have my own bike thank you very much."

"Time is not really the issue, Lamorna, Master Su is not going anywhere fast. She likes to keep herself shut off from mortal minds, be it locked in thought or in her tower. You see Master Su only lets in those who she thinks can offer her something, a trade if you will. She will give you what you need in return for that which she craves. The Master will ask a lot of you and you may feel shortchanged, you may want to end it all and bury your head in the sand once more, return to your desk and your slavery. You may lose all contact with her for a time, but she will patrol the halls of your mind. Omniscience is not something to be taken lightly, neither will she always display the sympathy you desire. I cannot recommend the path you have already chosen for yourself, Lamorna. At the moment you are in a state of crisis, this we have seen. Yours is not a course for good."

"I'm sorry I really don't have time for this. I've got work to do, I need to tidy my flat and my boyfriend is expecting me", Lamorna lied.

"Really? Lamorna. Is he really? And I suppose he is waiting up in the tower, ready to let down his hair so that you can climb and save him. Come now, it rarely pays to lie, my dear. Lies have very short legs and are rarely capable of outrunning the truth. I am quite aware of your living situation, who your so-called friends are, the colour of your bath towels and the contents of your refrigerator. Don't try telling tall tales to me; mine are the tallest in all the land", the gangly man claimed.

"I am sure they are. I just really don't think that I really want to see this Master of yours, you know? It isn't that this doesn't sound terribly interesting and exciting, it really does", Lamorna was trying her best to weasel her way out of taking a chance, "and I don't really get the impression that you are trying to trick me, despite your appearance of a Victorian swindler or conman. I just don't want to."

"Lamorna, think of all the things you have said 'no' to since you were a child. Don't you think it is time to balance things out somewhat? I am not sure if you realise what life is for, my dear. It certainly isn't there to sit around waiting to go to work and then collapsing onto your sofa once the day is done. I could say 'live a little', 'carpe diem' or 'be the change you want to see in the world', but I am not convinced that would have the desired effect either, my dear. I cannot convince and will not persuade you to come. It is your choice alone what you do. Your own agency is of the uppermost importance here. And with these words, dear Lamorna, I bid you good day and

Godspeed." He bowed once more, offered his hand and tipped his hat, picking up his tails as he turned and made to leave.

"I'm going to regret this aren't I?", she asked.

"Probably, either way", the man admitted while a wide smile beamed across his face; at least he was honest. "I can't recommend ignoring her call. If you leave her there for another twenty years bad things might happen. Life in a dark cell can do that to people. Others have tried giving her a helping hand before, it didn't always work out well. However, on this occasion she is coming for you. She will tease this greatness out of you too".

Lamorna nodded. The tall man gave her his business card, *'Xerxo, circus performer & ventriloquist'* were print-stamped on the black card in silver ink.

"Be honest with Master Su, she will know if you are lying. She will leave you by the side of the road if she senses you are being dishonest. It has been a great pleasure to meet you Lamorna. I wish you the finest of onward journeys. On your bike, lass! There's a clever one outside waiting for you outside", Xerxo gave a subtle curtsy and was on his way.

In the dull din of the cafe Lamorna was left sitting alone once more and reflected on the conversation. The tall man was able to wrestle every answer out of her, yet she didn't feel that he had really tried to push her into a corner. Little by little she had grown to like him, he had certainly been entertaining. She had little doubt that he was basically telling the truth. The only real information he had divulged was that Master Su, whoever she really was, wanted to meet her and that there was a bike outside she could use to get her there. Aside from the question of whether she wanted to go, she had a number of questions though which remained: where exactly should she go? What did Master Su want with her? When exactly should she go? Would Jason be angry if she didn't do any work on this particular Sunday?

In times like these Lamorna had developed a simple decision making process. She would assign yes and no to different sides of a coin and toss it in the air. If she was unhappy with the coin's decision she would take the opposite action. This worked well enough in most cases for her. Sometimes this was what it took for her to realise what her most desired outcome was. Of course, such doings lacked the finesse of constructing a detailed list of pros and cons, or writing a twenty-three page report on the subject, but it got the job done. She assigned *'going home'* to tails, *'Master Su'* to heads and flipped a fifty cent piece into the air, caught it with her left hand and placed it on the reverse side of her right. She slowly revealed the heads and let out a little laugh.

'Now then', she thought to herself and wondered whether it wouldn't take too much effort to lie to her boss, remain unseen and then, once she goes back to work the next day, continue to cover up the truth. Lamorna weighed up these truant thoughts in her head regardless. She didn't mind lying per se, it was more the whole effort behind it which she didn't feel up for. When her old friends had asked whether she wanted to come out, or friends on Platform asked if she wanted to visit, she would do the same thing - pure avoidance. She would ask herself, which is more effort for me? Lying, or going there and doing something that I don't feel comfortable with, with people I don't really want to see? Invariably she remained at home and saw a documentary, ate a frozen pizza, watched some clips on her phone and went to bed.

Lamorna started to ask herself in which ways this was different. For a start, Xerxo, the circus performer, was like something out of one of her fantasy novels, yet she couldn't quite place him. He was like a city sprite. In other stories it might be a woodland creature who appears from behind trees, tricksy and odd. Beguiling wayward travellers, corrupting their spirits and trading golden beans for the weight of their soul, a scrubby fawn perhaps. Whereas Xerxo was an exceedingly slick, dapper gentlemen who fully embodied the same characteristics. An urban aesthetic providing a useful veneer to his goblin magic interior; a fairy tale snake oil salesman.

Xerxo knew Lamorna well enough from a distance to assume that she would most likely choose *'flight'* if put under any real pressure. More often than not her friends would get antsy at some point in their conversations, on the phone or via message. They would do their best to persuade Lamorna to come and promise it would be a great time; whether she wanted it to be or not. They would accuse her of being lazy and a shut-in come the end. Eventually, they simply stopped asking. So in this instance Lamorna felt like she owed it to herself to say yes for once. She had more than enough overtime saved up at work and it was Sunday after all. She called Felix, feigning a coughing fit, telling him that she needed to take a personal day. She smiled as she hung up and paid her bill.

4 - LEAP OF FAITH

The sun was bright as Lamorna left the greasy spoon, she held her hand up to shield herself from the light. Her brown wavy hair was flailing in her face, offering some rest-bite from the rays, but annoying her just as much at the same time. As her eyes adjusted she noticed the rusty old Holland style bicycle propped up against the cafe window, with the word *'Renn'* in silver letters on the bike's frame. Had this been the bike the tall man was talking about? She peered into the wicker basket at the front and found a note:

Dear Lamorna,

Happy that you made it, the code is 1984. Master Su can be found in the tower of the setting Sun. Best make your way there now, but take your time, don't be early. The sunset is at 6.30 p.m.

Toodly-pip!

Xerxo

Lamorna looked at the letter a second time and scratched her head. She had enough problem-solving at work without having to decrypt secret messages; she began asking herself if this is what she wanted to do on a stolen afternoon. Rubik's cubes, sudoko and crosswords were always too much like work for her in her free time. Lamorna looked at the words again and eventually she started to get her head around it.

'Okay, if this is right, I have to follow the Sun. But it isn't 6.30 p.m. yet, so I have to work out where it is going to go down. But when I ride, it will change where I see it go down; West is relative, relative to where I am now. So I need to work out from here where I would see the sunset and then get there for 6.30 p.m. That gives me five hours, that's ridiculous, I could be there so much faster!

She looked down the long street towards the financial district and saw a collection of huge skyscrapers, some of which were over one hundred stories tall. The closest buildings were, however, somewhat smaller, perhaps half the height. 'The tower of the setting Sun', should she look for something roughly Asian themed? Use the whole city as a compass or a clock? Would the middle of the city rise up and create the shadow of a sundial? Sundials were one of the oldest forms of clock, after all. Or were old sand-timers and water-clocks involved too? Perhaps a whole hanging-garden, in addition. But perhaps the sundial wasn't such an idiotic idea. The Sun seems to travel in the night sky as the Earth spins and new parts of its surface become illuminated. Lamorna calculated, based on the curve of the sun's path that the Sun would go own between two of the larger towers and nestle behind a blue-windowed hotel building with the words 'Bluebird Luxury Apartments' written on it in dark grey lettering. On closer inspection it was non-illumined neon. Using her implants had its upsides too. She made a note of the hotel's location, it was only about a good hour's walk away, she reckoned.

Lamorna placed the note in her pocket, turned her head to the bicycle once more and saw the small padlock on the back wheel, rotated the dials with the code '1984' and removed the chain. She looked at the scratched black frame, the rusty chain, the worn brakes, the shabby saddle and was thankful that she wasn't required to ride it for long. The tall man, named

Xerxo it transpired, had mentioned not to get there too early. She wondered why? Could it be that the Sun would set somewhere else? Would she find a locked door if she were overly hasty? Would mute assassins cut out her eyes and post them in the Optix letterbox? She didn't much like the idea of sitting around waiting to be allowed in, even if she always had some kind of podcast or music to listen to. She could always grab something to eat while she waited and make a day of it if she felt like it. Her desire to get there ahead of time only increased with the knowledge that she had been told not to. *'Who was this guy to tell me how to ride a bike? I go cycling all the time, I would climb mountains if there were any around here.'*

Lamorna really was a keen cyclist, it was one of the reasons that she had managed to deal with all of the stress during her studies and now long into here career at Optix. It prolonged her agony, so to speak. There was nothing quite like the rush of tearing downhill, feeling her legs pumping as hard as they could as she rode over eighty kilometres per hour and the only thing keeping her upright was twenty-five millimetres of rubber and the subtle shift in bodyweight as the road gently curved in an *'S'*. The climbs uphill were a different kind of rush and Lamorna often found it hard to pace herself; she tended to leave the others trailing, if she went with anyone at all. She normally set herself a minimum speed at the start of the climb and never go below it, remembering a film she saw as a kid, where a bus would explode if its speed went under fifty miles per hour. By the middle of the climb her legs wanted to explode. Often she would then drop the minimum speed by two kilometres per hour or try and power through. The trouble with blindly powering through, she found out to her great consternation, was that if you were on a long ride, of say five hours, you still needed enough energy to get home. It is important to keep your carbohydrate levels up, prepare ahead, eat lots of pasta the night before, eat a breakfast of complex carbs and take enough bananas, gels and cereal bars with you for about   four thousand calories. On the first such long ride Lamorna did nothing of the sort, had just one measly cereal bar with her, had enjoyed a normal breakfast, no carb-loading the night before and basically broke down after two and a half hours. The final sixty kilometres were a special kind of hell for her. It wasn't just that her body was simply incapable of pedalling faster than twenty-five kilometres per hour, she felt the whip of her own stupidity lashing her as she trailed home. Pace was the trick.

Lamorna didn't imagine reaching such speeds on that piece of dreck. She only hoped that the spokes and the tyres would hold out. The thing had seen much better days, resembling a luxury saloon abandoned by the side of the road, becoming a plaything for local children, raccoons and vandals. She made another note of the location of the Bluebird Luxury Apartments and rolled the bike onto the narrow path. As she mounted the bike, doing up her jacket in the process she noticed the shiny silver bell with brass beater and gave it a ring. This brought a beaming smile to her; it was always the simple things. Renn was heavy, probably around three times the weight of her racing bike, which clocked in at a barely race legal 6.81 kilograms. The saddle was twice as wide as her own too, offering ample space to park herself onto it. Lamorna sat bolt upright on the thing too, this was made for people who liked to take in the sights while they plodded along, she thought to herself: *'I just hope nobody sees me on this thing'.* Giving the bike a shove to get it started, our protagonist slowly made her way down the road in the general direction of the finance district.

The bright spring Sun was shining in her eyes and she regretted leaving her sunglasses at home. It made it difficult to concentrate, normally the photochromic lenses would be fitted to her aero helmet while cycling. Normally Lamorna was so well kitted-out and she now quickly regretted her untypical spontaneity. Grasping for a solution she let some of her hair fall into her face, like blinders on a horse, struggling through. Her mind had been made up her mind to do this, so she was going to see it through; it was only an hour's walk away, after all. It wouldn't be too hard to cycle there. As she rode along the lunchtime traffic zoomed past; she wasn't used to that. Normally she could ride at about the same speed as the cars in the city, often getting frustrated by traffic just as much as the drivers. The problem with a racing bike in the city was the tramlines in the road, one fall had taken her into the side of a steel skip, but not before sliding along the floor and getting full-on road rash covering her leg and arm, as well as the slow acceleration of the cars themselves. She could hit thirty kilometres per hour in a matter of seconds, but some drivers would take half an age to do the same thing. She usually cycled in the country, but it took about twenty minutes to get there first. So she would sometimes just stay in her flat and use the turbo trainer there. Without needing to leave the confines of her four walls.

The route towards the financial district took her past street vendors selling souvenirs, food trucks selling falafel, soba and kebabs and as she made her way into the city centre there were more electronics repair shops, closed down haberdasheries and more restaurants. The grey buildings were fading into disrepair, the old signs were barely legible and there seemed not to be many people around looking to go there. She wondered who even took things to be replaced anymore? Why would you even bother? The last time she had the idea to get something fixed, her camera, the salesperson said that the manufacturer in Japan would demand one hundred and fifty credits just to take a look at the thing. He showed her the used cameras for roughly the same price and then she thought better of it. She had then spent about a month researching the optimal camera to purchase in her budget and then ordered it online, it arrived the next day, but she had recently found little time to use it.

The city was indeed a sorry sight, Lamorna had forgotten to turn on her Optix implants before she had left the cafe and realised that that was real life nowadays: people may or may not frequent the establishments, but Optix made them absolutely perfect. The veneer was enticing and each person saw it exactly as they wanted it to be. She was for a moment truly thankful that her company's technologies spared people the knowledge that everything was in reality crumbling in full view and truly grotesque.

As she pedalled along she thought about what the tall man Xerxo had said about Master Su. In the end he had not said much about her at all. It had been more the absence of information that had fascinated her about their conversation, than the enriched detail of knowing everything and anything in advance. She had a nervous feeling in her head, not so much in her belly. She ran through things she could say when she met the wise Master Su, pondering numerous ways to make a good impression, considering questions to ask her. As she had normally rejected most invites in the past years she had to admit to feeling a brave variety of elation at finally going gung-ho and being out doing something.

Lamorna was however tired of trundling along at a subjective snail's pace. Her legs didn't need to take it slow and she hit the pedals and picked up the pace. As she did this she also turned on her Optix; she had seen quite enough ugliness today; Lamorna simply couldn't stand seeing any more. As she gathered pace she finally felt the wind in her hair, the slight burn in her legs and the thrill of trying to match the cars for pace. This was indeed not so simple when sat up straight on such a clunky old cruiser bike, but she relished the challenge. There were races at the North Sea every new year where pro cyclists would ride such bikes and compete with gale force crosswinds as much as against each other. As she sped up the bike made a beeping noise, the kind a large truck makes reversing. She ignored it at first, but as it persisted it really began to irritate her. She had maintained her speed, roughly 25kmh and previously veered out of the cycling lane, the cars ahead of her were progressing steadily and she was just about keeping up. The bike was beeping away, but why? She wondered if it was a kind of theft protection, but then why would it only beep now? *'Was it a speed-limiter?'*, she asked herself. Well, if so, it didn't physically prevent her from going fast, for a bike like that at least.

Across the street, dressed in dapper charcoal suits and black ties two men were stood outside one of the many cheap restaurants. They saw to their astonishment a young woman hurtling down the road, matching the description previously given to them, her bicycle screaming with a kind of siren. The men double-checked their phones for ID and then confirmed that this was the one they were on the look-out for. Lamorna Cruickshanks, dark shoulder length hair, thirty-two years old, athletic build, about one meter seventy-eight tall, long face. They jumped onto their own city bikes and gave chase.

Lamorna was beginning to enjoy herself, despite the noise emanating from the bicycle. She had never let weird noises get in the way of a good race. One could be forgiven for making odd noises in the pursuit of a goal; grunting, farting, panting and shouting at oneself were the norm. On a racing bike as well as in the office. The beeping continued incessantly and it was indeed getting louder; now reaching the volume of a car's burglar alarm. The few people on the streets were looking at her as she whizzed past, they obviously had never seen somebody giving it some on such a decrepit old-fashioned bicycle before. One thing she didn't notice however was that the two grey-besuited men had gained most of the ground on her and were hanging three cars behind her. She had been told to take her time and arrive for 6.30 p.m., not to be early and she had wilfully ignored her instructions. These men had been on the lookout for someone looking to contact Master Su and would be reporting her whereabouts in due course.

Lamorna, her brow now full of sweat, was now waiting impatiently at a red light. She didn't understand why cyclists couldn't just carry on if they wanted to, it was only their own risk if they got hit. She tutted and frowned, glowered and huffed, but the light remained red for some time. It was a busy crossing with three lanes of traffic coming from all four directions. One for each month of the year and each hour of the clock face. The grey men behind Lamorna were readying themselves. Their mission, to sniff out Su's refuge, was top secret and they couldn't allow themselves to be revealed to her. Unbeknownst to them Lamorna was riding no ordinary bicycle. Its alarm had been caused by her exceeding normal speeds and also by her behaviour, veering from her bike lane and by her levels of cortisol. Through her sweaty palms the bicycle's handlebars were able to read the level of stress hormone in her body. Xerxo had instructed her to take it slow, to basically become invisible and to blend in. But this was not Lamorna's way, at least not when on a bike. The heavy black bicycle was attempting to communicate with her, but she was not yet able to listen. She was too goal-focused and she now had the bit between her teeth. Its warnings had started early enough and yet she persisted. When she raced past the men in suits she had given herself away.

Renn was not the typical rackety old thing, having long been a part of Master Su's collection of magical objects. Su had lent Renn to Xerxo for such occasions and the bike was more than happy to oblige. For it was a helpful bicycle, never too ashamed to get dirty and muck in. Being often stood outside in the rain, battered by winds, the bike was rarely cleaned. In most respects it was the opposite of Lamorna's racing bike. In one particular aspect it was quite unique: it was a sentient bicycle. It communicated through flashing its lights and sounding its siren. The channels through which it could express itself were severely limited. Master Su thought this however a charming aspect of the bicycle itself and likened it to a person learning a foreign language. At first they could only do the basics and that was sufficient for most contexts. Renn was, however, not able to move on its own accord. It required a rider to push its pedals and steer. It was much older than Lamorna realised, the rust was authentic, a sign of its living conditions, which also allowed it to better blend in; its mechanics were in more than pristine condition. Master Su was always sure to look after and maintain it, assuring Renn that the safest tools are the sharpest.

Due to Renn's sentient nature it would have been able to avoid detection, if had Lamorna heeded its warnings and heard the alarm, so now it needed to change tactics. Lamorna was approaching a left-hand corner at good speed, the alarm blaring, eyes ahead, the suited men on her tail. The sunlight was coming from her right side and without sunglasses she felt at a real disadvantage. As she took the corner she checked over her left shoulder and spotted the two men. She thought little of it at first, continuing along the road at a good pace, her own personal siren blaring, she was indeed quite grateful that she had activated her Optix implants, the colours appeared to her so much more vividly. She passed a few more stores, their signage now displaying a more pleasing shape and font, the smells from the food stands in the city centre wafting into her nasal cavity. Then, as she approached a zebra crossing she slowed slightly and checked behind herself again. The same men were still there, hanging about twenty metres back. She pulled up onto the pavement and got off the bike, its siren finally relenting, she got Xerxo's note out of her pocket again. As she read it once more a thought came into her head: *'If I am too fast, I will be too early'*.

She wondered what to do, she still had a good deal of time on her hands before 6.30 p.m. and the grey men were solemnly stood on the opposite side of the road trying to look inconspicuous. She spied a kebab vendor down the road and ordered herself a falafel wrap. As she stood with her back to the sun she took short glances to her left and noticed the men chatting together over a cigarette, their smart clothes blending in well with the garishly flash decor of the neighbouring shops. Lamorna then had a quite fabulous idea. She had recently seen a documentary about fiddle crabs which had a massive claw which it used to defend itself and assert dominance in their competence hierarchies, thus establishing mating rights and such things. But the thing which really stuck with her was their eyesight. In her private life she often took to looking out for things in the media and the arts which could be useful for her work and this species of crab was an inspiration to her now.

The crab would see in polarised light: its natural predators are herons and tern, and the crab could spot the bird against the sky despite the cloud cover and greyness of said bird. The grey-suited men fitted in so well to the swish upmarket shopfronts in the city centre, yet if she turned off her Optix implants she would see them for what they were. A black bird against a pale backdrop.

Lamorna quickly finished her falafel and made her way down the road, pushing the bike as she went. Renn was, of course, perfectly silent now, its alarm had served its purpose. Lamorna racked her brains trying to devise a plan. She wanted to get into the building without the men seeing her and needed to be cunning and spontaneous. The former proving less of an issue generally than the latter. She went through her mental archive of other nature documentaries as she made her way south-east closer to the hotel. Birds-of-paradise would inflate their chests, twist their wings and dance in courtship rituals. Zebra and tigers alike, despite being prey and predator shared the adaptation of resembling tall grass, even if in the case of the zebra it was not an environmental camouflage, but a herd camouflage with no particular zebra sticking out, should a predator attack. Chameleons adapted to their surroundings at will and this was the path Lamorna chose, with a touch of theatrics thrown in.

The men had noticed her movements and were subtly following her; they chatted amiably with each other like competing alpha male sales managers while discussing the previous evening's football results. As they walked down the road to her right side she noticed that their discussion was getting more heated, presumably one man had insulted the other's favourite player. She wondered if it would be possible to throw in the right level of distraction without garnering too much attention to herself. She muttered to herself all of her considerations; a rare externalisation of her thoughts. Her renewed view of the dull shopfronts and ugly pavement clashed with her until now much appreciated sense of aesthetics, yet her eyes now saw the downtown for what it was: overlooked and underfunded. The men were maintaining their distance, but they kept pace with Lamorna as she went down the road.

Renn heard and understood every word. Knowing what was needed and being unafraid to do it, it listened to the fragments of her different plans and doggedly locked itself where it stood.

The 'Bluebird Luxury Apartments' sign was now lit up in a resplendently vivid blue shade. Its light shone on the adjacent and opposite buildings, bathing them in a oddly warm and lively colour. The pavements were mostly empty and the blue neon strip lighting bathed the paving in a calming ocean hue. The orange tones from the sun provided a natural contrast to the hotels appearance and Lamorna already felt as if trapped in a simulation, or in a beta test of a new Optix skin.

The sun was close to setting behind the building while Renn and Lamorna made their way closer. Lamorna knew that she needed to throw off the grey men, but was unsure of how, her anxiety was beginning to get the better of her. As she pushed Renn by the handlebars it picked up on her increased levels of cortisol und knew it was time. Right there, around one hundred metres from the hotel Renn stopped in its tracks and automatically locked its back wheel. Lamorna began to release a volley of swear words at Renn; she was unable to budge it and was getting more angry. The weight of the thing was ridiculous, like a corpse. She briefly considered carrying it the rest of the way, unwillingly to let the thing go. It wasn't hers to give away and she felt a sense of guilt to Xerxo for just leaving it there. Whenever she borrowed something she was always very careful not to dog ear its pages or scratch it.

In that moment, as Lamorna was lost in thought, Renn flashed its front light twice. She looked at it again, unsure of what she had seen. Once again, Renn gestured for her to get moving. She recalled her myriad ideas for getting out of this pickle, taking it as a sign, thinking that the bicycle was a kind of gift from the universe; presenting her with a heavenly divined solution. In this instance it was of course no sign. The bicycle was telling Lamorna to get going, leaving Renn where it stood and for her to make her way to the Bluebird hotel. Without her implant activated she spotted a small compact blue car midway between where she stood and the hotel. She was curious to see what the standard Optix setting was for the car; most people left the default textures on for public spaces and other people's private property. They tended to invest in updates only for their own homes, cars, places of work and their neighbourhoods. The default setting displayed an extravagant limousine, the kind of which celebrities might be taken to a film premiere in the old days and which kids were taken to their first day at school nowadays. The long side of the car gave her a good chance to go unspotted while she mildly changed her appearance and then made for the hotel. She left the bike standing and slowly walked in careful, deliberate strides towards the sleek black limousine. Her now relaxed movements went almost unnoticed by her pursuers, their attention seemingly caught by the engrossing conversation they were having amongst themselves. Renn was left standing on the pavement outside an ice cream cafe, fading into the background as a Parisian in a Robert Doisneau photo.

Lamorna pressed herself against the car door, her face

wedged up against it and her legs shaking. She quickly decided to remove her jacket and do something she hadn't done since she was about twelve years old. She tied a knot in her t-shirt, exposing her trim belly, having pulled the bottom of the shirt up through the neck hole. She felt incredibly self-conscious and felt ridiculous for doing so, but knew she needed a disguise. She swiftly removed her black trousers too, struggling out of them as she did, and tied them around her waist as a kind of makeshift skirt. Now adequately transformed she checked whether the grey-suited men were looking in her direction, via spying them in the car's side mirror. She then noticed how the loud siren on Renn the bicycle had flared up once more, its raw irritating clamour for attention igniting the ire of many a passer-by. She saw her chance and ran the fifty metres towards the hotel building's entrance, all basked in blue.

5 - SU

Elated, Lamorna could see office workers inside the building, wearing grey suits and paisley ties, tasteful floral skirts and weightless neckerchiefs. She wondered to herself whether they were also spying on her, or whether they were just visiting. She hoped that Master Su had vetted the people before they were allowed into the building and trusted that they would do her no harm. She didn't really figure herself to be that significant anyhow. Her meeting with Xerxo and her impending one with this Master Su character had left her pondering otherwise. Had the men seen her entering the building? Were they about to rush in and apprehend her? Her made her way to the coffee machine at the far end of the foyer and placed a cup under the spout. She selected the button for an americano and kept her eyes fixed on the large glass doors. Still no sign. Renn must have distracted them, her disguised had made her invisible to them, or maybe they wanted only to ensure her arrival at the hotel. Regardless of the fact, Lamorna took her coffee and kept her view firmly placed on the entrance. The foyer was filled only with young professionals, in tight grey merino wool suits. She drank from her cup slowly, being careful not to burn her lips. Once she was finished, satisfied that she had completed this leg of her quest, she made her way across the foyer to the lifts. As she pressed the button for the lift Lamorna felt a tinge of anxiety. She detested being closed in such spaces and the fact that they had normally had no windows made it worse. Lamorna figured it was a common issue, yet that didn't make her feel any better; other people's problems didn't help her at this point in her adventure. She waited for the lift to finally come down to the ground floor, observing the numbers on the display slowly roll down from thirty-six to G. Lamorna pressed the button for the top floor. And patiently waited during the long climb up the tower.

As the ordinary lift doors opened they revealed an art deco laden apartment, coated in renaissance era paintings and minimalist marble sculptures. An eclectic mix for such a building, Lamorna thought to herself. The walls were covered in wood, seemingly carved on site; twisted knots of burl on each corner. The low level lighting came from hidden strips hidden in the walls, there were no mighty chandeliers hanging from the ceiling to finish the picture. Even without her implants on Lamorna's eyes were overwhelmed by the high fidelity detail and painstaking artisanal craft imbedded in the making of the room.

At the far end of the apartment waited a woman. The figure at the back of the suite was a hooded one. Dressed in a long white gown she gave the appearance of a tall swan. Her pale face, red lips and raven black hair gave an aura of an ethereal being. The dark eyes, framed by fine brows, tender cheeks with a small scar under the left eye each provided an uncomfortable juxtaposition for Lamorna. How old was she? Why had she summoned me, of all people?

The woman, more mother than crone, spoke clearly and without hesitation, "time isn't the issue here Lamorna, it is your perspective". The words' echo reverberated around the suite. The woman spoke once more, "each time you dwell on the past, your future is being consumed. You were thrust into this world, of that you had no choice. Yet what you now do, from this moment, is of your pure, unfiltered agency". Lamorna understood each single word, yet still felt like a twelve year old. It wasn't the woman's fault, although obviously learned, the robe told as much, the clarity in her voice and intonation gave the impression of a loving professor more than an admonishing matron.

"My name is Lamorna, I received a message to come and see you."

Lamorna asked the figure's name. "Su", she answered. "I have always been here, Lamorna. Though I have not been merely waiting. My entire life has led to this point, as has yours. Our meeting can of course be seen as a great cosmic coincidence, yet this would be folly. There is, of course, randomness in this very finest of universes, indeed only randomness. We are flying around the sun, rotating and twisting through the galaxy, the universe expanding at ever increasing speeds. The exact consequences of that we define ourselves. No one else can tell you otherwise, for they themselves are also flying through this universe at the same speed, but on a different vector. Tell me Lamorna, would you like me to repeat that?"

Despite feeling somewhat bewildered, Lamorna didn't flinch, she remained po-faced and slowly shook her head, "I've always wondered what motivates people to do something with their lives and I see people around me who get up every morning and proceed like nothing should ever change. Colleagues who don't realise the strain they are under who never bite back, never protest and rarely raise their heads above shoulder height. They are forever hunched over. Their faces fixated on screens, be they five or twenty-two inches wide. Afraid of biting the hand that feeds, or being struck on the back of the head".

"Indeed", Su replied, after some contemplation. "The world has become fixated, that is the right word. Yet it is a fallacy. The world itself is ambivalent towards us as a species.

Nature will always exist, just as the Sun burns at unimaginable temperatures. Animals have lived on this planet for hundreds of millions of years, all are thrown into existence unwillingly and die after somewhere between three days and four hundred years. However, mountains are formed at a snail's pace and are immovable. The idea of permanence is an illusion Lamorna. So, because of this each individual must fight for their own subjective meaning, their own goals in life, their own struggle. Most people prefer to ignore this mission, this struggle and their own meaning", Su continued.

"Which meaning?", Lamorna countered. "How can you find meaning in a universe which doesn't care if you exist or not, which throws you into life and doesn't give you the tools to master it?"

Su looked Lamorna straight in her blue eyes and held her right hand, "the meaning is yours to find. You are part of nature and it is your universe. The tools you forge yourself and the struggle is of your own choosing".

"I don't want to struggle, I want to be happy", Lamorna interjected, pulling her hand back from Su's grasp. "All of my colleagues have their families to go home to, their own houses, hobbies, dogs and cats. I have to find these things too before it is too late. My life has led to this point, I am thirty-two years old, I'm the best at my job, yet my boss keeps me from becoming a partner. Optix is my life, my colleagues are my family, the aquarium fish in the office are my pets. I don't necessarily need all of the other things in life that other people want, but I need to know it's all real."

Su asked, "why did you want to become an architect Lamorna?"

Lamorna shrugged while looking for the answer in her brain, continually coming up empty. She traced her thoughts back to her life as a teenager, as the eldest of two sisters she bore the brunt of her parent's discipline and learnt from their mistakes as well as her own. She knew when she was sixteen that she herself didn't want her own children, not despising them, just not wanting to lose herself in the same loop as her own parents. Continual meddling, fussing and stressing about what the children were doing, be it their health and safety, school, partying, shoplifting, fighting, exams or finding a job, building a career or starting a family.

"Lamorna, the question is not a trick. You became an architect, this is a great accomplishment. Yet you must know that this is not the end point. An architect only plans for what comes next, it is the builder who puts it into action. It is the tree which must grow when the seed has done its work."

"But how can I just completely change who I am? I have been doing this all my life. And to be honest I only just met you; why are we even discussing this?"

"I must correct you Lamorna. All your life you have been learning new things, taking on more responsibilities as a consequence, yes. All of these adventures were unexpected side-effects of your own ambition. It is the curiosity in you which has led you here. Your appetite, which brought you to me. This has all been your doing, you are in no need of a saviour, no desire for a person to hold your hand, your life has been a lot of work up to this point. Your struggle, your choices, your freedom. Mine has been a long life, or better said, many short lives. I was a maiden, a mother and a crone. I have been doted on, I have wandered alone in the desert, I have born life inside me, raised children and I have grown old inside, parts of me dying. It is this death inside which can eat you Lamorna, but it is the conscious dying-off and pruning of things which leads to new life, within and without. Below and above. You need to remember this idea of renewal Lamorna, let your ghosts die and rest. Especially those ghosts that dwell within your mind, who haunt you movements and lock you into your paralysis. What is the man who never forgets?", Su posed.

Lamorna struggled for some moments with the question, still dwelling on her innate ghosts. Eventually she mustered a response, "a man who never forgets is like an elephant."

"No. An elephant forgets all of the time", Su retorted, smugly looking Lamorna in the eyes.

"But they say that an elephant never forgets", Lamorna replied. Feeling that, although this conversation was taking her places she hadn't expected, this was almost a reality defining fact.

Su seemed impatient, her fine eyebrows forming a vivid 'V'. "First of all, who are 'they'? Secondly, how can this be proven?"

Once more the words echoed around the suite, as an avalanche repeats around a snow-covered valley. "Okay, it's a cliché. But it must have at least a drop of truth in it. Elephants are large mammals, their social behaviour shows empathy, for example they mourn their dead and they care for their young for a long time."

"Yes, perhaps too long", Su countered. "There is of course truth in the cliché, as in most. But you must look for it. The man who never forgets is not a large mammal with a trunk, living in Africa or India. He can live anywhere provided he can adapt to the situation. He must learn new things, how to walk, feed himself, talk, socialise, simple mathematics. He must learn to survive depending on the circumstances. A grown man can forget how to walk, because he does it every day. The process becomes irrelevant and can be forgotten. It is no longer of use to him to use his palms to raise himself onto two feet and toddle three metres into his parents' arms. He must forget this process and move on to learning how to talk. Once he has mastered *'mama, papa, want, nana, yes, no and yum'* he will learn simple sentences like *'mama, no'*. With any luck, one day he will write a successful job application and work in an office. And so there he must too adapt to the new circumstances, there it will no longer be necessary to walk three metres into his boss's arms. However, it will be of the utmost importance to say *'boss, no'*, even if this takes considerable practice. Some of life's lessons are doomed to repeat themselves and we will continue to face them until they are learned, by which time they will completely disappear and become a fully integrated part of ourselves".

"But how can he forget how to walk?", Lamorna was also becoming impatient. It felt like she wasn't being taken seriously and had begun to get antsy, gesticulating with her arms and pulling a grimace when forming her question; her voice rising steadily in pitch. "He just does it. He doesn't think about how or why."

"But he doesn't forget it. If he did, he would fall over", Su countered.

Lamorna felt like she was in with a chance of winning the argument, something she occasionally felt while arguing with Chamberlain.

"But indeed he does. If you were to ask him how he walks, he would be unable to provide an adequate answer. Alternatively, he would go on to construct an over the top quasi-physiological reasoning behind bi-pedal movement, detailing tendon-joint-muscle movement, nervous response and cochlear imbalance."

"But that doesn't mean he has forgotten it", Lamorna

vehemently added. "He has merely attained a greater understanding of things."

"Indeed, he has not forgotten it. Yet, he need not continually remember how to walk. Tell me Lamorna, who won the race: the tortoise or the hare?"

"The tortoise of course, everyone knows that story. The hare was arrogant, raced off at breakneck pace, had attained such a staggering lead over the slow tortoise that he lay in the midday sun, fell asleep, overslept and awoke in time only to witness the steady tortoise creep over the finish line before him."

"Good. What did the hare forget?", Su asked, holding her hands together as if in Christian prayer.

"I don't quite understand, he didn't forget anything, he was just arrogant, thought it was an easy win. He thought the tortoise was incapable of catching him, too slow to even match a snake for speed. His head was full of his own strengths, as well as the weaknesses of the tortoise I suppose".

"Molodets", Master Su said.

"Sorry?", Lamorna asked.

"Good job, Lamorna. Sorry, sometimes I forget who I am speaking to. There are others who come to see me, you understand. The hare believes himself superior and sees his own strengths and the tortoise's weaknesses. Excellent insight Lamorna. Indeed, the hare has remembered a good number of important things, yet he has forgotten even more critical things."

Lamorna poured herself a glass of claret from the decanter stood on the table. She took a sip, leant back in her chair and attempted to assume a relaxed posture. Assert more control and also relax her body at the same time. "Such as?", she eventually replied.

"His own weaknesses, the strengths of the tortoise and how they overlap". Master Su mirrored Lamorna's actions and took a large sip from her chalice.

"The hare is hasty, arrogant and impatient. The tortoise, in contrast, is contemplative, humble and striking only when the moment is ripe."

"Correct", Su confirmed and continued: "Of course, this is merely a fable", Su added. "Most times the hare would win, it is much faster, let's not get ridiculous. The moral of the story would be fiercely different if the hare had won this particular race, yet on this occasion the tortoise won and there are a number of reasons for it. The hare is arrogant, impatient, sarcastic and mean. He thinks precious little of the tortoise and this affects his preparation. The night before this particular race, having won one hundred percent of the previous races, he went out with some friends and had too many drinks, got home at 5 a.m., his partner berated him for this, they argued until 6 a.m. and then by the time of the race at 10 a.m. he just about made it out of bed and arrived at the race on time. His training the months before, due to his continued success, had also become more relaxed, he didn't need to earn it anymore, he had become fat, the previous hunger for excellence had left him entirely. He had given up fighting, for this was no longer necessary. He was content in a way, he was a world-famous sprinter, the best in his field".

Lamorna chuckled to herself, "in his field".

"Yes, indeed that is where hares live". Su smiled, but only one corner of her mouth turned skyward and she continued: "He did not bother facing proper competition anymore, he thought the audience were only coming to watch him, paying admission fees to see his personality win again. This accomplishes nothing other than confirming to himself what he is already capable of doing. Yet the premise of competition and sport is to measure oneself against others, to push each other forward and progress as an art. Just as artists are inspired by one another, the sportsperson strives to be faster, jump higher and carry ever heavier weights. This is to push the limit of natural human potential. This is however premised on competition, which requires participants of similar, yet not necessarily equal ability. The hare picked easy fights, ignored similarly quick animals like the fox, dog or pig and chose the tortoise, mouse and ant as opponents. He chose to punch down, like a schoolyard bully. He had forgotten and failed to recall a good number of things".

While Su was talking Lamorna had become distracted, taking in the extravagant furnishing of this room, the quality of the glasses, the beautiful joinery of the wooden table. Eventually she snapped back into this plane of existence and asked, "but how does that help me? My life may have led to this point Su, but how can the hare's fate concern me when I have completely other concerns?"

"Lamorna, the tortoises, mice and pigs of this world are of the utmost necessity. There can be no fox without chickens and no vultures without carcasses".

"Su, I struggle to understand what all of these animals have to do with my own predicament. What does this have to do with me?"

"You already understand this fable's relevance to your own life, Lamorna. You have lived it a thousand times. You race from one finish line to the next, yet do you reflect on the victories? Do you really progress on to more difficult challenges? How many tortoises have you raced against and won flawlessly? Lamorna, I do not mean to belittle your accomplishments. You are bright and talented, indeed a promising individual. Thankfully, you are here and are ready to discuss this with me".

Master Su was right. Lamorna replied, "The hare doesn't have anything more to prove, to himself or others. He could retire and be happy".

"Could he though? Be happy, I mean. His career has been that of a tyrant, punching below his weight, picking easy fights. A life of picking low hanging fruit is not something to write home about, Lamorna."

"But he has still got those victories, his trophies and memories" Lamorna countered.

"His achievements, given time, will be shown to be hollow. The gold medals will become cudgels to beat himself with, his career will mean nothing. The sportsperson still has half of their life ahead when they retire. Their body is no longer to keep up with the young challengers and so they leave the field. Then they are faced with the truth and the difficult questions".

"Such as?", Lamorna poured herself more of the purple claret into her crystal glass.

"What do I want to become now?" Su posed, holding Lamorna's gaze until Su's closed her eyes and reached for the now empty bottle of red wine. While Master Su stood up and went to the adjacent room to get a new bottle, Lamorna was left to contemplate the question. She felt ever so slightly puzzled, she understood the question, but thought the answer simple. "He is a successful runner, he is famous, wealthy and set up for the rest of his life. His life will not be that of a pauper; struggling each day to get food and a dry and warm place to sleep."

"Yet it is the pauper who has to live anew each day. Never having anything else to fall back on other than his wits and determination to survive", Master Su replied.

"But that is no life, that is a fight", Lamorna masterfully countered, by now feeling that she had Su in a clinch and was forcing her into a corner.

"The pauper is the not the richest person, by any means, other that they are fighting to improve their situation each day. Their fundamental needs are to be met at first, warmth, shelter, hunger. Should they do this, then they must be satisfied with their day's accomplishments. Do they want this for their life every day? In the majority of cases, of course not. Yet it is their daily struggle which is relevant here. I do not wish to romanticise the life of a homeless person, nor ignore the common societal conditions which allow this state to pervade. It is more that I wish to highlight to you Lamorna that they have a clear aim each day. They need food and warmth and so they act accordingly. Their morals are based directly on their needs and therefore their actions. They are aligned, focussed and hungry. Tell me Lamorna, are your needs, morals and actions aligned?"

The question felt like a gut punch, she wanted to fall to her knees. She hadn't seen it coming. She felt she had had the upper hand in this head-to-head and had pushed Su against the ropes. But Su's question struck the air out of her belly and left her crippled.

"Lamorna, each one of us has to draw a line somewhere. Often many lines several times a day. I can see that this is a struggle for you, the tears in your soul are visible to me; the weeping inside is not always a burden, it can be a way to grow. The question is simple. Are you doing what you consider to be right?"

"I guess so", Lamorna exhaled. Having held in her breath for far too long, as she felt the crevice open up inside herself.

"But can you know so? We are far beyond guesswork now", Master Su followed up with a swift left jab, tenderising Lamorna's right cheek.

Lamorna winced at the follow-up question, the one-two combo left her in a daze. She had barely recovered her breath from the first one and the lovingly decorated walls of the luxurious suite seemed to draw closer. Her senses focussed on Master Su, viewing her as through a fish-eye lens. Her view ignoring the periphery and focused on an enlarged view of her counterpart. "I have always tried to act according to my beliefs", Lamorna mustered.

"And what would they be?", Su responded relentlessly. The punches unceasing.

"Puh, I don't know". Lamorna folded her chin down to her chest, could feel the lacerations on her cheek, the blood dripping onto her torso, the bruises on her ribcage and gut. "I have always been a firm believer in 'do unto others as you would have done to yourself."

"And how has that worked out for you?", Su was smiling wide by now. Although she could see Lamorna basically on her knees and withdrawn, she knew that this was an important lesson for her and she would remain unrelenting. "Have you always acted in accordance with how you wish to be treated?"

Lamorna let out a low wheeze and held her head in her hands, not believing what had hit her. The questions themselves had not been the issue for her. She simply felt overwhelmed by their connotations. She drew in a number of deep breaths and ruminated on the question. "I suppose not in every case", Lamorna managed.

"And that is to be expected, Lamorna. No single person

can be perfect, it is not that aspect of human experience that makes life worth living. The imperfect nature of things is an intrinsic part of life, just as decay is an inevitable component too. A man is like an elephant in a good number of ways, yet most specifically in that it is bound to its nature, its imperfections and unavoidable death. That is not to say that we cannot strive to become more than our nature, and shouldn't try to attain a level of competence or appreciate our health. The point is more that these aspects are what makes life what it is: uniquely singular and yet together we must live with the choices we make and the lives we lead."

"What kind of life do you lead?" Enquired Lamorna. "Do you have family?", Lamorna was careful to watch Master Su's micro-aggressions, of which there were many. An upward turn of the left corner of her mouth, a scratching of her forearm and a flash of a frown, just to name the first three that Lamorna noticed.

"My life's goal doesn't involve family; my life I lead without such compromises or material attainment. I am here today, Lamorna, to lead and help you. Many moons I have seen and many stars have I guided", Su admitted, in the end through her teeth.

"But how can you do all of that if you don't have a family and children of your own? Who are you responsible for and answerable to?", Lamorna's tone becoming more direct and irritable.

"I am answerable to you, Lamorna, am I not? Is that not what this is now? A grand dialogue, a to and fro? And also I am of course, essentially answerable to my own conscience. There is no one else here, how should there be any other way?"

Lamorna nodded in accordance, stood up once more and added: "So how will we proceed? What about us? What is this? Some meeting of minds?"

Master Su smiled, her eyes glistening and happily took Lamorna's hands in her own. "Our adventure is just beginning. We have a lot to see and many things to accomplish. Come with me, I have something to show you."

Master Su gracefully gestured for them to stand up and take in the sights. The top floor afforded a wondrously spectacular sight and Lamorna gladly took in the great view over the city. The panorama window offered a black and orange view of the skyline, the riverboats coursed downstream and the great skyscrapers jutted out as smoke stacks in Victorian England. Even without her implants activated Lamorna could see the beauty of the city, at this macro level it was resplendent in the evening twilight.

Su popped open the new bottle of red and poured the purple liquid into their glasses. Su motioned for Lamorna to take a seat, then proposed a toast: "Lamorna, in all of my years on this Earth, it is for this day that I am the most thankful. It is on this day that we form our alliance, our sacred bond and our word. We have long sought for truth, honour and meaning. Lamorna, I want to support you in everything you do. I have watched you for a long time from afar, as is my way. Many refrain from approaching me, but you came here of your own free will. I may seem steely and cold to others, but you have seen the warmth and kindness. Do not mistake my words for mere flattery or niceties."

Lamorna quickly scanned her brain, "is this really the first time we have met, Master Su? It is a feeling I can't describe adequately".

"Indeed. Perhaps it is not. And the feeling may be new to you." Master Su agreed. Her deep set eyes lighting up with a fire. Master Su was of deep learning and had lived in many places, met many other learned people. But in Lamorna she saw a special potential, something which Lamorna herself was unaware of. "Lamorna, how do you think I should best help you? Should I remain a distant benefactor, as von Meck was to Tchaikovsky?"

Lamorna once more felt provoked by the direct question, unused to such honest enquiry, although by know she felt more than sufficiently tenderised. She sat in silence for a few minutes; Su's patience was not tested. She knew that this silence was necessary to listen to the inner self. Lamorna, however, was not used to this practice and did everything she could to not answer the question, but without showing too many outside indications of her distraction. For Lamorna was a master of distraction, a hobby collector, an information hoarder and an emotional recluse. She had a myriad of coping mechanisms for dealing the stress in her job, but when faced with such questions she found her brain functions going haywire and sending out SOS messages. Lamorna simply did not know how to answer. She tried to analyse Su's expression, in the brief moments when she could look her in the face. What did Su want? She asked herself. Lamorna was careful not to let Su inside. Her own levels of protection firmly established and well fortified. By showing vulnerability she was hyper-aware of being left exposed and potentially a target. But how could Su help her, and did she want to be helped?

"I don't know, Su", Lamorna managed to rustle up, as a bare minimum, scratching the back of her head as she spoke.

"Well, I think that for a start we need to define the matter at hand, lay out reasons for it, outline possible solutions and then apply the right ones", spoke Master Su softly.

"I suppose that sounds about right". Lamorna looked at Su and smiled weakly. Someone else was actually on her side and helped pick up some of the formidable slack, she felt a slight relief. Her own burdens lately becoming too much to bear: The loneliness, the workload, the sheer pressure.

"First of all, we have you, Lamorna. You have been focussed your entire life on getting more information, believing that this will help you one day. You have been spreading yourself out too thinly. You have not been thinking about what you have denied yourself in life, you have not kept in mind what is good in you and you have not been reflecting on what has been happening every day."

"Every day?", Lamorna, latched on to the last words, feeling that they were the simplest.

"Every day. Every day you live your life. Every day you do things which define who you are. Every day you collect more information without transmuting it. Without processing it. Information without application is useless. That which you do not need, you need to let go. This is the first lesson. Empty your mind", as upon a great mountain, Master Su looked down at Lamorna.

Lamorna nodded, her head hung low. Then she said: "Su, I am an addict, I need this hit of information to keep myself going. How can I live without it, when it is such a part of me?"

"Explain, which part of it is you?", Su countered.

"All of it. I want to know everything. Well, not everything, but I can't stand not knowing something that somebody is talking about. I am not a dumb person and never will be. I hate that feeling of ignorance and feeling small."

"To feel small is the first step towards wisdom". Su smiled at Lamorna and took her right hand, stroking it lightly. "You are but a grain of sand in this whole universe".

"In fact, there are more grains of sand on this planet

than there are stars in the entire universe". Lamorna countered.

"Indeed, but does knowing that make you feel any bigger, Lamorna?" Master Su thoroughly enjoyed sparing with her new apprentice.

"Of course not, but if I am so small, how am I able to change things? It is not like I can just keep to myself and pretend that everything is fine and that nothing needs to be corrected."

"That is exactly right. Lamorna, it starts here" Su pointed to Lamorna's chest.

"Here? Don't you mean in my head?"

"Quite the opposite", Master Su replied. "Your head is the result and cause of most of your problems. You need to free yourself from this and learn to listen to your self. Your self does not reside in your head. Your real self can only be understood by looking deeper into your soul. Look deep down and dig for more. You may be shocked and appalled at what you find. This journey is dark and foreboding, painful and long. The shadow inside you is waiting to be discovered, full of things you are blissfully unaware of. You will reveal to yourself deeper truths, festering capabilities and knowledge. The key to unlocking that potential is something best done with guidance and I will do my best to support you. Yet, this is a path which you alone must walk. You will incorporate your shadow self and integrate these hitherto aspects of your personality until you are transformed and born again. Then you will move on to your male counterpart, Lamorna, your animus. You may be already aware of him, lurking beneath your shadow, all those aspects of self which you will work on for the rest of your life. Your determination until now lacks focus. This will be your life's work, amongst many other still to be characteristics of your very self."

Lamorna was now far beyond being able to keep up with Master Su's monologue and allowed her to continue. This path would indeed be long, she accepted.

"Your second lesson is to reflect on the day you lived. Do this every night: which activities took most of your time on that day? How did you react or feel? Try going chronologically through your entire day, every little step. Do not try to judge yourself, merely describe the events. You can also go backwards and recount everything; sometimes you will find that your actions and mood had direct causes. Such meditation will aid your inner reflections and support your shadow integration. The third lesson is to think about yourself. Which positive characteristics come to mind? It is imperative that you only think on the positives, not to fool yourself, but to reinforce the good. Finally, bring into your mind to which plans you have for the following day. These can be normal tasks or appointments, or you can set yourself goals or wishes. For example, you could wish to be surprised. This could open you up to more spontaneity, dear Lamorna. As I have seen today, your are quite the improvisor, your journey here to this tower proved that to me. The way you dealt with my agents outside was quite wonderful. Back to the surprise, it could be that somebody from your distant past calls you from out of the blue, it could be that a new song plays, it could be that a bird visits you. But be open to that experience, allow the randomness of the universe to enter your life. This embrace of life is probably the most important aspect for you to change. If you only focus on long-planned events and only reflect on these, critiquing their success, you will remain stuck in the loop. You need to see outside of your current life and realise that you are part of this human nature, allow yourself to be surprised, disappointed, loved, wounded. And look back, but move forward."

Master Su looked over at Lamorna only to check if she was still paying attention. Once she had confirmed that, she continued as before: "The next lesson is this: On complete faith I would like you to take this and keep it. Do not lose it, do not use it until you know its purpose. It is not a trifle, Lamorna." Su showed Lamorna a wooden box, marvellously fashioned in olive wood. And swiftly opened it to reveal a round ball, a perfect sphere of sand no bigger than a golf ball.

"What is this and what should I do with it?", Lamorna quizzically enquired.

"Your intuition is strong, Lamorna. You took the words directly from me, as if drawn out by magic", Master Su replied with a smirk. "Put it in a drawer and forget about it. I want you just to trust me. When the time is right, when you are at ease with yourself and all is set, you will place the ball in exactly the correct place and all will be revealed." Once more Lamorna was alarmed at the vagueness of Su's instruction. Again, Su followed up with a change of subject: "We will meet again Lamorna, you can send for me when you feel it is the right time."

"Oh, okay. Sure. I suppose I expected a wonderful retelling of this ball, its significance and much fought-over history. But, yes. I'll look after it, sure thing. Does it require watering or feeding? I'm not very good with house plants or pets, I'm afraid."

Master Su now stood and opened her arms, her blue gown now spread wide and she smiled a crooked smile. "Not at all Lamorna, just do as I said. Kept secret and safe, it will in due time reveal its purpose to you. Remember only this: *'I am as small as a grain of sand'*, it will serve you well."

Master Su stood up and then accompanied Lamorna back to the lift. They exchanged pleasantries and made their farewells. Lamorna didn't really know what else to say, but was sure that she would again have the chance to ask Master Su for more revelations when the time came.

Having reached the ground floor once more the foyer was almost completely empty. The tall night porter bade Lamorna good night and with the wooden box in hand she made her way back to her flat, this time on foot and with her Optix implants activated; she needed some sense of normality once more. One hour with Master Su was quite enough for now.

Master Su's background was complex, of course, whose isn't? The closer we look at a person, the more detail we discover. Said detail is made up of a million folds, turns and pixels. Each grain of someone's make-up can, in turn, reveal a thousand truths. This was never more true than with Master Su. Su trusted deeply in the universe, regularly holding midnight discussions with the moon and stars, looking for truth in them.

One night in the undefined past, as Master Su was wandering alone through the forest, she came across a lake. The water was shimmering a ghostly white, the moon's reflection found distorted on its surface. Su sat on a tree stump, the forest recently cleared of deadwood and the flat surface offered her a restful perch for her contemplations. She meditated every night. Usually she would stand in front of three red candles and pray to the moon and stars; asking for inspiration, connection and a chance of redemption. On that night, as she sat on the stump she saw bats dashing over the shimmering lake's surface, their nightly hunt for flies and pond-skaters providing a majestic theatre. The bats blew in dark ellipses, a dance held by three or four of them, their movements elegantly coordinated and precise. The fluttering of their fragile wings gave an erratic appearance, but their bodies held the line true and their sight was focussed on their targets. As we all well know bats do not see you like you and I, they rely on echolocation for orientation and navigation. The scatty movements of their prey made this a challenge to them, a challenge they could have avoided. For there are other insects ripe for eating, their search needlessly complex. However, the bats had chosen their targets with this in mind, they needed to maintain their skill in the hunt and not go for low hanging fruit. Their innate ability to see with their ears was one fascination for Su, who imagined a blind genius who understood every word ever said, regardless of language, like a towering personification of Babel. She imagined such a figure wandering through the forest whispering to the bats and betraying the flies exact location, assisting their midnight feasts. A bearded man, shabby attire, lovingly wrinkled eyes and hollowed cheeks, tall of stature and battered of shoe. Master Su felt inspired to create a new tale and made notes as she sat and imagined the blind woodland man. Her rumination on the bats and the blind man took her into a fantasy realm; a world resplendent with miniature messengers for a forest king. She unpacked her notebook and began writing, the words flowing out of her hands as conduits for thought:

The Forest King

The blind man
Sees with his ears
A bat's echolocation
A seer's reconciliation

He towers over all others
His beard hangs low
He is careful what to show
For he does not hear it

He feels every word spoken
Forms landscapes in his mind
His past and future he cannot hear
Only the present is at his feet

And what he says is formed in ways
That you can see just what he means
He does not stutter an utterance to you
He means everything and it rings true

He'll build a tower in the sky
Firm and steady, ready for you and I
And we will climb it and rejoice
In the sound of his wise voice

Master Su's pen dropped from her hand. And she imagined the sound of this voice; a booming, oaky, smoky drone would be typical, she believed. But in Su's head she created a more unique timbre. The sing-song mountains and valleys of a foreign tongue, some deep and some high frequencies. Unpredictable sentence structures and errors in declinations. His gait should be also not that of a phlegmatic, steady older man, but that of a lithe panther, lolling of shoulder and unpredictable. As she imagined him, she called him into being. She envisaged her own shadow-self. Master Su picked up her pen again and was inspired to write of this shadow:

My Soul-Brother

We walk the same streets
We trace paths unmeeting
Not allowed outside
Selling out ourselves

This knife entwine
This life mine
This life yours
Our shadows part

Blood collecting in pools
In our hearts' chambers
As we cut the strings
and hear the explosions in the sky

Forget not
Into oblivion
On these shores
The woodman and the firebird wait

Already she could feel this shadow-self more and more tangibly within her; her animus, her male counterpart. She had long searched for a friend with whom she needn't even have to speak to; to be understood innately.

Master Su's musings on her animus and the woodland man led her to think of the blindness which was pervading modern society. This led to her true purpose. Her forest thinking opened her own eyes to the dire situation in the world. As much as she was guilty of slipping into her own fantasy world, seeking refuge, control, inspiration, at least she was aware of that fact. She was retreating inside, into her imagination as she did it. Master Su was under no illusion, magicians and sorceresses came to prominence in her stories, but she knew that they were not real. She was alone in the forest, in the deep of night. Yet, even in the middle of the day there were only dog walkers, looking for a spot for their dog to defecate without them having to clear it away afterwards. Her ancient ancestors had come from water as fish, climbed the trees as apes and now everyone had fled the forest, fled the reality of nature and sought the warm bosom of technology. The eyes we were given enable us to see so much, storms and rainbows, birth and death and everything in between. The problem now lying before Su was clear. How could we tear the world away from seeing falsified images? The idea of media manipulation and propaganda was nothing new, but now everyone had eye implants which gave them their own rose-tinted, or whatever colour-tinted view of reality. As each person saw fit, they would see their subjective reality, neglect the reality of life and all of its peaks and troughs and routinely, no, consistently trick themselves into believing that all is well, everyone is happy and we are in a wondrous state of progress. It reminded her of the duck and cover advice against the threat of nuclear war and the fingers in the ears denial against hearing the truth.

Master Su saw the culprit as Jason Chamberlain and his Optix technology. Su saw the the idea could have come from any number of different countries or companies. But this Optix technology was implanted in each and every citizen on the planet at birth nowadays; governments the world over had endorsed the technology. It's roll-out spreading across the globe at an unrelenting pace, no single country was able to deny its broad appeal. There were over two billion victims already.

The people of the world were being manipulated, tricked into believing that society was in a better state than it was. Their ignorance being farmed and utilised by Optix, fed into their vast offshore data warehouses and being regurgitated into each person's visual experience. Optix had long passed being a company which only made the world appear brighter, more colourful and new. It was also clear that, in the wrong hands, the truth could be prevented from being revealed. Media outlets, one of the first industries to invest in the Optix augmentations, reporting on urban disrepair, poverty and war were caught in a dilemma. Their ability to report neutrally was compromised, their motivation to show the truth was initially still there, yet once the early adopters and then early majority had their own Optix implants installed, there was no more poverty, ruin and destruction to see. The general public turned a blind eye to all of the bad in the world. It was a safer, cleaner, brighter future which the people tricked themselves into believing. This absolute denial of the truth made Master Su angry about the cowardly nature of the people. They needed to be forthright in facing danger, authenticity and risk, as Michael fought the terrific dragon.

Another critically existential problem came in the disappearance of imagination, the realm of fantasy and the exploration of fiction. It was no longer necessary for people to dream up a better future. It was, of course, still possible to be truly creative and to imagine something truly unique, but these people were usually preoccupied with short-term relief and hedonistic, superficial pleasures; taking the easy way out, absolute avoidance. It was no longer necessary to invest in the real, tangible long-term future when your eyes could be told that everything was okay. Optix had scoured the globe for promising creatives who could be employed as content generators. These people could entertain the world's population. The other half of the wicked operation involved the worker ants, the *'meta-architects'*. Their job was to maintain and develop the nuts and bolts of the operation. Each cubic metre of the world had to become individualised. The standard surfaces were available to all, immaculately painted public buildings in a perfect sandstone colour, which in reality had faded and needed maintenance. But if people wished they could have it painted black, pink, white. All it required was a premium subscription and an architect who could change the textures and colours. The trick was to cater for every whim and make people feel like they were special. The content creators did a fine job in identifying trends and manipulating them as such so that a great majority shared a similar taste, thus reducing a degree of cost and risk, while at the same time increasing predictability. It had worked in clothing fashions for decades, where the colours for the upcoming seasonal collections had been decided industry-wide two years in advance. They needed to make the people feel like it was their own individual choice and that it reflected their vibrant, unique and informed personality. With that free will had become a mere illusion.

The enormous army of developers was also a worldwide phenomenon. Chamberlain had established his own academies of programmers all over, using government grants and subsidies to expand at a great pace. The so-called architects continually created a falsified reality, ever morphing and drifting further and further from the truth. This expansion of the Optix technology was first targeted driven by young people and trend leaders. But the integration of the technology across all demographics was made possible through careful negotiations with industry leaders and lobbyists in the fields of medicine, the military, policing and economics. For the middle-aged, it became a standard treatment for those requiring reading glasses. They would see sharp in the near, middle and far distance for ever more. The police were able to utilise the polarised light filters to better catch criminals. Marketeers were able to fully customise advertising and products to suit every single potential customer. As the technology became more sophisticated it was possible, as a result of corrupt long-term negotiations with the UN and humanitarian organisations, to have the technology implanted into new-born children. Such early installation was found to support improved cognitive development, early motor skills, improve school grades, long-term income and this would therefore also increase tax income for each individual government in the long run. The financial benefits were overwhelming for each individual state and, without exception, every member state signed up.

On the state, continent and global level Optix became the standard. The reputation and reliability of the technology unquestioned. However, some rebelled, campaigned, fought and lost their lives resisting the technology. Some political opponents were silenced, some quite normal citizens simply disappeared. They were however very much in the minority, either dying of old age, being invisible or simply fading into the background and lacking the ability to form a cohesive resistance. The remaining people went underground, rejected the implants, remained true to reality and used their own sense of imagination and discovery. Where they were exactly remained a secret, for fear of discovery. One of these people was Master Su and she made it her mission to help the blind rediscover their vision, within and without. She had made plans to groom potential leaders for change, setting structures in place to lead a resistance and change the world.

In time long before our story, Master Su looked once more at the bats flying over the lake, though most of them were still not satisfied, the flies proving elusive despite their best efforts. The most successful bats kept their focus on one particular fly, ignoring the swarm, and didn't give up. They simply flew away when they had enjoyed their fill. Su had to find a potential candidate from within. She needed to thoroughly scour the planet for members of Chamberlain's organisation with the potential to change the course of human existence. By finding an insider with a tortured conscience, Su would be able to exploit aspects of the technology and use them against Optix, bring down Chamberlain from inside his own baby.

One night in the Bluebird Hotel Master Su sent out her feelers online via Platform for potential candidates. As we well know by now Lamorna was her most promising result. Others were also considered, but either lacked courage, knowledge, intelligence or were already too outspoken against the direction the Optix organisation was taking. She needed someone who could be trusted. Someone who, ideally, was already entrusted with a good deal of responsibility in the organisation and also knew the famous Jason Chamberlain personally. She whittled the candidates down to a shortlist of five and created an account of her own on Platform. As probably already guessed by now, the name of her profile was '*Pepper*', a bit of good old fashioned spice.

Master Su needed to be careful in her approach. She first set up an account with some nerdy meme content, some pictures of various meals and videos of concerts so as to lend her account some authenticity. It wasn't difficult, but Su needed to bide her time. These candidates were pros and they would sniff out a fake account on Platform quite easily if it simply seemed to spring fully formed out of the ether. The posts needed to be curated, paced and seem genuine. So Su, AKA Pepper really did go out, share memes, watch live bands, getting nearly deafened in the process. She kind of enjoyed it, she hadn't done so many of these things in her youth and liked the idea of making up for lost time. The material of her baggy blue jeans was blown by the bass frequencies at the loudest of concerts, but she most of the time she stood awkwardly at the back of the venue with her arms folded.

The memory of the deafening music reminded Su of the bats. Theoretically, she could close her eyes and just about locate the loudspeaker from which those bass frequencies were emanating. But Su stuck to the task at hand and remained diligent. She slowly started liking posts belonging to the candidates, watched their video posts, but still remained careful, cool and aloof. Once this had progressed for a number of weeks she would formally ask to follow their public accounts and to her great satisfaction, having judged their characters thus far correctly, they followed her in return. And so began a tentative back and forth, some simple exchanges here and there. Master Su would leave comments on their photos and started messaging the first three candidates; she left Lamorna and another for a while as she deemed them the most promising of the five and didn't want to risk losing them by making noob mistakes in the chat. She approached them with questions on music, it was a perfect way in. Their discussions went off in different directions; philosophy, art and music were the most common topics, Master Su was careful as to not leap in head first and broach the topic of an Optix-led dystopia, brainwashing humanity and leading to the death of free thought. After a time she allowed these contacts to die down, Su maintained a degree of interaction with them, not wishing to simply drop them. She still recognised their potential, perhaps there was a chance for a collaboration in the future. These contacts could ally with those in the underground and create an uprising to help bring down Optix.

Lamorna, however, was different. She seemed to practically live on Platform. Her *'close friends'* list on her profile seemed to be limited to people she could only feasibly know online. Su made sure to do her research into them too, in case more colleagues at Optix were to be found there. Her caution was in the end unfounded. Lamorna had contacts in Poland, Sweden, Brazil, Finland, Russia. From all over, yet few people from her hometown in Cornwall and nobody from work. Master Su found this most promising. It wasn't only the pure abject loneliness that she could sense, it was a spirit yearning to fully reach out and establish meaningful contact. This was something Master Su could empathise with. Su's own young isolation and loneliness, combined with being overworked were also very much things Su could sympathise with. Looking back Su thought that Lamorna was such a good fit, not because of the lonely soul, but the very clear hunger for truth, which Master Su saw as her duty to assist Lamorna in attaining. The world was behind a veil for generations of people, the newborn would never know anything different, unless Master Su's work was done. Lamorna would be they key to the door, or indeed the door handle itself. Master Su had a particularly vibrant imagination, sometimes finding patterns, objects and scenes which became a motto, target or inspiration for her. None more so than a door handle which she once found near a ruin of a monastery. The brass handle, curved like a treble clef, lay among the ivy near a decrepit loose stone wall. There was no archway, doorway or indeed door in the vicinity to which it belonged. Su even enquired at the nearby chapel whether it was theirs, even going as far as speaking to the caretaker. He had never seen it before and he explained how all of their handles were stainless steel and the caretaker allowed her to keep it and sent Master Su on her way.

Su took the brass door handle with her wherever she went, just in case she found the fitting counterpart. It was only about twelve centimetres long and she always found space for it; it was simultaneously a problem and a possible solution for her; her own symbolical paradox. It weighed heavily on her mind and she, after a time, became frustrated with her lack of progress. Had she scoured the right territories? Had she spoken to the right people? Could they even see the compatible door if it were right in front of them? Despite the taxing nature of her mission, the door handle being only a small part of this, Master Su was resilient, focused and hopeful. The door through which Su would then go involved opening the people's eyes to the reality of life, seeing the beauty and inelegance of being. To feel the true surfaces and not to feel an artificial synaptic response generated by engineers hunched over desks. This real life which Master Su was fighting to redeem was indeed her true purpose. And she had to start with individuals, seeking them and then beginning a dialogue. Expanding a network of like-minded souls and helping humanity to find itself once more; she needed to act cautiously and protect her own identity, by adopting the Pepper persona online.

It was with Pepper that Lamorna opened up. Without any shadow of a doubt Su she knew that Lamorna wouldn't have been able to communicate so freely had they met in person sooner. They exchanged messages via Platform for months on end before Su instructed Xerxo to make contact with Lamorna and to pass on the message, also leaving Renn outside for her. Xerxo had been a dear old friend to Su, having helped her out many dark years before she had become a master and learned to live freely.

Pepper had become an important social connection to Lamorna, Su was aware of that, nevertheless she struggled to reconcile that action with her conscience. Su saw this untruth, this lie indeed, as a necessary, lesser evil in order to establish contact with Lamorna in order to earn her trust and to set her on her path. A possible earlier meeting with Lamorna she rejected out of hand, at regular intervals. Su preferred to test Lamorna's resolve and to audit Lamorna's true desires and motivations.

Of course, Master Su had a problem when it came to a physical meeting with Lamorna. She could see how Lamorna was too busy with work to just make time for friends, despite them writing to each other and needed to force her hand. By getting Xerxo involved and the magic bicycle Renn, a riddle and a lavish penthouse apartment she was able to coax Lamorna better into believing in the cause; of this she was quite sure. It was a good job that Master Su could use a proxy for the second meeting along with Zho.Kinn, AKA George. Su was sure to use another apprentice of hers for the mission, a particularly promising one who was schooled on the topic of *'Lamorna'* well in advance and had complete access to all of Su and Lamorna's chats on Platform. Master Su was a meticulous planner, after all. The time was nigh, Pepper would be called into existence.

6 - PLATFORM

Three days later Lamorna sat eating breakfast inspecting the wooden box. She looked at the fine olive wood finish, the beautiful dovetail joints and the curved edges. Real expertise went into making it, without question. But for the life of her she couldn't fathom the reasoning behind the ball of sand. It held itself together by an invisible force. She could hold it in her hand and it didn't come apart, neither did grains of sand come off. Yet it was most certainly completely sand, the weight distribution would have been all off if it had a metal, rubber or wooden core. These weren't merely sand grains stuck on to a golf ball or anything. She thought on a number of science fiction stories she knew: *'Was this a key, a soul gem, a camera? Was it an heirloom from a distant galaxy, an often fought-over quest item, poised to trigger an interplanetary war?'* She carefully placed it back into the box and then stuffed it into her drawer, preferring to ignore it.

Lamorna made her way to the sofa, pushing t-shirts and socks to the side. She wrote to her Platform friends Pepper and Zho that morning; they didn't live all that far away and she needed to finally go out and see people. The meeting with Master Su had shaken her out of a century-long slumber. The interaction had been like that with some kind of alien, a being from another plane entirely. Yet at the same time it was as if Su had always been either five steps ahead or behind her the entire time, trailing or leading she could not say.

Zho and Pepper she really had each known for a good number of months, it must have been three or four by now. At first they exchanged opinions on photography or music and that progressed to an almost daily exchange of messages about all sorts. Until she met Master Su, Lamorna only really discussed her work or her hobbies with them. Lamorna's previous reticence about suggesting a meet had been born out of the fear of rejection and then embarrassing herself. She imagined that they wouldn't want to meet up anyway, had better things to do and more interesting people to see. Maybe they did. Maybe she was just being neurotic. In any case Lamorna figured that the risk was worth taking. What was the worst thing that could happen? Either they say no and things continue pretty much as they were or they slowly drift apart. If they did indeed begin to lose touch then that was going to happen anyway and she didn't need to waste her time second guessing what might or might not be.

In her daily work she had to hold too many different possibilities in her head and she didn't need that in her private life she surmised. *'I need to take more risks, live a little and put my neck out'*, she told herself. As a kid she hadn't really taken the first steps when it came to making friends and as a result was most probably seen as being disinterested and reclusive. Maybe she just didn't need many people to surround herself with. She certainly wasn't one for larger gatherings, always feeling awkward around new people and struggling to find her words; her eventual mutterings merely being a lo-fi version of what was going on in her head. By the time the words could come out of her own mouth, her own thoughts were already three steps ahead. Forgetting vitally important information in a conversation just as it might be relevant, yet remembering irrelevant snippets of trivia and shoehorning them into the conversation. Yes, that was Lamorna's superpower. Maybe she was also just overly choosy? Did the prospective friends need to mirror an aspect of her personality in order for them to be of interest to her? Did she select them like one may clothe themselves each morning. Not capriciously and dropping them daily, but curated, into a certain style; combinations of complimentary colours, or at least shades of faded black. Put together like a well organised menagerie of glass animals, kept for special occasions, not for daily play.

She made her way into the park, Zho and Pepper were stood chatting on the bridge as Lamorna approached. Pepper was clad in an oversized black hoodie with the name of a random American university on it, the logo faded from repeated washes. She stood hunched and her black hair was lank and greasy. Zho appeared much taller, had a heavily receding hairline and the kind of flat arse and meaty paunch only a middle class, middle aged man could have.

"Hey, you guys!", Lamorna merrily greeted them.

"You came at last", Zho replied and they each hugged Lamorna. They took a walk and observed the beautiful trees and bushes growing there, Lamorna was somewhat manic and skittish. They seemed to have similar Optix versions installed and could share and compare their views on the colours of the leaves, the shape of the trees and the arrangements of the flowers. Soon they got to talking about Lamorna's work, her exhaustion and her struggle to deal with the workload Chamberlain was expecting of her at Optix. She ran through all which was on her mind that day, only skimping on the finer details of her meeting in the cafe, the sentient bicycle and meeting a sorceress.

Pepper was a trained photographer, very quick-witted and in a not dissimilar predicament to Lamorna in that she was under appreciated at work and yet stuck in the hamster-wheel. They exchanged inspirations through music and shared thoughts on topics like art, ethics and politics. They had been sharing these thoughts for a few months, lived about forty kilometres from each other and had incredibly not yet met in real life. Lamorna had half-heartedly broached the subject, but Pepper had preferred to keep the meetings online; she must have had her reasons and Lamorna respected that, not wanting to push too hard and risk losing one of the only friends she had.

Pepper told of her new hobby: Every Tuesday and Thursday she went kickboxing and simply envisioned her boss's head being beaten to a pulp, whether by hand or foot. That was her way of venting, saving hundreds on therapy.

Zho.Kinn, real name George Keane, also had problems sleeping, just like Lamorna; his job as a university lecturer kept him awake for long hours at night and he also basically ran on fifty-percent Adderall and fifty-percent pure diesel caffeine. He gave Lamorna a pack of sleeping tablets he used so that he could manage to get the four hours of sleep he needed to function. Lamorna was thankful of any help she could get.

They mused and whimsied deep into the evening, laying out thoughts for a much fairer, more enlightened world. Their discussions were tinged with sarcasm, irony and criticism of existing structures. In a pique of creative fervour and on a whim they wrote up a list of new commandments for a better world:

1. *You shall not betray your friends*
2. *You must not betray yourself*
3. *You should buy fewer things, reuse them and then recycle them*
4. *Think for yourself, question authority*
5. *The first minister's word was law (Zho is president, Lamorna is the vice, George is treasurer)*
6. *All new members must follow the above rules*

The list went on and became more and more far-fetched and ridiculous. They were painfully self-aware that their tendencies reached into totalitarian territories and they leant in hard. It was all just a game for them and they each quickly forgot to write a real manifesto or print pamphlets.

They worked well, a balanced team. A kind of three-legged stool. Where even the shortest leg helped the stool stay upright. They had those kinds of long silences which were never awkward, they just were there, like the pauses in a piece of music or ad breaks between episodes. They made their way to a collection of elegant recliners, looking out over the pond in the middle of the park and spent another hour sharing short stories, mostly about being happy to be outside and finally meeting, not being alone in their respective flats. Lamorna told a little about meeting Master Su, how she had opened her eyes to a few things; holding back from divulging too much. She asked them if they knew that feeling of being verbally pummelled into submission by someone. "I'm just glad I'm self-employed", Pepper giggled as a reply. Perhaps Master Su was just another con artist, just laying in wait for another victim. Or maybe she was a person to provide a well-placed spark.

Coming back to her friends, Lamorna told herself she needed to do this much more often, the four walls had been getting ever closer over the past few years and she was rarely out with anyone, even just on her own. This park was not far away and it was ridiculous that she hadn't spent much time there before. The evening whimsy gave way to tired reality and they each went their separate ways. Like two lovers who rolled out of bed and left their night behind. They promised each other they would meet again a lot sooner. Three or four more months would really be too much time. Lamorna had been growing frustrated at having these great talks, yet never meeting the people she was having them with, finally, that had changed. And that change wasn't something she felt all alone. Upon arriving home Lamorna kicked off her shoes and flung herself on the sofa, put on a film and passed out soon after, George's tablets really worked wonders.

7 - LAKE SWIMMING

A good week later, after a difficult night's sleep Lamorna was awoken by the beeping of her phone's alarm. It was 8.30 a.m. and the sleeping tablets she had procured from George had left her feeling groggy. She supposed that is what happened when you fell asleep only at 2.30 a.m. She felt like her limbs were manacled, but her head was acutely sharp and wide awake. She had arranged to meet Master Su in the nearby forest after lunch and she had some chores to do beforehand. Lamorna showered and made herself breakfast, half-heartedly tidied her flat, moving books from one table to another and stacking the washing-up into one orderly pile of plates, bowls and cups. The last week at Optix had been nuts and she had heard enough of Chamberlain's rantings at the Alpha team. She would leave the proper cleaning and washing-up for yet another day; Lamorna had already worked enough and it was time for the weekend.

By the time lunchtime approached she felt pretty exhausted. What did she even do until so late into the night? She must have spent at least three hours messaging Zho and Pepper on Platform, reviewing their commandments and plotting world domination. If she were the leader of a cult, she would be sure to do a better job of it than Chamberlain, she chuckled to herself. Lamorna warmed up some pizza from the previous evening's take-away to eat for lunch, ate a couple of apples to go with it and then got ready to meet Master Su. Lamorna donned her hiking boots and a warm jacket, it had rained a lot in the night and the going would be soft. She got on her bike and took the short journey up to the forest.

The rain had left plenty of puddled pools of water to

ride through and Lamorna revelled in splashing through them. She didn't care how dirty her trousers got, she had been wearing them for seven days straight without anyone else noticing anyway and they could do with a wash anyhow. The short way to the forest took her past tall blocks of flats, looking like towers of strong bamboo out of an anime or flag poles. Her own flat was in a smaller building and she was happy not to be stranded high up on the thirty-sixth floor like Su. If absolutely necessary, Lamorna reasoned, she could climb out of her flat and down the side of the building, if and when she needed to make a quick getaway. She often had such fantasies and thoughts of quickly having to flee. A fall from the third floor would unlikely be fatal, although some serious injury would be possible if she misjudged the factors and her calculations were off. Thoughts of escape came to her quite unprompted and typically revolved around some kind of natural disaster, rather than a home invasion. She was aware of the wind and rain outside in the dark hours of the night, having grown accustomed to trusting her ears rather than her eyes.

The path took her between residential zones, the buildings rising high between as she rode under tree cover, turning off her Optix implants she realised they were only street lights. Without her implants on she soon felt a queasiness in her gut, a general feeling of uneasiness. The world seemed so much sadder and only consisting of grey tones. Each street corner was run down, the shops which were open had faded posters and signs stuck to their windows with tape; print advertising had almost faded out of existence, disappearing like images on bleached fast food menus on sunny shores. This form of advertising had been all but completely replaced by a personalised visual marketing, catering to your every desire, chosen and curated for you and fed directly into your immaculately gilded trough.

It was, as mentioned before, a quite short ride for Lamorna, travelling east towards the forest and its gently rolling hills. The mist had come over in the night and the dew was still hanging on the snowdrop flowers as Lamorna approached. They were shimmering in the midday sunshine still, having remained in the shade until now. The beauty she observed in the forest was like fire to the ice of the dull urban cityscape. The midday light shone down through the Douglas fir trees, the bracken and moss provided a warm blanket on the forest floor. It looked so comfortable and inviting that Lamorna considered going back to bed and taking a thick slice of the moss with her, its bright green buds making a most tessellating pattern as a bedcover. Or even better, she could just gather the bracken and moss right there and build herself a hovel in the depths of the forest.

Lamorna spied Master Su in the mid-distance, who was stood waiting in her sapphire blue robes, which was in fact a thick wool coat with open gaping sleeves, tapering up to the shoulder. Su was stood with her arms folded as Lamorna dismounted and locked her bike to a post. As she did she was reminded of Renn, the autonomous bike, and wondered where it had gotten to. She hadn't seen it since her journey to the Bluebird hotel, a journey which felt like it had taken place a decade or so before. For when Lamorna was with Master Su time was a great irrelevance. For one thing, they paid it no mind. The day, their meetings, the topics they discussed melted into one. Their discourse had its own flow. There were moments and indeed passages where nothing was said; their views cast over the lakes or in the tree canopies above. Other times each one of them was bursting with five topics each, simultaneously which needed to be written down and remembered for later, lest the chance forever disappear and the bud of an idea be lost.

Each time they met, however, it took a bit of a run-up for them to start their conversations, as if it needed the cranking of an old vintage motor. More often than not Lamorna, exhilarated from a swift bike ride uphill, would info dump on Su and get a thousand words out a minute, not holding back, telling Su of all possible things. The banalities of work, the frivolities of play and a quick run-down of a plethora of different philosophy and sociology podcasts. Lamorna would seemingly monologue and rant, while Master Su patiently listened, sometimes mustering a smile, often not. While Lamorna was regaling tales of deadlines met and describing some new music she had discovered, Su was reminded of her own work; it had not been easy to leave it behind as she absconded into the forest with Lamorna. Exactly what Su's work entailed was lost on her companion and collaborator. Lamorna prodded and provoked, looking for chinks in Su's considerable armour, to no avail. While she was acutely aware that it involved the care of others, a form of education perhaps, necessitating deliberated planning. She was never truly able to penetrate Master Su's authentic self in the forest. The protections that Su had built up over the years kept out such prying endeavours and she was able to deflect, redirect and ignore most attempts at digging deeper. Some people Master Su had come to know in her life, logically, assumed that this cold, harsh veneer was constructed to communicate disinterest and ambivalence, even dislike.

But this was not the truth. These protections had been constructed for her own self-preservation. As a child of a loveless set of parents, who mostly spent her young life fighting, Su was quick to retreat to her inner world. She had no siblings to really speak of, her school friends also lacking in terms of quality and quantity, her interests were too specific and unpopular. Master Su very early learned to connect with the written word, studying hard in alien worlds, enchanted kingdoms and fantastic legends. Even in her meetings with Lamorna, thirty plus years later, she would wax poetic on stories, literature from far flung lands, from hills far away. Lamorna, after her initial info dumping on Su, would settle in and listen to a tale or two, invariably shaking her head and admitting ignorance of such stories and was beguiled by them. Forest spirits who would protect visitors, witches granting wishes, nymphs pulling unsuspecting bathers underwater, giants who smote their enemies upon rocks, birds of flame soaring to the sun.

"Lamorna, there are some stories which are truer than you believe. Despite their setting and flights of fancy, despite the moral of the story ringing true and all of that, they actually happened. Do you believe that to be possible?", Master Su asked while sipping yet more claret from a plastic beaker.

"I would have to hear it, to believe it", Lamorna replied.

And so Su told Lamorna of a particular tale of a fair maiden trapped in a cellar, kept hostage by a mountain ogre for many years:

"There once was a closeted woman who lived in a far away kingdom, shy of sunlight and life. Having been taken from her parent's cottage as a young child by a mean old ogre, she had been ripped away from all warmth and love. The sweet, sensitive girl had spent her entire life underground, bereft of all she held dear. The pain and doubt that she had experienced in all those tender young years had become her normality.

The young girl had since turned into a woman. Although she had spent so much time in the cellar dwellings where the ogre kept her, she had not furnished the walls with images or icons of comfort. She had not made it into her home. Her wish for decoration, for finesse and sophistication she was saving for her next life. She had known no one else but the ogre, wide and dominating figure who rarely let her out of his sight. On occasions when the ogre would leave his own home he would tether a chain to the woman which kept her tied to her desk. How she pleaded with the ogre to take her outside, how she desired to see the outside world with her own eyes again.

In the past she had only made one attempt to escape. While the ogre was on a foraging exhibition in a neighbouring land she had made contact with a passer-by. Through her small window, just below the ceiling, she began a conversation with a small boy. He had been in the garden rummaging for food in the allotment. When she spoke to him he quickly ran away and was never seen by her again.

To break out the woman needed help from outside. She had tried conversing with others, but that time the wicked ogre had warned the townsfolk from talking to her. 'She is a cold witch who will eat your children, prey on your elders and cause your harvest to rot', he would tell them. From that day onwards she only heard their timid footsteps and faint whispers.

On wet days the rain from the street ran down into her cellar, on snowy days the light would be completely blocked out and eventually the window became overgrown with plants. When the sun did shine there came some faint, obfuscated light into her life, where there was otherwise none. She lived from day to day paralysed, in her mind, body and soul. She asked herself how she could get out, how to change the townsfolk's weak minds, whether she could charm the old ogre. Her window was sturdily built, the door was always bolted. The townsfolk had ignored her cries for years as a maiden, ever since her first attempt to escape; due to the ogre's warnings she felt more feared than the ogre himself. She sang songs of joy and painted pictures of hope, wrote poems of love and elegies of redemption. Yet the people did not listen. Her bitter life was left unchanged.

She turned her attentions and efforts to her captor. She tried to charm and enchant him, soften his stone heart, woo him. Yet, for all his obvious superficial disadvantages as an ogre, he was no fool. He knew she felt no real love for him and was quite aware of her attempts at manipulation. As a young ogre he very quickly had become aware of how others saw him and so his ugly, stumbling facade he used to mask his inner being: that of a quiet and intelligent beast. They were both utterly isolated from town life and this prevented her from opening her heart to him. He also knew not how to show any love, a prisoner of his own rocky demeanour.

The captive woman spent her time in books, learning of the local wildlife, history and geography. The ogre had allowed her this simple pleasure; his own intellect compelled him to provide her with books. She buried herself in them, reading five or six at a time. Tales of valiant heroes, horrific monsters, sentient birds, unclimbable mountains and deft deception. The birds took her interest, able to fly huge distances, whether alone or as part of a group. She learnt of their feeding habits, social behaviour, breeding patterns, migrations and nesting areas. She herself hatched a plan.

The poor woman's weekly rations were brought at the start of the week, early in the morning while she still slept. The food she had to prepare herself. In recent times she had implemented a new tactic: She kept back some of the berries and seeds, having picked the nicest ones and she left them outside her small cellar window, knowing that some of the local birds fed on them in winter. After a few weeks she noticed hit was the very same crane bird that always came to visit her: Upon its beak was a small black speck. As the weeks passed the woman eagerly awaited her visit from the crane, until in mid-winter it was nowhere to be seen. She feared that it had died, got lost or *forgotten the way. Then she remembered the information from her books and the long winter migration. She had to wait again until the warmer months for the bird to come back. The woman had already waited a long twenty years under the ground and she passed the time with her books, even writing some of her own."*

Lamorna enquired: "Why didn't she cry for help? She could have gone on a hunger strike or threatened suicide."

Master Su, looking didn't look up. She merely stated in a low voice: "The woman was focussed on true, living freedom. At all costs." Then she continued the story:

"Once the snow had cleared and the morning dew took its place the ground came to life again. She could see how much lighter the days became by seeing how much of the mould on the opposing wall was visible. Other than reading and writing the woman had been busy. Knowing that certain foods were inedible to cranes she had constructed a message to be hidden inside an eggshell. After the first cool weeks of spring were over she started to leave food outside again for the returning cranes. For the first weeks there was no sign of them, nor the black-specked one. Yet still she placed the seeds outside, along with some vegetable peel. Come late spring the bird came back to her. The next week she carried out her plan: the eggshell she very carefully wrapped with carrot peel and left outside her window, the crane took it in its beak and flew away. Yet more weeks the woman sat reading and waiting in the cellar, thankful for the longer days, bringing more and more sunlight."

"Surely she could bribe someone to get help for her. Or offer payment for them to help her directly. I still don't understand how she could remain there for so long." Master Su ignored Lamorna's complaints and went on:

"*Across the town stood a large castle which also housed an academy of wizardry. An apprentice was walking of a morning and stumbled across an ailing bird at the side of the road. He inspected the large white bird, for it was the crane which had visited the captive woman, and saw that it did not seem injured. The crane panicked when he came upon it and moved to fly, yet it was unable to. The wizard recoiled in fear as the crane frantically fluttered its wings; he flinched and wanted to run away, but he felt drawn to it. The crane struggled and gave a whimper, he wanted to place his hand on its side and comfort it. He knelt down and wrestled with his fears, wondering how to best help the poor bird. He had not yet learnt any restoration magic and felt unable to outright heal the thing. He hesitated and then stood up again, pacing back down the road. 'I must help it' he told himself, 'It needs me to do something'. His sweat was pouring down his back, beneath his thick novice robes. And so he very slowly began to move closer to the bird. As he did so the crane spread out its wings to their full width and made to fly away. The wings flattered and vibrated, making the air around the apprentice wizard flurry and dance. At last the crane took to the air and landed a short distance away, in the process revealing a perfectly formed golden egg. The glistening brilliance of the egg took the wizard aback and drew him in closer. He made to pick it up and then saw that the egg was beginning to crack open. It moved, as if the egg itself was alive, not a bird inside, but the shell was the exoskeleton of a further being. The shell split further open until it laid open, like a lily, revealing a small rolled-up piece of parchment inside, which on it read:*

> *Buried beneath the ogre,*
> *dwells a maiden in her deepest hell.*
> *Turn the lock and handle with care,*
> *Let down your auburn hair*

The apprentice did not know what to make of the riddle. He understood on the surface that this was a call for help, or a joke, perhaps even a trap. However, his natural curiosity led him down a trail of further adventure. Regardless of risk or possible error he knew that it was his time to be bold, for his trials were coming in the academy and he needed to be more forthright with his spell-casting. He took the riddle back to his master in the academy and watched the crane fly away."

Lamorna turned to Master Su and asked: "Are you telling me that the woman's message landed at just the right person's feet and I am supposed to believe that?"

"We don't tell the stories of those women whose efforts forever failed. By sheer definition this story is something extraordinary and wild", Su responded. "It would be neither newsworthy nor special if we learned that this young girl had neither been kidnapped, nor held captive. Not abused, nor rescued. This is her story and there is no parallel for her. She survived that. She found the help she needed. She made sure of that. She cast the necessary spells and made the necessary sacrifices. Can you do those things, Lamorna?"

"But that is just a fairy tale, people do not get kidnapped by trolls and kept against their will in real life. There is no goose laying golden eggs". Lamorna retorted, growing frustrated.

"Crane."

"Yes, a crane. People today have a choice. They don't need to do what other people tell them, they don't get sold off into marriage like in the medieval times."

"Quite true", Su responded. "Yet, people can become trapped and forced to live without light for years on end; fed only on scraps and be completely without hope. It is for them that we continue to tell these stories, lest they forget this parallel reality they are living in, blind to the truth laid out before them. Please allow me to continue, dear Lamorna." And thus she did:

"*The apprentice wizard, upon reaching the academy, climbed the stony stairs, opened the door to his chambers and sat in his red leather chair. His feet were weary from the pace he had maintained underfoot. The wizard was unsure where to start. The business with the golden egg, the crane, the ogre and the maiden kept him awake all night. In his mind he wrestled with the words on the parchment. Knowing of no ogre, nor having seen any records of golden eggs, he had learnt from his master to look at problems the other way around and so he started trying to read the riddle back to front. Sat in his dark chamber he whispered the words 'let down your auburn hair' to himself. He was immediately reminded of a tale from a neighbouring kingdom, where a captive was held in a tower for a long year. Eventually, once her hair was already reaching the floor, she had the cunning idea to collect the odd bedsheet and then tie them together once she had enough ,whereupon she managed to escape her prison. The king still had a reward out for her return, as far as he was aware. Should he collect bedsheets? Should he grow his hair long? And where was the secret messenger? He had no way to find them. But then he reminded himself to maintain focus on that line of the riddle: 'let down your auburn hair'. He thought of all of the possible connections with the words contained in the line itself. Hair, rhymes with hare, a rabbit. Lower a rabbit down into a cave, perhaps? Auburn, golden, red, glowing, burning, afire, arson. He played with the images in his mind. Linguistics and conjuration were his favourite combinations of academy subjects.*

The apprentice wizard moved onto the penultimate line: 'turn the lock and handle with care'. That could have something to do with fragility, glass, decoration, brittle bones, some kind of withering thing, he told himself. Without doubt there is a threshold to pass in order to free someone, or something. Some kind of boundary, no doubt particularly well guarded and dangerous. When it comes to turning a lock, perhaps there is a deceit, a picking of a mechanism to be done, some thievery and trickery involved. The wizard looked back on his hitherto closeted and carefully led life. He inevitably became a wizard, just as his father wanted, he had rarely given his own path a thought. Now he was faced with an adventure, risk and novelty. And he was scared; facing the crane had been scary enough for him.

The lines 'dwells a maiden in her deepest hell' and 'buried beneath the ogre' were clear enough; merely scene setting. But who was to be saved and from whom? The lack of an ogre in the town befuddled him, wracking his brain as he scratched his scalp nervously. The ogre must be a shut-in, a lonely figure tired of being stared at and having stones thrown at him. Theoretically at least, the maiden would be even more of a problem to find, unless there was a clear link to some kind of monster, brute or bully. The apprentice grew weary and decided to ruminate on the lines while drinking some tea and changing into his bedclothes. The hour was late and he had his trials coming up. He cycled through the four lines in his mind as he closed his eyes and imagined an underground prison, guarded by a beast, a fair princess held against her will and an enchanted door handle whose spell was needed to be broken. He dreamt of fairies in golden cages mounted on trees, sea nymphs guarding an underwater palace, a great sea monster circling the depths and a mermaid kept against her will. The apprentice further dreamt of hands hanging from trees, blinded old wizards and talking oaks. His dreams mixed and melded together and as he woke in the morning in a flurry of bewildered excitement he leapt to his feet and shouted out of the tower: 'I have found it, I must to the library. There I will find my answers to the riddle!' And so he alighted to the vast library in the castle. He ran from his room as fast as his young feet would carry him, almost forgetting to don his dressing gown beforehand."

Master Su looked over at Lamorna, who was lying on her back on the forest floor with her eyes closed. "Carry on", said Lamorna. She was as far away from falling asleep as was possible. It was difficult enough for her at the best of times, let alone whilst lying on roots and damp ground, but that was of little concern at present.

"The apprentice, upon reaching the library, stumbled on the thick carpet laid out at the entrance, let out a loud 'oof' and apologised to the two other wizards in the room. Even though it was only around five in the morning, there were always other wizards in the library. It was as if there weren't enough dusty beds to go around. As he perused the shelves until his eyes fell upon a special book in one of the far bookcases. He discovered a book waiting for him on the shelf of legend and lore, handwritten and barely touched. Its spine was red and regaled in golden lettering: 'The Tales of Wonder and Mystery'. After plucking it from the shelf our dear young sorcerer scanned the ornate lettering, ignored the foreword and concentrated on the titles of the stories. The book contained around forty stories, of towers, mermaids, snow covered islands and also ogres. Naturally, he swiftly turned to the story of the ogre and read its contents as if hungry and unfed for days. Here the tale provided him with enough insight into the beast's nature to understand their innate jealousy, greed and aggression. Their weakness to shiny objects and lack of flexibility would be aspects for him to exploit.

Satisfied with his near immediate findings, he turned back to the contents and was about to close the red book and rest it back onto the shelf whence it came, when he spotted another story: 'The Red Rope of Hell'. He made for the corresponding page and found it to be completely blank. There was no single word visible to him. He felt the surface of the paper and felt no bumps, ridges or lines. There was a subtle blemish on the page in the vague shape of an arrow. Following the direction of the arrow he felt a small flap and lifted the page, revealing a secret compartment embedded in the pages. Inside was a dark red velvet pouch, with the initials 'RRH' embossed onto it in gold lettering. He lifted the pouch out of the book and felt movement inside; a wriggle and a squirm. The apprentice recoiled in fear and let out a small yelp; sweat appeared on his brow. The pouch continued to slowly morph in shape whilst in his hands. It was little more than one hand's width in size but it was quite heavy. Full of fear at that point he remembered his master's words: 'Those without fear have no reason to be brave'. He summoned all his courage and pulled at the cord to loosen the knot. Peering inside he saw a thin red rope which glistened even inside the dark red pouch. The resplendent sheen of its surface gave it the appearance of movement, a kind of mesmerising coiling. The apprentice reached into the pouch and the rope began to move and coil around his fingers and then wrist, swiftly making its way up his forearm; like a small sea snake slithering silently. There was absolute silence in the room, the kind when a bad joke is told or the announcement of a loved one's passing is made. The other, older wizards were none the wiser. The apprentice only breathed in, sucking all of the air he could into his lungs for fear of it being his last breath.

The rope, about three quarters of an inch in diameter, continued to climb his arm. It moved with a silken elegance, reaching up now to his shoulder until his entire arm was covered with a red, vibrating glow. At one end of the rope, coiled around his thumb was there was an enlarged knot, the loose ends of which formed the forked tongue of a snake. As much as he tried he could not loosen the grip of the rope. Neither did it react and squeeze him any tighter, nor did it relax. It remained joined to him and held him close, as if being held by a good friend. The horror of the situation was now plain to see and the other two wizards shared a glance and merely tutted at the poor young apprentice's plight, who fought and tugged at his arm and the red rope of Hell only held him tighter. His yelps were falling on almost completely deaf ears. The more he fought it, the tighter the red rope of Hell gripped him. At a loss at what to do he collapsed against the bookcase and slid down until he was sat on the floor. He just sat looking at the red rings of thread which made up the rope, all of the glistening strands of that magnificent object. And then he realised that it too had relinquished its tight grip, though with every movement he made, the rope would move and ripple and be ready to grip him hard once more. The apprentice pocketed the pouch and closed the red book, 'The Tales of Wonder and Mystery', and placed it back on the shelf. He gathered up a stray dark blue gown hanging on the back of one of the old red leather armchairs and made for the door."

"This wizard's apprentice sure knows what to do, doesn't he?", Lamorna surmised. "He knows exactly which room to enter, which book to lift from the shelf, to which chapter to turn, how to find the secret compartment and to allow the rope to climb his arm."

"He is the figure of our story. If he had done it any other way, it wouldn't have been worth telling. In a parallel world somewhere we would hear the famous tale of a young wizard who couldn't escape that particular room, never found any magic book and died a wrinkled old man without having experienced such adventure. But that it is not the story we are weaving, Lamorna dear."

"Or maybe he would have died of a heart attack there and then. Also, if he had stayed in the castle forever, he would not be worth writing about. Is that what you are trying to tell me, Su?", Lamorna returned.

"Only partially, for every person has a story to tell; a

young man turns old in a number of different ways, be they mental, physical or emotional. The point is what do we need to take from this particular tale? The rope plays a role, also the wizard's naïveté, as well as the ogre and the trapped woman. In the tale of the young wizard trapped in the castle there is also much to glean from, but we must save that for another time." Master Su made herself comfortable once more and continued her story:

"Closing the heavy oak door behind him, our hero, the young apprentice wizard took the stone steps downstairs and went to his chambers. He only then removed the brown robe and stared for a time at the now still red rope of Hell. The young man attempted to remove it carefully by lifting the knotted end now resting on his palm, to no avail. The comfortable tension had reached a steady rhythm with his own breath. The apprentice could see the rope contract and expand with each of his own inhalations and exhalations. The surface of the rope seemed to transition from vermillion to scarlet with every lifting of his chest. He gazed at it, feeling every rise of his rib cage and minuscule loosening of the rope. Transfixed, he eventually fell asleep.

The next morning the sun shone through the small crack under his door, his own room lacked a window. The shuffling of feet, the scraping of wizards' staffs and the hustle of morning ritual gave life to the castle corridors. The apprentice arose, washed himself as best he could with the red rope still attached, and redressed. He again donned the brown robe and made for the great hall, where breakfast was waiting for him. Thankfully it was someone else's time for serving duty this week and our intrepid mage was happy to have enjoyed a long, restful sleep. It was long after sun-up and the hall was mostly cleared, save for one long table where a handful of wizards sat. They were a mix of apprentices like himself, as well as adepts and master wizards. While serving himself a bowl of gruel he was asked about the red rope tied around his hand by one of the novices. He made an excuse, telling of a new experimental treatment for joint aches in the restoration school of magic and changed the subject; asking of the novice's progress with his fire magic exercises. That particular apprentice loved to tell of his latest achievements and the apprentice was able to eat in relative peace. Upon bidding the others good day he set out on his own adventure, with the red rope of Hell.

He left the castle on horseback and took the path along the lakes to the city. He passed meadows, streams and the grand forest. His path was winding and rough, his horse was no longer the youngest or fittest and it required some considerable spurring to get it up to speed. The warmer spring weather was, however, at least to the horse's taste and they made decent progress through the countryside which lay between the wizards' castle and the town itself. He held the reigns with both hands and watched as the red rope around his left arm remained comfortably and symbiotically linked to him. The red of the rope was glistening in the sunshine, his cloak since relegated to his saddlebag. Outside the castle he did not feel the need to disguise or cover his arm. Amongst his peers it would have been another issue to be discovered with his whole arm covered in a red rope, their eyes also being more learned and inquisitive. Among the small folk he had no such reticence to show himself. The apprentice soon viewed the spire of the cathedral in the distance. The relative quiet of the early morning at the castle was giving way to the hustle of the first simple buildings on the city outskirts. A tannery and a falconry were the first he passed, some simple farmhouses too.

He enquired at the first farmhouse regarding the ogre and the witch, to no avail. The farmer and his wife were not eager to talk with the out-of-towner. At the second house he knocked for long minutes on end and then eventually spied a lonely farmhand tending to the old goats in the yard. Their brief discussion was amicable enough and happy to talk, but the farmhand had not heard anything of the odd couple. At the third house he knocked again for a long while, peered then into the yard and yet no one was in sight. He pushed at the front door and it yielded. He remained on the porch and felt ashamed to even contemplate entering without permission. The red rope of Hell shone more brightly as he stood in the shadow of the roof. To his great surprise the end of the rope gestured forward towards the door. Shocked by the rope's continued sentience he took a step back, in doing so he merely encouraged the rope to push the door open further. The rope then grabbed the edge of the door and pulled the apprentice into the farmhouse.

Inside he found a cosy homestead with a lit fire, mead on the table, a comfortable bed, some leather chests and well-stocked bookshelves. He asked himself whether the inhabitants were able to read, but then a figure came to his attention parked in front of the fire, lying still. He spied the crane and wondered to himself if it were the same crane as before. He struggled to remember any defining features of the one he had met at the side of the road the previous day. This crane had seemingly found itself a warm home to rest. It turned to face the wizard and it opened its beak and made a chattering sound. It continued for some time before it shook its head and raised its wing to where its forehead was. Then it began to speak: 'Please excuse my rudeness, kind sir. Yesterday I was unsure whether you could be further trusted with this mission and I was reluctant to open my beak.'

'What is this grand sorcery?!", exclaimed the apprentice.

'My good man', the crane continued, 'we are well met indeed, yet yesterday you did not carry the red rope of Hell. Today I indeed observe your readiness and willingness to complete your task, as it is you who has been chosen.'

'You know nothing of me, crane. How can this be? You are talking to me as if thou art a human; you have memories of me and the past. This is madness'. The apprentice looked gravely concerned and made for the door in panic.

'Do not leave, kind magician. We are linked by this rope, this fate', the crane countered.

'Such madness. I have learnt a great many things in the academy'.

The crane, chuckled: 'Yet you remain a lowly apprentice. Your path has just begun, there are many secrets awaiting their discovery. Shadows are awaiting light for your finding and dreams are there for your interpretation. Tell me dear apprentice, are you aware of the history of this rope?'

'The chapter was empty, there was nothing to read. I only know that this rope is not a typical one; it is more than it seems', the apprentice replied.

'Indeed, it seems it is not alone in this fact. I could of course go on drawing any great number of parallels. Naturally we are all underestimated in a plethora of ways, including the underestimation of ourselves. But the point I want to make is that a rope is a great number of things. It can connect as well as separate.'

'How so?'

'Well as well as tying together, which I am sure you gathered, it can also be used to hang a person. Thereby severing their spinal cord, separating them from life, love and family. It can be used to bind, capture, tame. Yet it can also direct, steer, be used to build with. These tools are not obvious in their purposes. In fact the more obvious the use, the less flexible they are. Of course an axe can chop, but a good one can also be used as a hammer. Not to forget the many uses of a blade for shaving, chipping, marking and so on.' As the crane talked and talked it could see that the apprentice was becoming more impatient. 'Dear wizard, what do you suppose this red rope can be used for?'

The apprentice wizard had in fact grown somewhat weary at the crane's explanations of rope; he was well aware of a tool's *flexibility and variety of use. He then considered the rope on his arm and took in the red rope's details. It was a finely wound thread of deep colour which transitioned in the light into a vividly vibrant hue. He could imagine it being used for ceremonial purposes as well practical ones. In a theatre or at a royal wedding. He knew of its name and the idea of Hell couldn't escape his mind, along with the riddle delivered by the crane on the day prior. He pictured fire and suffering, a devil and its minions, cries of pain and unending agony. What would the rope have to do with all of that, he wondered. Given the apparent intelligence of the crane he posed this very question.*

'I cannot be entirely sure, but legend tells us that this rope is made of the very heartstrings of countless souls who dwelled in the very bottom of Hell. The filthiest of the depraved and insane. Once harvested, their hearts were dissected and spun into a fine thread and then into rope. Eventually, after many centuries, it found its way, literally, into the 'The Tales of Wonder and Mystery'. It has passed hands through many generations, it was believed lost to time and has been lying on the shelves of your academy's library for time beyond memory. As such the ancient rope is made of elaborately manipulated organic material: twisted muscle fibre. And they have their own memory and agency. They can contract and expand and repair themselves. In many ways it is a miracle of engineering. Yet, we can safely assume that it was not made by human hand, don't you agree?' The crane anticipated the eager nod from the apprentice and then continued: 'The devil has many names in our stories we tell each other, in some stories the name is not even committed to paper. The rope is magical in nature and will not reveal its use to its wielder until the time is right.'

'I suppose I will have to trust that information and try to find this ogre's house. Most likely I will be able to use the rope to lasso a unicorn, tie up a hungry wolf or hang a fire-breathing dragon by its tail.'

'Dear apprentice wizard, you are a most swift learner and invariably right. However, it is the upmost importance that you do not underestimate your task, the rope is only a tool; it will not do it all for you.' The crane, which seemed to have a smile on its face and also spoke with a lightness of tone, then reminded the apprentice that he had only solved a part of his problem. The object to be used was one thing, he did, however, not yet know who he was to rescue, where he was to go, from whom and also why. 'Are you capable of solving the rest of your puzzle alone, dear apprentice?'

The apprentice was by now sat on a simple stool and held his chin in his hands. 'I don't think so. I don't want to go and knock on all of the doors in the city. I wouldn't want to risk an outright fight with an ogre and even when the deed is done, what do I need with a maiden?'

The crane gave noises of agreement and seemed content. 'You continue to surprise me. To knock on all doors and make a lot of noise, facing the ogre directly and run off with the witch do not seem at first hand to be prudent ideas. I believe you wise to question such tactics. It requires courage to ask yourself these things and to admit to yourself that you are not well-equipped to fight an ogre.'

'Do you believe it would be courageous of me to run away and leave the rope here with you? To pass on the note to the next person who runs into you? To forget all of what I have learned of this rope and the witch and ogre? Isn't it just better to know when to cut your losses and run?'

'Perhaps', countered the crane 'but I think there are other options'.

'I believe I know what you are getting at, crane'. The apprentice raised his head off his hands and sat up straight. He swallowed awkwardly after feeling his voice break slightly and could feel a queasiness in his gut. 'Do you think you could help me? If it were not too much trouble. I couldn't do this alone; I don't know where to start.'

'Esteemed apprentice, indeed this is your necessary courage. It is more difficult for you to ask for help than to go it alone. Tis' a simpler task for you to knock on every door and die at the ogre's hands than for you to conspire with another and forge a plan. For this reason I waited for you, both now in our talk here in this hut and yesterday at the side of the road. I needed you to see it for yourself. For it is this fear you have, to stretch out your hand and risk rejection. We will go forth together and I will show you the way.'

Thus did the crane make its way with the apprentice through the city streets, taking care to avoid the more trodden alleyways and thoroughfares. After a while they came upon the market district with its smells of fish, leather and balms. The market was bustling and the crane gestured to the apprentice for him to take it in his arms, which he did. As he crossed the marketplace he even received a number of enquiries as to the freshness of said crane and a couple of offers. The crane was playing dead as to not arouse suspicion; the apprentice fobbed off the questioning locals, answering that he needed the crane for an important wizarding experiment. They took a left after the market and reached the last landmark before the ogre's house.

'We cranes have great memories, we remember almost everything. We know the quickest routes from north to south and back again every summer and winter. For us to find the way back to a house in the city is much easier'. The apprentice was no longer surprised at the crane. Once it spoke to him the first time he was rapped with fascination and hung on its every word. 'This is where I will leave you, dear apprentice. The house before you belongs to the great ogre and houses the witch. My family is waiting for me by the cathedral and I will return to them. I leave you with this: You may be connected in some way to this rope and to this witch, yet do not forget that this rope is a tool to be used, you are its wielder, it is not your master.' With those words the crane bade the apprentice farewell and took flight, never to be seen by the apprentice again.

     With a small salty tear in his eye, the apprentice took his last tentative steps towards the ogre's house and inspected the outside walls and windows; there were not many of them facing the street. The simple grey house was covered in a simple render, parts of which were cracked and ready to be peeled off. The small windows upstairs were sealed shut, while the ground floor ones were covered from the inside with wood. The house seemed deserted. It was part of a terrace of houses, so the apprentice was unable to see behind it. He took another look at the boarded up windows and also at the old oak door, whose heavy knocker was in the shape of a bull's head, inhuman in size and wrought in iron. He moved towards the door and gripped the knocker, deliberating whether to lift it and see what awaited him. Unsure of whether this was indeed the right path to take he gently allowed the knocker to rest in position and removed himself from the door. Looking left and right he then made his way down the row of houses looking for its end. He had the idea to look at the back of the building and see if there was a more clandestine way to enter. He passed a good number of houses as he went in the left direction; most houses were in a slightly less dilapidated state of disrepair. But this was no expensive part of town. The filth and ruin was almost palpable; the streets were reeking with the foul smell of all manner of possible fluids and solids.

     After a number of minutes he took the corner and was able to walk along the back of the small gardens behind the row of houses. He then realised that he had no way of know which house belonged to the ogre. Looking at his left arm he realised that he could return to the front of the house and measure the distance using the red rope. He pulled lightly at the end of the rope and to his considerable surprise it completely complied with his will. While alone behind the houses he began to lay the rope down on the ground in order to measure its length. He tied one end to a tree at the back of one of the gardens and *began walking. He estimated the rope's length to be about five metres long but as he continued to walk the rope twisted and glistened, seemingly extending itself. So it was to be. The rope's construction, the supple heart strings, allowed it to stretch and increase its length seemingly without end. His problem now was to work out which house was the ogre's."*

"How is he going to solve that conundrum?", asked Lamorna, as she took another handful of roasted pistachios.

"Well, there are almost always two sides to everything. Be they right or wrong, black or white, dead or alive, yin and yang. And so it is for houses too, now pay attention; we are getting towards the end of our tale." Master Su, inevitably, continued:

"The apprentice noticed the sun slowly setting, it had been a tumultuous day with the crane and he began to feel tired. He knew that the best way to solve the problem would be to go back to the front of the house and then measure from the house door to the corner, before turning to the back of the houses. But for that he would need the cover of night in order to not arouse any suspicion. He allowed the rope to coil around his arm once more, put on his brown cloak and made for the nearest ale house. Our young wizard turned heel and returned to the market district and swiftly found himself a suitable establishment.

Upon entering the Stolen Mare his first impressions were hopeful, there was a mixed lot inside the ale house and it was full of dark crooks and corners, dark woods and full of mighty casks of ale. He ordered a pint of brown and nursed it until well past sundown. The fellow patrons mostly kept to themselves and he was careful not to rest his arm on the bar and unwittingly provide a view of the red rope of Hell. The Stolen Mare seemed to be an inn for a quiet night and not the kind where punch-ups and swindles were common. Nevertheless he needed to keep his wits to himself and not give anything away. The red rope of Hell would entice too many questions, would draw too much attention and he didn't want to risk anyone trying to take it from him. The young wizard ordered a few more drinks in the course of the evening as shady figures came and went. He kept an eye out for anyone from the wizards' castle, but truth be told he was more anxious about bumping into the ogre or another speaking crane. The apprentice spied a number of hooded figures lurking in the dark, more often than not each sat on their own, each busy with a long pipe. This seemed to be the perfect kind of establishment for sipping on a beer and keeping secrets. He had struck it lucky.

After finishing his third tankard he thanked the barkeep and made his way out. By then most of the windows were bereft of candlelight and only the city's pigeons and some distant fighting could be heard. Walking back to the ogre's house he was careful to avoid any groups of people, taking the odd side street where necessary and waiting for others to pass. He was soon back at the house and when he did arrive he kept walking on past it, without stopping. Once he reached the corner, which would have taken him behind the houses, he scanned up and down the street for anyone who might interrupt him. The coast was clear. He carefully loosened the rope from his arm once more, went to another tree near the side street at the end of the row and tied a good hard knot.

Again checking all was clear he slowly paced his way back to the ogre's house. Step by step he counted the one hundred and three paces which led to the door. Upon reaching the door once more he heard a tinny rattling, like metal on metal, his heart began to beat faster and sweat formed on his brow. He anxiously looked around in a fever, having come so far our fine young magician did not want to be halted or discovered now, at the last. The noise relented somewhat but he could not be sure where it was coming from. The young apprentice put his ear to the door but that did not provide him with any clear indication of the sound's origin. This disappointment however reminded him of his original plan: To make his way to the back of the house having noted on the rope how long the one hundred and three paces were. From there he made his way down the side-street and found a similarly positioned tree and walked the same number of steps along the back of the row of houses.

The reverse side of the ogre's house looked much like that of the others, falling apart and lacking any kind of loving attention. There was a small overgrown allotment where vegetables grew, some already wilting, having been denied any form of green thumb. He looked at the rear windows, they were boarded up on both floors, the house must be filled with darkness. Despite his grave concerns he continued to proceed with caution. The wizard slowly approached the back of the house. With each step he took he could feel the thud of his heartbeat. Every breath leaden and a struggle.

He hadn't originally planned on any of this; he only wanted to study and progress to the level of master wizard, learn some tricks, finally meet like-minded individuals; people who just wanted to quietly learn how magic works. Now he found himself on an adventure; a quest. Quite amazingly he was talking with sentient creatures, attempting to fool an ogre and rescue a fair maiden. The simple facade of the building disguised the sophisticated protections the ogre had employed. As well as the windows being boarded up, they were locked. The doors, front and back, could only be opened with a unique key; alone in the possession of the ogre. The apprentice got to the back door, tried the handle. Nothing. He looked around for other possibilities, a ground floor window cracked open or something of the like. Again, no luck. He then stubbed his foot on some brickwork outlining a simple flower bed, which itself was over grown with nettles, shrubs and some wilting daffodils. The brickwork was laid out in a rough D-shape, each last brick meeting the house wall. As he looked closer he saw that there was a partially hidden opening. He peered yet closer at the dark postbox-like slit at ground level. Then a voice emerged from the darkness, 'is that you?', the woman asked. The apprentice was reticent to answer. Could it be a trap? Was the ogre masking his voice? He pretended he instantaneously vanished and slowly retraced his steps towards the back door, like a stalking cat.

'I know you are out there, I have heard your loud heart beating for the last five minutes, you should really get that thing looked at.' Again the sorcerer was unwilling to let any words leave his lips and he began to panic. Playing dead now will not help me, I suppose the only way is through.

'My master says it is normal', the apprentice replied. 'It's nothing to worry about. I have a lot on my plate right now and stress can cause that kind of thing.'

'Do you think that is why you are here?', the woman asked. 'That stress brought you here, that duty led you to me? Never mind your reasons, I am glad that the crane was able to pass on my message. You see I have spent many seasons here in this hell and I am about ready to leave, my bags are packed. The ink is dry on my farewell letter and I am delighted that it is you who heeded my call.'

The apprentice had not expected this. He imagined a young maiden, of marrying age perhaps. A helpless thing, frail and afraid. In his books these figures were more often than not naïve, lacking guidance, ignorant to the demands of the world. Those moments spent talking to the woman in the cellar provided him with the clear impression of talking with someone more enlightened, steadfast and focussed. And so it was. For this was no waif or princess, but a sorceress herself. She knew what she wanted and what she needed.

'Young apprentice', she began, 'tell me what it is you carry'.

'Carry?', he spluttered, as a hiccough.

'Yes, dear boy. I asked you to bring something to me. Something precious, useful and eternal.'

'Er, I did, yes. How could you know of it? This rope is something beyond the knowledge of most of my wizard colleagues; it has been lying in a book for years, if not decades. How could you...?'

'It is quite simple, dear apprentice. I have read about it myself. The books in your library are many and they are indeed delightful. Yet, they are not the only books in the world. Nor is it the only library. The ogre indulges my thirst for such literature. He thinks that it keeps me here. But I knew that there was no way out for me without that object you have coiled upon your arm. It is told of in many different tales. From the far east and in the deep south. The northern legends boast of a shipwright who held his fleet together with it. In the west we believe it to be made of heartstrings from the most wretched dwellers of Hell. One thing is sure. You will place it in my hand and allow me to free myself. Your job is done dear apprentice and for that I thank you. I no longer require your assistance."

"Wait a minute", Lamorna interjected. "You are telling me that the apprentice went to all of that effort to rescue the princess and then she doesn't need him any more? Is that even fair? How can she do such a thing? Doesn't he deserve more? A reward? Maybe they can ride into the sunset with each other in the end?"

"Maybe they will, Lamorna", Master Su explained. "But as far as she is concerned, his is work is done. She doesn't owe him her life just because he saved her from the deepest, darkest pit of darkness. Her life of enslavement and servitude is over. She need not traded captors. Why should she feel indebted to him forevermore simply because he gave her a red rope? Would paying this emotional debt in kind not be yet more imprisonment? As you will see by the end of the story, a happy ending depends on when you end it."

"The apprentice turned a ghostly complexion. He had not expected this. He felt the air in his lungs compress and pull him down hard to the earth. His breathing grew heavy and he felt a panic in his heart. Just in that moment the red rope of Hell loosened its grip on him and slivered to the ground. He fell to the floor to grasp at it, but the end of the rope rose up, the ends balled together in the size and rough shape of a snake's head and hissed at him. He fell on his back in shock and witnessed the rope glide along the ground and slip between the grating which covered the opening to the woman's domain.

'Thank you apprentice'. She took the rope in hand and marvelled at its lustre and detailing. The dark room of her cellar, lit with only a few small candles, barely enough to read with, was now aglow in a majestic hue. The rope began to hum and sing a low tone. The woman was now visible to the apprentice through the grating. Neither was she long of hair, ready to be climbed down upon, nor was she asleep in a glass casket, nor hidden behind thick bushes of poisonous thorns. She was in a cellar, with empty bottles of wine lying in every corner and she looked quite frayed and singularly determined to finally escape the overbearing ogre who had made her life until now a complete misery. She allowed the rope to coil from her arm, around her torso and then down her leg. One end of the rope she kept in hand and the other made its way back towards the small opening. It wriggled its way towards the wall, then slithered upwards until it reached the grating. Then the woman spoke the following words:

> Unbind in me that which was lost
> Free me from the prison 'twich I was tossed
> Open the gates and release the fire
> And let the brutal ogre feel my ire

The red rope of Hell formed a knot around each fork of the grating, until each individual heartstring, straining under the force, could be seen my the apprentice outside. She repeated the words once more and the rope let out a great crack and then a wailing shriek. The rope was now under immense tension. Then the woman could be seen in the centre of the room, the other end of the rope had formed a helix around her body, which flowed like a red river of illuminated blood. With great concentration she then grasped the rope with two hands in front of her and pulled with all her soul. She heaved the rope and the grating began to shake. The apprentice, watching aghast from the outside, could only see what looked like liquid fire inside the cellar room. He feared for the woman's very life, even if something told him, he should be more concerned with his own; whilst quivering, he thought to himself that surely the ogre would awaken now.

The red rope of Hell, then resembling great whips of flame had wrenched the heavy wrought iron grating out of its frame and the window was now fully opened. The grating clattered to the cellar floor, the woman still regaled in red light. The great tentacle-like arms of flame reached outside and grabbed the closest pairs of trees in the garden, the apprentice recoiled and jumped out of their way. The woman was then pulled out through the window by the flames and now finally stood in front of the apprentice.

'We are bound, dear apprentice. This rope tied us together for a time. Intuitively you knew its import and did that which I could not. And as your counterpart I was able to use it as you could not. Our bond will remain unbroken. You will see. We are not the same, we are two halves of a greater whole. What I lack in instinct, you are missing in courage. What you have in humility, I lack in flexibility. We are fortunate to have met. Not everyone is so lucky. Yet our paths have merely met here, in the middle. Like the centre of an eight. And for your great service I am ever thankful. Now I am free and feel a great lightness. You now have the heart of a lion, my dear. I will leave this red rope with you; I trust that you will do the right thing with it.'

'I....will', the apprentice managed. He could finally see the woman in all her splendour and felt great terror in his heart. 'Will I see you again?'

'Perhaps on the great plains, across the ocean or in the weeping sky'. She then took his hands, kissed him lightly on the cheek. Her face then turned to the moon. 'I will leave now. It is not important whether we meet again, be it in this world or the next. This deed you have done is more than enough for one lifetime. Hold your breath and count to ten. Start again.' With those words the woman disappeared and began the start of her new life, wherever that may be. The apprentice stood, now empty handed and looked up at the night sky, cursing the woman who slipped out of his life as he did. He vowed to himself that he would use whatever methods he could to set things in balance.

Upstairs in the house the ogre had been polishing his favourite collection of gemstones, a hobby of his since his childhood. The gemstones were the only things left from his war-torn and now long destroyed homeland. He had made his way to this kingdom many years ago and had taken in the young woman after her family had been killed in a massacre. She had been too young to remember. He kept her as he best knew, like his gemstones, in darkness. He was greedy and his actions had been ruled by fear. The massive tumult downstairs set him in motion. He instinctively stood up, grabbed his axe and ran down the stairs. Once he arrived at the cellar door he began the arduous process of unlocking all of the convoluted mechanisms, which had kept her inside for so long. Eventually he finally succeeded in opening the door and was greeted with the greatest chasm of emptiness. He sank slowly against the wall and held his head in his hands. His pitiful sobs only drew the attentions of the apprentice. The woman was gone. The ogre looked into the apprentice's eyes from the dark cellar room and they met each other

116

with further emptiness and loss. The ogre remained until the end of his days in that dark room and the apprentice spent many aeons looking for the woman. The ogre eventually succumbing to his loneliness."

"Are you trying to tell me that there was no happy ending here, Su? The woman got her freedom, that's all we need to know, right?", Lamorna asked, a little concerned as to whether she had missed something and perhaps passed out on the forest floor. She sat up and turned to Master Su.

"That's absolutely right, dear Lamorna. The long years spent in the darkness led to her only craving the light. She needed only a crack, a glimpse, then she seized her opportunity and grasped it. Her heart had suffered long enough and she then needed to define her own little life. No-one would be able to hold her back. And I never thought that such stories were pure fiction", Master Su admitted to Lamorna. The morals of the story were always so clear to her: A woman needed not to be saved, only to be given the tools necessary. A woman can free herself and need not become indebted to a master or husband. Such stories had kept Su warm when growing up, her young life, mostly solitary, often in hospitals for various ailments: broken bones, infections, muscle spasms, migraines, absolute heartbreak.

Lamorna leapt into a monologue of her own, having listened long enough to Su's wise tale. "I have to tell you about my dilemma, Su", she began, her voice breaking slightly and her lower lip quivering as she did. "I don't know what to do anymore. I've given all I can working for Jason and all he does is provide me with more projects, more responsibility for more people in my team and even tighter deadlines. I just feel like I have so much going on in my head that I can't even hear myself think. I don't even know how I feel about these one thousand things anymore; I can only recall cold facts. I can't remember the last time I felt particularly strongly about anything in particular. I get home and all I can do to keep myself sane is to stick my head in the sand, a perfect hiding place. I don't even remember how long it has been this way! When was the last time I just stopped, took a moment, realised what was happening to me and then thought about how to change it?! I just stick on my music, do anything to distract myself, I pick up the guitar, turn the volume right up and just abuse myself with pure amplitude. I don't care what I put in my body, I survive on frozen pizza and vitamin supplements. I have no real friends to speak of, I don't go out, I dive into films and games in an attempt to ignore whatever I might feel. I feel guilty when I think I might miss out knowing about anything and at work I can't miss a deadline and that drives me on to meet every single one of them, it is a permanent tension in me which I am painfully aware of, but of which I just can't let go. It is as if all of these different projects and responsibilities pulling me in twenty different directions, like twenty horses tied to my limbs and body with twenty ropes and I am permanently fighting to hold them all back. It is an unbearable tension which I can feel in my bones." Lamorna barely made eye contact with Master Su. Then, slowly, she turned towards her.

"The sad fact is that I have been training all my life to hold the horses back, so I know I can do it, I am strong enough, not exactly stupid and pretty determined. I have to hold them all back, lest they tear me apart. But for how long, Su? How long can I hold back? What if they become fifty horses? What if the horses work together and they pull smart, ripping me as I struggle to coordinate myself? What if they become smarter than me, more determined and stronger?"

The moonlight shone on Master Su's pale face, she waited and had let Lamorna talk. Once she saw that her companion was finished, Master Su answered in a deeper voice, in a more measured tone. "Lamorna, the solution is simple. You need to cut all of the ropes at once. You can't sustain it. It is impossible. With time you will adjust to the new tension and more horses will come, as they have in the past. You will, as long as you take the reins, always acquire more horses. The metaphor is a good one, but the solution is almost literally in your hands, or more accurately: it is out of your hands. You need to let go. Of all of the horses. At the same time."

"Fuck", Lamorna's head whacked back down against the ground, she was unable to look Master Su in the eyes. She didn't disagree with her, she just didn't feel like she could just give up.

"Yes. It is astounding that you have held them back for all of this time. It is a wonder of the human mind and body. But it is risking your soul, Lamorna. Without delay and without regret or feelings of guilt".

"I don't understand." Lamorna remained on the cold forest ground. She was fluent in understanding body language and didn't think that Su could be fooled by pretending to posture and pout, to argue or deny she was utterly spent.

"I know. How could you understand? You haven't trained your feelings before. When have you ever truly reflected on your feelings? And I don't mean cognitively Lamorna. Of course you understand what hormones do to the body and you are painfully aware of some important principles of psychoanalysis and how the mind processes emotions. But you have not allowed yourself to feel these things before.

"I don't know what it means to feel? Do you really

expect me to believe that? What do you mean? I do it all the time? Like when my cat died, and when I hurt people, I feel bad. It isn't something alien to me."

"Lamorna, you keep it to yourself. You bottle it all up inside and blame yourself. You don't give yourself the opportunity for it to come out. It is like a pressure cooker and it's on a long program. You are afraid of taking the top off and finding out what has been brewing all this time. Yet this is precisely what you must do."

"There is nothing that I *'must'* do, other than facing death, Su. You are beginning to sound like Jason."

In an instant, grim-faced, Master Su replied: "Yes, maybe you must face that before you will learn. But I can't judge you for that. It is not a joke when you consider ending it all. I have a strong understanding of what can lead a person to that darkest and most desperate of places. When faced with such terrible absurdities and unbearable burdens or tragedies, it can be a very logical and understandable response."

Lamorna remained unmoved, tears now flowing from the corners of each eye. She had indeed considered killing herself: By electrocution *(too unreliable)*, by throwing herself in front of a train *(too traumatic for bystanders and train drivers)* and finally by throwing herself from a high motorway bridge into oncoming traffic *(see train)*. Even in death, she was thinking too much of others and how it might look. Doubtless a common concern. She often asked herself how many of her thoughts were truly original. Master Su could see the tears, but did little to comfort Lamorna directly, preferring to continue with her reasoning: "What I can't judge is whether or not Chamberlain speaks a degree of truth in his judgements. My point is that you avoid the conflict and the interaction. By busying yourself with novelty and trivial things you permit yourself respite from the stress of your work at Optix. You create a new facade for yourself, a kind of cocoon into which you retreat. Nothing but the light from your screen permeates its shell and you remain safe. You are not the first to do this. It is a very logical response for someone who is afraid of loss and a tried and tested coping mechanism. The best action to avoid the pain of loss is to never have contact with the outside world. By retreating inside you control the risk, protect yourself from humiliation, rejection, judgement and isolation. Which is, of course, self-defeating. You are a smart woman Lamorna, who am I telling this to?"

The cold air carried Master Su's voice over the water of the calm dark blue lake. Lamorna could only summon a short murmur and exhalation of breath; dark feeling of inertia embedded in her heart.

"You see, Lamorna, even now, with everything laid bare, I need you to rise up and fight me. Push me and pull my hair back, scream at me and kick me. I want to see your blood boil and fire in your eyes. Will you not give me that satisfaction? Will you not get yourself out of this? I fear not; instead, I see you forever trapped, as if held between powerful magnets and you can only stand and passively observe. You are in your own prison, like the poor woman from the story. What are you waiting for? A magic mythical book and an apprentice who will come and free you? Where is your bewitched crane and hairy ogre? Where is your magic wand?"

"Do I need to really make my own wand? I mean you are all dressed up in your ridiculous robe. Is that what you want of me? A copy of a copy? A facsimile image of a fairy tale sorceress?" Lamorna began to rise from her lying position, now on her knees in front of Su. She began to feel the blows of this humiliation, this dressing down and couldn't accept the idea that she was a failure. "Do you think me your lackey, disciple or a project?"

"This is all very good, Lamorna. You need to push back, especially against me. I am not your equal. We are not the same. You are like an apprentice to me, it is true. But in order to ascend you must push back against me, with a renewed ferocity. Without this you will remain ignorant of what to do next. You need to harness the full breadth of anger within you and create a conduit so that it can regularly flow out of you. Not all at once, but a little, every day."

"So, basically, you are recommending I join a dojo. Thanks for the enlightenment, dear Su."

"Again, Lamorna. You are deflecting. Yes, of course a dojo would be a good idea for some people, but probably not for you. This form of physical aggression and violence can be of great benefit. But would you stick at it? Or would you sign up for six months, learn to kick-box, attain a passing proficiency, then stop going regularly and then give up? I think we both know the answer."

"Too many people", Lamorna provided as her answer.

"Perhaps, but you need to find something to do just for yourself and do it every day. Be it writing lyrics for a black metal band, telling stories of brutal murder, or running until your legs burn; embrace the pain in your muscles. This can be your outlet. Now this is of the upmost importance, you must do it for yourself, not for anyone else and not so that you can continue to work for Optix at a good level until you are too old and are carted out of there, sold for glue like poor Boxer. Also, you need to tell yourself what is wrong, write it down. Don't keep it inside, let it out. You know what else you could do, Lamorna?". Su continued, "you could get up each morning and go to the mirror in your bathroom and speak to yourself about what you need on that particular day. You may feel tired, you may want to go for a run, it could even be that you want to just curl up in bed and do nothing but weep. But, look at yourself deep into your eyes, without flinching, do not break the contact and promise yourself something. You deserve to show up for yourself each and every day. Nobody else can do it for you. It is not that every person must truly fight for themselves, that would be too egotistical. It is more that in order to really listen to yourself, you must give yourself that attention."

"You're telling me to look in the mirror and tell myself to do something?", Lamorna, looked a little underwhelmed at her wise master's advice this time, not quite grasping the gravity of it.

"Lamorna, this is not a triviality. Each day is a new start, the saying goes, correct? And you will always have your ups and downs, regardless of how much progress you make. You need to look into your own soul, the very essence of your self. This takes much practice. This requires discipline. It also sharpens the mind, allows you to listen to your soul and the final connection is for you to activate the Gamma-aminobutryic acid neurotransmitters."

"And how would one do that?", Lamorna enquired, her tear ducts by now dry and her cognitive mind again tuned on to the sound of long science words.

"The key is to look yourself so deeply into the mirror that you see your authentic self and then once you settle on a word, or a phrase, a thing you need to give yourself today, you high-five your mirror self, sealing the contract."

"But that is ridiculous; I'll have to clean my bathroom mirror almost every day", Lamorna argued.

"Come now, Lamorna", Su began, "we both know that is not a priority; neither your cleanliness nor the knowledge that you need to make important changes to how you live your life. You cannot and must not run or hide from these things. They will not go away, they will only fester and worsen if you do not confront them! You need to look at your mirror image and mean it. High-fiving yourself produces a dopamine response, you don't need me to tell you that is a good thing."

"I'll give it a shot", Lamorna promised.

Master Su had the wonderful habit of Socratically stinging Lamorna like an inquisitively stubborn wasp. The venom was nothing sinister; it should function more like an inspiration. All of the uncomfortable topics that Lamorna preferred to ignore and distract herself from were laid out in front of her for the reckoning. During her observations, as she had watched Lamorna still from afar, Su indeed saw much potential in her personality, or better said personalities. For Lamorna was an adept mask wearer as it transpired; adapting to the situation, environment and surrounding people where appropriate.

***

"Which Lamorna am I meeting today?", Su stung her with one cold afternoon; they met roughly every week by that time.

"Don't start with that today, please. It has been a hard day. Chamberlain is demanding that we let go several of the new colleagues because, as he says, they are just too stupid. I've never fired anyone before; it's going to ruin their lives!", Lamorna lamented.

"It wouldn't be your fault, Lamorna, if it is his decision. Maybe he just wants to test you", Su replied.

"How would it be a test?", Lamorna looked quizzically at Master Su.

"To see if you have what it takes to make the difficult

sacrifices". Su, looking over the lake, lowered her hood and gave careful consideration to Lamorna's response.

"Do you really think that Jason doesn't know that I can be a tough person?", Lamorna was getting impatient with Su.

"When you let people go, from your company, from your life completely, it isn't about being tough. It is about doing what you deem right for the organism in question. For Chamberlain it is, hopefully, about the future of Optix, its financial and technical prosperity, otherwise it would just be flexing muscle and creating suffering. In the case of cutting people out of your life it is much more complex. With those people there is, except in very rare cases, such as marriage, no formal contract or legal document involved. When you lose a friend, disown an uncle, or leave a partner, you are creating a wound not set by any kind of legal parameter, with notice periods, compensation or written warnings. You can feel terrible loss and emptiness even though you know it was for the best and the stages of grief are rarely followed linearly Lamorna. You can jump from deep sorrow to brutal anger, through negotiation and acceptance and back again within a one fifteen minute period and still come out of it with a crooked smile on your face". Master Su's faced was in that moment a special angle of crooked.

"Is this something you have experienced yourself?", Lamorna enquired, observing the soft wrinkles on the corner of Master Su's mouth as they twitched slightly and she contemplated her answer. Lamorna was learning to read Su, who was a cautious communicator, rarely divulging much information about herself or her other relationships, unless directly questioned.

"I am experienced in these matters and have made some sacrifices, yes. You are no doubt looking for a more detailed response, Lamorna. And as such I promise that I am generally more than happy to divulge as much supporting information as I deem helpful to you, where appropriate, however I feel it unsuitable timing for me to monologue on matters of my own heart at this time. Let it be left to the imagination for now. When it is time I promise that I will explain all. This is linked to the things that brought us together of course; I have not forever been holed up in the Bluebird hotel and neither do I plan on remaining there for long. Yes, it is a place which affords a great degree of comfort and discretion to me, yet I seek more humble and homely abodes. A dark wet cave for example". Su applied a deflecting chuckle to her last statement and waited in anticipation of Lamorna's reply.

"Would you say that you are also a kind of hermit, Su?", Lamorna felt like getting in some of her own jabs, deciding to give as good as she got with Master Su nowadays; Lamorna understood that this was part of her training.

Master Su seemed pleased with her young apprentice. She weighed up a number of responses in her mind: *'that is projection, my dear.'* Being the first one which came to mind. *'Of course, my shell offers me armour against my enemies, warmth in winter and protection from the elements'*, came next. *'I travel light, so yes, it suits me well'*, then came into her consciousness. *'I like moving house; I get to see new places'* and *'I like a good workout'* followed. Su then decided against a verbal response and simply smiled and nodded. Su knew the time and place to defend herself, when to attack and when to avoid conflict; for the latter this was such a time. Most of all she was happy that Lamorna had the insight and courage to ask such a question.

"Back to the matter at hand, my dear", Master Su took the approach of redirection in this instance, "we were in the middle of discussing loss and separation. There is of course a great degree of difference between firing someone and the separation of a romantic relationship."

"Naturally, one is incredibly painful. The other makes things awkward at Christmas and weddings", Lamorna let out a wry smile.

"Indeed, it can be very difficult to inform others when you have left a relationship. Often more difficult than being fired. Such wounds need more than pure, indefinite time to heal. They require nourishment, help from friends. There will be a period of time when the person will try to convince you to accept them back into your life. They may wrestle with their own conscience about whether to tell you. They may write letters, hire a mariachi band, come to your home in the middle of the night and beckon you, hoping to woo you with a siren's song. They may however just do all of the above in their head and lack the courage or energy to do so. To proclaim such robust love for someone, even after separation is putting your self-worth at great risk. It is not about accepting defeat, it is about not being willing to lose that person from their life, which is of course, completely understandable. Think on the old Trojan War: Menaleus was unable to let Helen go, he may have been jealous of Paris, but it was the enduring love he felt for her which drove him to wage a ten years' war against the Trojans."

"Surely it was hubris and greed which drove him to attack Troy. He was cuckolded and couldn't accept that Paris was the more attractive prospect for Helen". Lamorna knew the basics of the story, she was unsure about the muses and the prophecy of Paris falling in love with the fairest woman in the land, it sounded more like a fairy tale to her.

Su continued: "If we had been there to see it, we would

have been able to observe how it could truly be love which drove Menaleus. Love has the power to wage a sustained campaign of such magnitude with such great personal and material cost. The love he felt for Helen gave him hope. Yes his pride was hurt and one could argue that the sunken cost fallacy played a role. If the events unfolded as told in the sagas, the power of the tale lies in this enduring love for the woman in his life."

"If you look at it from Menaleus' point of view, he was completely justified in his actions", Lamorna posited.

"If your actions are truly grounded in love, they are seldom hurtful. The question is: How much pain did Menaleus cause in his pursuit of Helen and what were his realistic chances of victory?", Master Su wondered whether Lamorna really cared about the collateral damage.

"Is it really about pain though?", Lamorna looked quizzically, gathering her thoughts as she attempted to answer her own question on Menaleus' justification for war. She played with the skin around her fingernails, like pulling at a loose thread. "If it was for love, then surely he would do anything to win her back".

Master Su was not convinced of the all or nothing tactic: "If he really loved her, he would have sought a dialogue with her. Menaleus would sit down with her, having sent envoys to broker peace treaties, he would have asked her questions and tried to understand why she left him in the first place. Menaleus did none of these things, so how can we be sure that he did this for love?"

"We can't. Perhaps ego", Lamorna remarked.

"Indeed, and fear of losing face. To truly love someone you need to give them their own freedom of thought and space, support them, respect them, be open with them, be willing to let them grow, set boundaries and trust them. Most importantly you must be willing to let them go if you truly love them. This is the greatest test. To accept that their true path and life's happiness could be without you, as much as it may break your own heart and kill your ego."

"That is quite a picture you paint. Can that really be put into practice?", Lamorna enquired.

Su smiled at Lamorna, the faint crow's feet around each eye coming into view "That has to be the goal. For what is it that you love about the person? Why would you want anything but the very best for them? What would you not give up for them? Your home, your wealth, your job? Even your own family and friends. If you love them enough, you would do anything to ensure that their heart's desire, that which their heart truly burns for and requires, is fulfilled. Even if this means that it is not to be with you, but another, as in Menaleus' case. The situation is different if you are to leave them, naturally." Master Su continued, her hands taking Lamorna's right hand tightly: "If you leave them because you love another, then it is important to help them understand the need for you to leave. It could be that it requires deep meditation on your part, before you know what your heart truly needs. It may be that the knowledge that you will cause them almost unbearable pain will prevent you from wanting to go through with it. But you must be merciful, again, like a good king. You must be honest firstly with yourself and then with the person who loves you. This I have naturally experienced myself; I have made many sacrifices to become the person standing before you now and such sacrifices leave massive scars on your soul. Be truly honest with yourself in terms of what you want and then, once you have followed through with pulling the trigger, you must learn to forgive yourself. Such loss can destroy a person, leaving them to pick up all the pieces. It can be a period of chaos for both parties. Your feelings will make you doubt that you are doing the right thing. You will sometimes desire to turn back time, or to have cut yourself in two to live two parallel lives, both with and without them. But this is folly, dear Lamorna. The chaos of feelings is something which itself must be processed. Give them also the space and time that they need to heal. This is the mercy I spoke of. The separation must be clean and not lingering. Their thoughts and grief must become a source of energy for them. That tumultuous chaos of emotions, as violent as when a tsunami floods coastal towns, will wrestle control from them, until they regain it. It is the water that drew the people there, salt of the tears is the same. The desire to rebuild their lives must come from them alone. But to feel alive and to love means to feel that pain. And also, you sometimes have to kill the things you love."

Whilst listening to Master Su's excursions on love and break-ups Lamorna's thoughts wandered; the closest thing to a partner she had was Jason Chamberlain. She was practically married to Optix and that family home was more like a prison for her. "Does Optix need to be brought to the ground?", Lamorna came out with.

"All is fair in love and war, as they say, dearest Lamorna", Su offered. "How well you find parallels, how practically minded you are, these are important considerations. Of course, this is your decision. Optix and Chamberlain are such a large part of your life. Have you ever thought of leaving before?".

"To be honest, I haven't. And as much as I can't stand it there, I don't just want to give up." Lamorna's response was as honest as it was brief.

Master Su looked at Lamorna and saw so much of her

in herself. Su had been in a similar position before, feeling like a prisoner, and she knew that it was easier to change where you are than to revolutionise your surroundings. With that thought in mind she launched into a new diatribe: "A simple bomb will not work, Lamorna. You cannot change a culture with violence. Guns and swords are not the answer here. Look to the water. It moves through everything and leaves a path." Su then tried to redirect the conversation: "Coming back to our analogy, when the tsunami's waters have cleared, the survivors will go through the debris and weep, they will look for their lost ones and will despair at the waste. But they will rebuild. While grasping at beams and corrugated steel they will band together and build a new life for themselves, while finding constant reminders of all which was lost. Overcome with guilt, regret and, as the waste clears and the stillness enters their life again, they will feel the empty pang of loneliness. It is this emptiness which must enter before that gap, the weeping chasm and vacuum standing in their heart, can be filled and replenish their soul. For them that abyss will feel like the end of all things."

Lamorna looked concerned, "I don't want to cause a tsunami, or to leave a path of destruction".

Su held Lamorna's hand tighter and forced a smile, "Then give them hope. Without hope it could well be the end of them. The tinder for the fire must be that burning desire to reach back from the edge of the abyss. But once they begin to seek order from the chaos after that tsunami has hit, the adrenaline will have subsided and they must face the terrible reality of being alone. The abyss will then seem like warmest and most inviting thing in their lives at that moment. The pure, magnetic nothing will be waiting with open arms to hold them and they may seek its embrace in those darkest of times. It is at times like these where you will want to help them the most and what you do right there in those moments is of profound importance. You cannot be responsible for what happens at Optix after you leave. You need not remain there for fear of hurting people's feelings. Optix is a beast feeding on ripe souls, Lamorna. It has taken enough of you, the world, already."

"It really has, hasn't it?", Lamorna mustered. She had spent most of the evening lying on the forest floor and was ready to peel herself of it when Master Su suggested the same.

"It is time for us to head back, Lamorna, let's see if we manage to arrive home safe before the sun rises. And that you change your life before the horses pull you apart."

8 - CLINICAL

"She needs blood! Her pressure is down, thermics are low, patient is not responsive!". The clear voices in the emergency room covered the clattering of the trolley as Lamorna was rolled in by three attendant doctors and a pair of nurses. "Get her sedated; she's in shock!". Lamorna's brutalised body lay on the trolley as if beaten by a herd of bulls. Her legs were broken in several places above her knees where the car had struck her. Her head was bloody from the landing. Bystanders would have barely seen the car coming. Lamorna hadn't seen it at all. The last thing she saw when leaving her office building was a row of trees beckoning her into the park. Alas they had not been there before, only appearing in her mind. Chamberlain had manipulated her implants.

The bleeps and sirens fired in Lamorna's head, the pain was unbearable. The bright lights of the emergency room seemed to be drilling like laser beams into her brain, ripping through whatever was left of her; tearing at her grey matter and leaving all detritus lying on her retina for her to behold. The lights also seemed to serve an important purpose: They prevented her from wanting her to open her eyes and see the damage done to her once fit body. Until the morphine kicked in Lamorna was able to experience the sense of being a human milkshake, she felt merely a bag of bones, all pulp and no form. Her experience of hospitals had been mercifully limited up until then, a life lived without too much risks had its upsides it seemed. At first she understood the feeling of slowly drifting off as a numbing lullaby. Such a wonderful lullaby would calm a screaming tiger. Lamorna resisted the chemical handcuffs intent on subduing her, but finally she drifted into a blurry in-between world, forever trapped in the office at Optix, remaining in the hamster wheel of thought which had helped cause her accident in the first place.

***

Lamorna, emboldened by her previous meeting with Master Su had woken up early and rode her bike to work. She wanted to confront Chamberlain and tell him that she wanted to work on more protections and user welfare. Lamorna clocked in and made her way to the seventh floor. Upon arrival there Lamorna whispered to Felix that she needed his support. She wanted to call an emergency meeting and gathered Alpha team members and Chamberlain together. They met in his office.

"Jason. This isn't easy for me to say. You know that. That is why I need to get us all together today".

Jason Chamberlain's eyes looked at Lamorna like a cat never lets a dog out of its view, untrusting and ready for violence. "Lamorna, just come out with it and don't waste our time. As you know the deadlines aren't getting any further away and every second we sit here we are wasting valuable resources".

"That's just what I mean Jason. You treat us like robots, no, like bound slaves and just expect us to do your bidding, unquestioningly. I don't remember a time when it wasn't like this. You expect us to give absolutely everything to Optix, to work evenings, weekends, on the bus, under the shower, at the dinner table. My brain is always on work time, always working on upgrading the plans, improving the user experience. And all you can do is whip us harder. Even the Romans knew that the people needed cake and games too, not just blood and fire".

"Be careful now, Lamorna. Don't act as if you aren't the one choosing to give it all. You worked your way up. You stay on and your damn perfectionism is what drives you. You can't just leave things undone." A sardonic smug firmly established itself on Jason Chamberlain's face, where before only disdain and slight disappointment was to be seen.

"Jason, this toxicity, this poison has been carefully curated and fed by you. Don't put it on me. You treat us like cannibals. Hungrily waiting for the next one to fall, so they can be devoured and have their place taken by the next. You won't be satisfied until you are sat alone, if at all. The Alpha team will be a distant memory and you can fool and manipulate the world on your own, and charge a hefty fee for the privilege."

"If that is how you feel, then I think you should leave Lamorna. You had a good run, but you really haven't been the same recently." Chamberlain laughed her off, turned to the other Alpha team members and just shrugged his shoulders. "It isn't like anyone is held hostage here, you are all free to leave whenever you want. These might be turbulent times, we are forging a new future for everyone and that is always going to face resistance, even from within. I can't fault Lamorna for her courage in calling this meeting today, she had something to say and she went ahead and did it. We don't need sheep and sycophants here at Optix, we need critical thinking and insights into how to improve our organisation if we are going to help humanities perception of reality and build a better world. So I say to Lamorna simply *'thank you'* and think it would be best if she took some holiday. She really has worked hard to contribute to what we have here and we need her back to her best. As in music, the pauses are just as important. So, Lamorna, I want to send you off for a four week holiday to the place of your own determination. Be inspired, be lazy, be you. Leave all difficult thoughts of Optix behind you, regroup and reenergise! We will accept you back into the family when you are back". And so Chamberlain, having successfully polished the turd in front of him, folded his arms and forced a smile.

Lamorna felt blindsided. How did he take that so well? She wondered if she had missed something. A tear formed in her eye, her body was lying to her. It thought Chamberlain actually cared. His offer of holiday was merely to get her gone. She wasn't stupid enough to start believing her body's responses just yet. "I'll go Jason. And I don't know when or if I'll be back. But you can be sure of one thing: I will not return the same person. I have had the wool over my eyes for too long and I see you for the greedy wolf that you are. My advice to the rest of you is to wake up before you are devoured too."

With that Lamorna made her way to the lift and made her way to the ground floor. The relief was in her bones, a weight lifted, a euphoria even. She was sunken in thoughts of revolution and retribution as she made her way through the foyer. The glass doors framed the beautiful green path outside and she could practically feel the wind in her face already, she hastened her steps and made her way through the doors. As she felt immersed amongst the beautiful green oaks and firs she heard the brutal crash of metal on flesh, screeching brakes and screams. Those were the last things she remembered.

***

The heavy sedation had worn off and Lamorna lay in her hospital bed reading. The heavy pain medication was still in full effect though, she had a button to press whenever she needed more. It was her favourite thing. She could slip into a painless sleep and any thought of Chamberlain, the accident or Optix would fall away from the edge of her consciousness. The first days faded out of time and memory, she simply wasn't there. The countless surgeries, consultations and the handful of visits had completely passed her by. It was as if she had not even been invited, such was her state. The pain was dulled, as was her reality. She slipped in and out of life.

As the first week drew on she finally had the chance and wherewithal to concentrate on a good book to distract herself. The nurses had gone to the hospital library and picked up a smattering of different novels for her. As a single female they disappointingly and inaccurately figured she would appreciate a couple of *'finding yourself'* stories about recently divorced women travelling to a foreign country, learning an enlightening new skill (a foreign language, cooking, arts) and meeting a Pablo, Stavros or Jean-Francois. She flicked through the first one quickly enough, it barely touching the sides as she practically swallowed it whole. Finished and feeling a saccharine sickness, she threw the pulp fiction to the side and looked at the rest of the pile. Thankfully, there also lay Asimov's *'Foundation'*, a well-thumbed science fiction classic about building a better and brighter future by dealing with inevitable crises and Erick Fromm's *'To have or to be'*. She decided on the latter and made her way through it. It took a good bit of time for her to get into the book itself. The basic principle was already clear to her. To be is indeed to be: to experience, to do. And having involves collecting objects because you want them. Yet, as Lamorna dug deeper she realised that life, if you don't pay attention, can itself turn into a collection of things, a collection of *'having done'* things: Milestones reached and achievements attained which you can cross off a list which now belong to you. To have a university degree, to have musical instruments to have a partner. Yet these things should not be about ownership, per se. To love is a verb, to learn is a verb and to play music is a verb. She distantly recalled words spoken by a far spirit.

All of these things require activity and are never completed or finished. There is with every door opened to you by knowledge a new room with twenty doors waiting for you to discover how much you didn't yet know. But you can never truly own this knowledge, it is merely passing through you. The music played on an instrument is heard and felt, it flows through your fingers when played on a piano, gliding into your ears and of those of the people around you, affecting mood and temperament. It has the power to completely change your world. And lastly, to love is something only ever done actively, never something you can nail down, as this can only kill it. If you love something or someone, you have to allow it to fly on the wind. If it returns to you, then it loves you. If they are never seen again, then you have a choice to continue loving them or not. Yet you cannot command them to come back and still hope that they love you. Lamorna's romantic relationships had generally been short-term things, never really reaching that level of connection that she would term romantic love. She hadn't taken the time to cultivate it, never really felt that spark from the outset. She had always been focused on her career. Now she felt as if everything had been built on sand, unable to carry the weight and provide the stability she needed. As soon as she noticed that the book was causing her to dwell on the feeling of loneliness she pressed the button and the pain, as well as her mind, went away.

***

During her stay in the hospital she had a number of different patients with her as neighbours. First of all there was an older lady who very much kept to herself. Gladys had fallen down the stairs in her council flat, breaking her femur. She had spent the majority of her life living alone, her first and only husband dying after only a few years of marriage due to a heart attack. Having lost him and then becoming a reclusive alcoholic she subsequently lost her job and fell into the care of the welfare state. Lamorna struggled to strike up a rapport with her in the first days, as she was in a lot of pain herself.

On the fourth day Lamorna plucked up the courage to ask Gladys about more than just the obvious. If she wished to know anything about her injury she need only observe the massive plaster cast. "Gladys, have you been to the hospital much before?", she carefully prodded.

Gladys let out a micro-grimace, betraying her emotions, "when I was young, I spent a lot of time in these places", she replied, the corners of her seventy-three year old mouth turned down. Gladys visibly welled up with tears as she turned to look to her left to look at Lamorna. Without really trying Lamorna had struck a nerve, a wounded part of Gladys's psyche. As she apologised for the seemingly direct question, Gladys waved her concerns away and proceeded: "When I was a young girl, about six or seven my mother was taken ill, she overdosed."

"I'm so sorry, I really didn't mean to pry. I always manage to put my foot in it. Did you know she was taking medication?" As the question left her lips Lamorna wanted to shoot herself. How did she manage to somehow ask an even more stupid question?

"It's okay; I haven't thought about it for a long time. I hate these places and try to avoid them like the plague!"

Gladys joked, the corners of her mouth flashing up for a brief half-second. "I detest the smell of cleaning products and the decor is horrible".

"I have to agree", Lamorna stated, but then wondered to herself why Gladys had not simply changed the wall colours, floor coverings and pictures herself. "Do you keep everything white?", she asked.

"I don't have any eye implants if that is what you mean. They can see what you are doing all the time and you end up spying on yourself." Lamorna thought it a bad moment to bring up her profession, but brought it up nevertheless. Telling Gladys only of the basics.

"I pity your generation", Gladys managed. "I think young people like you are coerced into such technologies, without any conscious decision of your own. You have grown up being told that everything needs replacing after eighteen months, people as well as your devices, that only the absolute latest version is acceptable, that you don't need to remember anything yourself and that Big Brother is just a TV show. In my day we read books, saved up our money to buy things we needed and rarely threw things away. If it broke, we fixed it. All you do these days is what the adverts tell you to do, hardly stopping to think. It's all a pile of tripe, all of it. People shuffling along like brainless sheep, only reacting to the latest corporate propaganda. Tell me Lamorna, what are you doing here? I mean, how do you spend the days here in the hospital?"

"I read. I don't have anything with me, I didn't plan on coming here", Lamorna looked sadly down towards the foot of the bed, where her lower legs used to be.

"I've heard that one before", Gladys answered, the corners of her wrinkled mouth now slightly less downturned.

"Things are never good if you have landed up in a hospital like this one, Lamorna. You remind me of a quote from Joseph Campbell. He said: *'It is by going down into the abyss that we recover the treasures of life. Where you stumble, there lies your treasure'*. It was the same for Bilbo, Batman in the comics and for you here and now. This is the chance for you to pick yourself up and find out how to live, and truly live. What you do defines you, who you are is created every day. And your actions will be what you are remembered for. So, there comes a time when all you need is your memories, providing you have enough of them. I have never been able to sit still; after my husband died I never wanted to remarry. I have done so many things in my life and I wouldn't want to bore you with them deary, even if we seemingly have much time on our hands. But rest assured, I will die one day safe in the knowledge that I used my time here on Earth to the full. I climbed a lot in my thirties and forties, before my joints began to ache, then it became too dangerous. Then I took up cycling and that took me all over Europe. I always had a group I could join - you have to maintain such friendships when you are a widow, otherwise people will slowly forget that you exist".

"That's not only the case with widows", retorted Lamorna. "I don't really hear from many people nowadays, wouldn't really want to either. I don't really believe that anyone can truly know what another person is going through. We have been together in this room for the past week and only now are we really talking to each other."

"Exactly!". Gladys began to smile. The first time Lamorna had seen her do that during her stay. "I don't follow", Lamorna admitted.

"When it comes down to it, there is very little that you really need, Lamorna. That includes people. You need, at any given moment, very little, a bottle, a book, a pair of glasses, a pen, a phone. Hardly anything at all. In order to complete different tasks we need tools, be it a hammer, wrench or saw. The builder, butcher and baker need these things to do what they do. But, nowadays pen and paper have been replaced by touchscreens, but all of these people have forgotten how to do things with their hands. Changing a bike tube is impossible for them, broken down cars have to be taken to IT specialists and nobody tends to their gardens anymore, they just wish for everything to be blooming and colourful all of the time. Using their blasted implants instead of getting their hands dirty. They are just fooling themselves."

Lamorna nodded in agreement and continued to feel shameful about her role in all of it. Until recently she had only thought about how and never about why. Gladys spoke further and Lamorna's attention began to fade. There was talk of giving up, young people and rabbles. As their talk progressed Lamorna had the feeling that her neighbour wasn't the lonely old lady she had assumed she was. Gladys was a rebel, but didn't know in which direction to bark.

During the next week she and Gladys spoke more and more often about the mindset of their fellow humans, drawing on their life experiences and opinions. Gladys firmly believed that the human race was setting themselves up for a big fall. She went on to explain, "what happens if there is no more electricity? Not only will the transportation, lighting, machines stop working, but the water won't be pumped anymore, people will not know how to make a fire, be unable to cook or keep warm. The few people who actually go out into real forests and camp are few and far between, most of them just use programs or apps for that and imagine they are among the trees for the day and then go to their bedroom and supposedly sleep in a tent, on their own comfortable mattress. They are all merely fooling themselves, their children and each other. We are all making ourselves more and more impotent. In my time here I have been helpless, I have been fully reliant on all the good people here in this hospital. Without them coming to rescue me I would have died of thirst, with no one to check on me or come by. We have lost that sense of community; I like to know what is going on with my neighbours, I offer help, I ask questions. As you can probably imagine, all I get in response is negative and the kind of faces that tell me they have already seen enough of me in those ten seconds and they would rather sit in front of their TV again. When I go home again that is what I will be surrounded by again Lamorna, absolute apathy".

When Gladys departed, her leg being strong enough to support herself, she left Lamorna with a parting gift. It was a red silk scarf, which Gladys had worn for the majority of her stay in the hospital. "The silk is strong, soft, but able to carry heavy loads. Don't be afraid to use your strength Lamorna, even if you are unsure how. One day you will need all of that strength, and more. You will find wells of power deep beneath you which will enable you to overcome so much more that you imagined. This is just the start".

They enjoyed a short embrace and Gladys was gone. The next morning Lamorna, with some considerable effort, pulled herself into her wheelchair for the first time on her own and wheeled herself down the corridor, passing rooms left and right with injured patients. She gave a measured nod to the passing nursing staff, seemingly at the end of their tether and hardly able to muster a half-hearted response. She deeply admired their resolute dedication to their work. Even slightly envying the absolutely necessity of the work they do; in contrast to the literally superficial nature of her work at Optix.

Lamorna went looking for further career inspiration and her first thought took her to the hospital library. She made her way past the non-fiction section, her usual haunt, and perused the contemporary fiction section. There were so many new authors she had never heard of, her preferences lying among old classics. The hospital had hundreds of worn and dog-eared books, how many people had spent their time here lost with their head in a book; a time machine made of paper? She reached for a particularly worn book, reasoning that it must be good if so many people have held it in their hands. She thanked the librarian and made her way back to her ward, book on her lap. It was a quiet morning and the breakfast trolley was making the rounds, but Lamorna didn't have any appetite; she was sick of the same jam all the time. It was as if they had a great surplus from the previous year which needed using up. She made her way back to her room and called a nurse to help her back onto her bed.

Shortly after her new neighbour came in kicking and screaming, his face was bandaged up with a thick gauze and both arms were in plaster. His name was Carl and he had been involved in a motorcycle accident, as Lamorna later discovered. New skin had been grafted onto his face, his open helmet had offered little protection from the road rash suffered on the left side of his face. Both arms had taken the brunt of the force when his bike crashed into the side of a lorry which had sailed through the crossing. Carl's eye implants had somehow malfunctioned, the RGB values had been incorrectly calculated and Carl had mistakenly gone through a red light.

"I'm so sorry", Lamorna let out, once Carl's medication had kicked in. "You must be in so much pain, is there anything I can do to help you?"

"Just leave me alone!", Carl snapped. His face, half

covered in medical muslin, folded up as if he had become a snarling lion scaring away a cackle of hyena from its prey.

"Okay, no problem. I'm sorry for bothering you". Lamorna understood that sometimes it was just best to shut her mouth and move on. In this instance she stayed right where she was and sat in her bed looking right ahead. She looked into the hallway and saw nurses and the occasional doctor rushing by; the trauma ward was always full of noise and she found it very difficult to concentrate. Carl's shrieks had changed to low moans, but she knew that he was still in agony. She reflected on the last book she had finished, Fromm, and realised that what Carl felt right now would pass, that this experience he was having was his and no one else's. She tried to empathise with him, herself also being a traffic accident victim, this was not too hard. But she hadn't lost the left side of her face, this was something else. She had also retained the use of her arms, suffering only mild abrasions. Lamorna had lost her legs. The car accident had completely shattered her femur, fibula and tibia. Her knees had been destroyed and her ankles had resembled pulverised snooker balls.

When the surgeons told her that they needed to amputate both legs she had wept. She had always been sporty and fit. She struggled to reconcile losing her legs with her sense of self. She would take the stairs instead of the lift, jog in a real forest and not merely on a running machine while running a forest program on her implants. She tried to negotiate with the surgeons, doctors and nurses. She pleaded with them to reconsider and for them to rebuild her legs. But they refused; it was more economical in terms of surgery and physiotherapy to provide her with Synaptix prosthetic limbs attuned to her nervous system; they would allow her to walk again.

Surgery was completed without any complications, but

the first days were torture. As ever, it was the terrible feeling of helplessness and the loss of control that were the worst. In sessions with her physiotherapist her implants would sometimes glitch and she would fly to the floor. In others she would simply lose her own balance. Over the course of her sessions she struggled to adapt to the new legs. They were one of the mid-level models, covered by her health insurance. They had a creme coloured hue to them, were relatively sleek and had a twenty year life expectancy. They were made of a carbon fibre substructure with a polymer skin, the circuitry aped that of the human nervous system and connected mid-thigh with the end of her legs. Unlike in the past, the connection was made with electromagnets. Lamorna's upper thighs had been prepared with a new interface, resembling an old electrical razor's cutting surface. She hated them, she felt less like herself.

The first day she completed a walk back to her room unaided she felt like a fraud. She had seen old action films where the hero gets paralysed and completes eighteen months of rehabilitation in order to heal their broken back. They had become a singularly focused individual, wholly intent on getting their revenge. Their struggle had remade them, forged in a crucible of pain and slow progress. The fight to overcome the greatest of hurdles, the anguish and agony, the setbacks and the victories were devastating yet redemptive. She had gone through none of that and experienced a heavy bout of imposter syndrome. She wished for more. She sat down on her hospital bed, without help, looked down at the legs, visible below her black shorts and gave out a sigh. Reclining on the overly soft bed Lamorna closed her eyes and pictured herself outside of the hospital.

In her mind she stood on a beach. The wind howling in her ears and the waves lapping at her toes. The chill of the ice cold water gave her a thrill, the wind almost knocked her off her feet. The rush of the elements struck her senses. She felt at home. The white noise generated by the ocean calmed her and she felt at peace. The sound filled every fold of her earlobes, satisfying her need for a loud kind of silence. Her real body, lying on the hospital bed, slowly relaxed and her hands went limp. In letting go she was able to take control of her thoughts.

Her complete view was now of the sky, full of slow moving clouds and she was stood on a cliff. Ahead of her only the blue and white amalgams of a world flying past her. The white faces, like spectres, the ghostly echoes of her past. They just floated by. She pictured old friends, and saw them go. Her parents both swept past. Su, white wisps trailing behind her, faded from view too. Finally she saw the visage of Jason Chamberlain. His cold eyes belied his otherwise youthful features. She had a hard time letting that one pass; her anger began to well up inside her.

After a time Lamorna woke to a piercing scream. Her new roommate was sobbing in her bed. Sandra was a woman also in her thirties, maybe early forties. As she later found out her husband had recently left her, taking the kids with him. She had tried to kill herself with pills and alcohol. Sandra had been found by a friend she had recently spoken to on the phone; a white foam had coated her mouth and she had been completely unresponsive. Sandra spent most of her time in bed. She normally pulled the covers over her completely and wore ear plugs around the clock. On the rare occasion that Lamorna had a proper conversation with her Sandra reported that she needed to isolate herself from the world, that she never wanted saving and didn't want to exist anymore. She had lived a quiet life, worked hard, been there for others, said her prayers, paid her taxes. Yet she found one morning that there was nothing left for her and the emptiness completely overwhelmed her. Lamorna wasn't sure how to deal with her; in the end she realised that Sandra needed her own space and she mostly left her alone. Sandra's thick brown curly locks were all that she ever really saw from then on. When Sandra eventually left they didn't share anything more than an empty glance.

Her final companion was called Sven who had suffered a skiing accident and subsequently been brought by helicopter to the hospital. A problem in his Optix programming caused him to fly into a tree, the latest textures had not been updated in the remote mountain village where he had been staying. Sven had suffered a severe spinal injury preventing him from ever being able to walk again. This had been the latest in the line of very many setbacks for Sven during his fifty-three year long life. An only child to relatively old parents he grew up in an overly protective environment and had some catching up to do. After graduating with full honours in mechanical engineering he quickly became a success in his field, yet he lacked the ability to stand up for himself and promote his own achievements. Lamorna would, despite her own troubles, talk at some length with Sven and endeavour to find some light in his story. Sven was difficult to talk to. He often trailed off mid-sentence and would try on other occasions to change the subject. At first Lamorna found Sven very hard work. She tried daily to talk to him about the broader scope of mechanical technologies in the future, given the emphasis on software based advances in recent years. He tended to remain focussed on manufacturing and production line technologies and was seemingly unable to see beyond this. There were days when they would rarely speak at all.

Roommates came and went, but Lamorna's constant companion was the written word. She used the opportunity to visit the community rooms, where she would meet up with her other *'book club'* members. She had, once able to leave her room, made a habit of sitting outside in the spring sunshine and reading for hours at a time, losing herself in the works of Fyodor Dostoyevsky and Haruki Murakami. Their books explored the soul of man and played on her conscience. She tended to dwell on past mistakes, playing through past and future events, developing contingencies and alternative timelines. While reading the Brothers Karamazov she learnt to truly understand the three-fold man. One of the brothers was a pure rationalist, whose entire being seemed focused on disproving his devout brother's belief in God. This gentle brother loved from deep within; seeing the holy in everything. The third brother was a passionate fool, unable to control himself and this led to no end of trouble for him, as well as for others. Each brother suffered massive setbacks and this struggle came together in their relationship with their father. Their father had huge debts, was a remote personality who rarely interested in their wellbeing and something of a maverick. He was more interested in chasing the lover of the passionate son than in organising his own affairs. Lamorna could relate most strongly to the cold rationalist and at first understood his attacks on God and his brother. As she grew to better empathise with the devout brother's outlook she began to see the utility in a belief of the divine aspect of life. The third brother, the wild, passionate fool, was, most likely, the furthest removed from her natural character. He was all about taking risks and living for the moment. His passion overwhelmed him and he flew into fights as often as loving trysts. After the first half of the long book she felt as if she truly knew the brothers. She felt as if she could foresee their next moves. She was invariably wrong in her predictions, yet she enjoyed the second-guessing and hypothesising. She began to wish for a fourth figure who would incorporate the characters of all three. A figure able to see the divine, the rational and the passionate parts of life. This figure would be able to not only mediate between the three brothers, but also see a clearer path to be taken, a bolder way to be followers, without the weaknesses of the other three. The self could only be complete once the body, mind and soul worked together, integrated and aligned.

Her meetings with the book club were typically unspectacular affairs. In the spring sunshine on the terrace, outside the entrance to the hospital, patients would go to smoke and mingle. She took a bottle, a long book and her sunglasses. It did her so much good to bury her head in a book, '1Q84', a Murakami novel, she devoured in a matter of days, its thirteen hundred pages read more like three hundred. She lost herself in their little worlds, be it Osaka, St. Petersburg or Mexico City. During the first five days or so spent outside she didn't talk to a soul, so focused was she on her books. After a warming-up period another young woman, a red-head with round glasses and a long pony tail would sometimes greet her and sit at an adjacent chair. This was the founding of the book club. Anja was singularly-minded, learned and quick. At first she and Lamorna would simply read next to each other and not say a word, for a couple of hours on end. Then as the days passed they would sometimes read together by the pond and recommend music and books to each other; by the end of her stay in the hospital Lamorna had twenty new books, thirteen music artists and four comedians to discover. After the first week they were joined by a tall, balding man called John. He was also a keen reader and fit right in. His calm and relaxed demure belied a deeper cutting humour which slipped out completely unannounced.

During the evenings they would meet as a group of three and read, then one after another they would lay their books down and signal that they were ready to talk to each other. This behaviour continued for a couple of weeks; unspoken agreements, giving each other space and enquiring about just the right things at the right moments, intuitively. Lamorna felt at home with them, nothing was forced. They didn't pour out their life stories to each other and they each knew that their brief time together would most likely be like a holiday romance: Nice while it lasted, with no promise of riding off into the sunset with one another.

On the day Anja left both John and Lamorna were scheduled for a group therapy session and skived off it to enjoy one last cocoa with their parting friend. After Anja was discharged Lamorna and John spent more and more time together, between physiotherapy and during group meetings. He had a keen knack of asking pointed *'why?'* questions at opportune moments, which Lamorna had learned to deal with in her talks with Master Su. He further challenged her thinking processes and aided her reasoning. In the final week John and Lamorna began a passive expansion of the book club. At mealtimes they sat with a slowly growing group; going from two to five. One particular person, Ronni, was in her early twenties and studying philosophy. She told John and Lamorna of her death wish and her need to feel nothing, to feel free of pain. Lamorna had never heard anyone else tell of their wish for death before, she at first listened: "I just want to feel at peace", Ronni stated, stone faced. "I just don't feel the joy that I used to as a young girl; there is just nothing that particularly makes me happy".

"When did this start?", John asked, careful not to judge or discourage Ronni.

Ronni continued: "I'm not sure. I remember that feeling would sometimes come up when I was still at school. My few friends already had boyfriends and I would be the one who just tagged along, with my notebook and music. If I slipped away and died, I am sure nobody would have noticed. That's when it started and I haven't shaken it since. It has slowly festered and grown in me, inexorably taking control of me, boring itself into my bones. I just feel like I want to experience that absolute calm of death, where there is nothing left to make me question myself. I mean, am I fucked up? How can you fix something which has wrong circuits, put together backwards. I'm sorry, I don't want to draw you guys into this."

"You know, when you are dead you won't feel at peace", Lamorna coldly stated, after a minute's thought. "When you are dead there is nothing, no pain, but also no calm, no peace. There is only a void and even then none of us will experience it. You say you want to feel free of the pain, the relief, but you won't get to experience that. You'll be gone and the stark contrast will not be felt by you. Only grief will be left for your loved ones and your body will decay."

Ronni didn't really say much as a reply, she didn't want to agree with Lamorna, that much was clear. Had Lamorna been too confrontational? She had her own clear opinion on the matter. Lamorna half thought that Ronni was looking for a reaction, but a good number of people in the hospital had already faced death and the darkness it brings. Ronni preferred to sit with her notebook and made some scribbles. She had taken to writing her own poetry recently to work out some things for herself. She was trying out some stream of consciousness stuff for herself, no doubt some of it would work. After a few minutes of further silence John added his own view on the issue of death.

"It never is as complicated as we think it. One day you are gone and after that you don't feel anything anymore; everything you wanted, loved, hated and wanted to escape is no longer there. That can be exactly what you need if life is truly unbearable. Without light nothing can live. Otherwise, the feeling after death is of a complete nothing. The difference is the feeling before death and knowing that you are ending something unbearable. That is your release. But whether that is something that you can enjoy as a feeling of peace is another thing." He and Lamorna didn't feel it their place to talk Ronni out of it, there were much more qualified professionals to help her properly. But they listened and that was what mattered. Ronni became a permanent fixture of the book club and they would meet of an evening and even write poetry in parallel.

Lamorna's physical therapy sessions were more of an after-thought, the evenings with her new friends were of much more use. On her own final evening Lamorna was surrounded by the members of the new book club. She, along with John had previously passed the leadership of the book club onto Ronni (in a formal ceremony, naturally). Lamorna was happy to have a gang again, for the first time since school; which made the parting even harder. She knew that this fleeting relationship was never going to be long-term, which was why she initially preferred sitting outside alone, unwilling to risk connecting with anyone for the fear of loss when the inevitable parting came. She had learnt some valuable lessons in the hospital: alongside her physical recovery she had learnt to open herself up to new experiences. She had not voluntarily been to a church service in over fifteen years, she had tried hot water therapy and eaten meals silently in a room full of a hundred people. Most of all she learnt that it was ok to show her frayed edges; everyone in the hospital had gone through different things and were treated according to their needs by the doctors and nurses. It was better not to speak to some people, even with the people she got along with she realised that some questions were better not asked. She took risks, formed bonds which may, or may not last. Yet this did not stop her from being unapologetically fearless in doing it in the first place. She understood the importance now of living outside her head and outside of herself.

9 - KINTSUGI

Despite her unapproachable outward appearance and overall cold demeanour Lamorna indeed had a relatively trusting, borderline naïve personality. This partly came from her somewhat protected childhood; a child of the ocean. As a kid she spent most afternoons down at the cliffs and on the beach. The mile-wide sands lay out in front of her offering a hundred different ways to play, the grains offering billions of different toys. She didn't remember there being school holidays at the time, as she was at the beach most afternoons after school anyway. She would leave primary school after lunch, go home and do the small amount of homework, mostly maths or writing and then take the short walk with her mum and sister to the water. She remembered the many palm trees lining the way, walking past older locals and always smiling at them.

Lamorna also had one seemingly ancient neighbour, Jinny, who had about thirty cats. They would sometimes visit her and drink tea and eat biscuits, in hindsight, maybe they were cat biscuits. She never saw Jinny outside of her house; she was just happy with her cats and heavily scratched leather furniture. She had about seven little leather footstools in her living room, but Jinny didn't seem to have any other family who came to visit. Each time they visited Lamorna's mother asked Jinny if she needed anything or if she wanted to come down to the beach with them. Every time Jinny handed over a short shopping list, with sellotape, milk or cat food on it. But she never came along herself. Lamorna wondered what Jinny did all of the time, whether she talked with her cats, whether the cats talked back and whether she was just waiting for something. Lamorna remembered something that Jinny had told her once, she was seven years old at the time, not long before Lamorna left to move up country. She said, "This will always be your home". At the time Lamorna assumed the old lady was extending an invitation, to come for tea and biscuits whenever she liked.

"This is where you are from, this is where you are, this is where you will be", Jinny had followed it up with.

Lamorna enjoyed riddles and she took that one home with her, asking her father what Jinny had perhaps meant later that evening. Her father, who had just got back from work and lacked the patience required in that moment, said to Lamorna, "to be honest, love, I think that woman next door has been eating too much cat food and needs to go out and get more fresh air. She is pent up in that place 24/7 and you guys are the only people she ever sees. If she just went to the bingo or got a darn dog, she wouldn't need to confuse you pretty little head would she?"

"But, Dad, what did she mean, this will always be your home?", Lamorna's little face looking up at her father's.

"Ah, I guess she just likes you. Lamorna, she is an old lady, I don't know how old. But she looks about eighty. She only has her cats, I don't know how many. But she doesn't have a husband or any children. She was living here before we moved down here eight years ago and she was already alone, with just as many cats as now, maybe more", Lamorna's father seemed desperate to end the conversation quickly.

"Do you think she meant that I should visit her more often? Me, Rebecca and Mum go there most days already and she kind of creeps me out."

"Listen, ask your mother about what you should do, I need to get changed, have a shave and then it's dinner time."

Lamorna wasn't exactly satisfied with her father's response, that much she could remember. Looking back she appreciated that he had taken any time at all to give her a halfway adequate response. He was often quite visibly stressed when he came home. He would typically return from work around 6 p.m., dinner followed shortly after and then the evening would be spent around the home entertainment system. There was rarely much talking. Their weekends were however broadly harmonious affairs; often spent on the beach, where her father could relax, swim and play ball with Lamorna and Rebecca. Regrettably, talking was just not a priority. Was this why she had always felt the need to prove herself and impress Chamberlain?

As Lamorna grew older and started working she began to sympathise with her own father and would rarely have enough energy after work to go and see her friends. Little by little she lost contact with former school friends, her course mates at university had also mostly kept to themselves and she started working shortly after. Her school friends were mostly of the nerd-lite variety, like herself. They were a kind of loose conglomerate of awkward types who out of weak solidarity stuck together in the years leading up to the school exams.

When they met in the lunchtimes at school they would chat about music; their next trip into the big city to shop for new albums; they would discuss their lessons at school and what they thought of the ridiculous level of teaching. Some of the teachers seemed better suited to sitting in the rows with the students. Others should have been taken away and locked in padded rooms. This mutual tolerance among school colleagues withered with the passing of school time, like the abandon a moth gives to their cocoon, its purpose long served. The most energy Lamorna could summon to tend to the friendships after a number of years was the occasional social media message on a birthday or when someone inevitably got married or had kids. With the advent of Platform things got easier to follow how people were getting on with their lives, but she just didn't feel the need. It wasn't so much that she and her friends had used each other at school, but there was no living connection keeping them in each other's lives. Lamorna had a strong feeling that their purpose no longer existed, that some things are for the past and others are for now, and some others are best left for possible futures. And besides, imposing herself on formerly known people was much too awkward for her. Would they feel the same?

Her peers at university had been a different story. First of all, she and her four flatmates had been randomly thrown together in the first year, in a high-rise building and a shared flat. They had come from all over the country and each tolerated the other, by and large. It felt more like a social experiment: *'Come and see five people cope with living away from home for the first time and have no choice in where and with whom they live, for one whole year!'.*

With the benefit of Optix and some basic architecture principles Lamorna would have been able to create five individual realities for each of the occupants to make their lives more tolerable. She would have started by making the hallway appear wider, brighter and more airy. Secondly, the walls should have been sound-proofed, or at least made of more than reinforced cardboard. After one particularly messy night out a guest of one of her flat mates managed, while coked-up, to thrust his head through a wall. On other nights she could simply hear the thuds and low moans of couples having sex. This didn't bother her that much, she simply turned her music up and made her own thuds.

Further augmentations she would have made to the drab beige walls, filthy bathrooms, the mould-ridden shower, the filthy toilet, never free of traces and the constantly unwashed dishes in the kitchen. This was the biggest cause for conflict in the student flat too. Nobody wanted to wash up. For eighteen year olds it should not be a big thing to clean some plates, pots and knives. However, it turned into a demented competition to see who could tolerate the most disgusting level of floating debris and mould in the sink. Lamorna wasn't innocent in this practice, she being particularly stubborn, simply made toast each day, losing a good bit of weight in the course of the year. She embellished her diet with bottles of vodka and red wine, typically chemically produced bottom shelf rubbish which was only fit for making mulled wine. Nevertheless, she would eat a few slices of toast, drink half a bottle of vodka and go out to some bars on a Friday night. While her other four flatmates always went to dance clubs, she preferred dingy pubs with sticky tables, wooden walls and a jukebox.

Her favourite was The Hatchet, apparently the oldest public house in the country, hailing from the thirteenth century. The doorways were certainly hobbit-friendly, if not for giants. The tiny bar pumped out great glasses of brew for a few groats and the bearded folk sometimes danced on the tables. Lamorna felt at home among like-minded souls. These people knew how to have a good time, just as her flatmates knew. But the pace of it was more to her suiting; she could nurse a pint of black beer and have her own kind of peace. The din of factory-produced dance music and the breakneck chugging of shots replaced by near deaf barmen, Thin Lizzy and a measured and relaxed appreciation of scotch. She would come back to the flat in the early hours as if with socks stuffed in her ears, just about managing to swipe her keycard to unlock the front door and crawled her way upstairs to the flat, often bumping into other inhabitants of the building on the way back, who had been out at similar pubs, although nothing beat The Hatchet. They arranged to meet up the following week, inevitably forgetting, until they stumbled into each other the very next week and the process started all over again.

***

Lamorna's education itself was something of a secondary affair. She had endured school as much as anything; it started off alright, but once her teenage years kicked in she realised how unintelligent her teachers were. They seemed only interested in and well-informed on their specialist subject, refusing to tangent onto other topics. Her biology teacher was unable to discuss artificial intelligence with her, barely able to teach her class without the use of the text book for the definition of key terms. Her history teacher refused to speculate on parallels between totalitarian governments and large corporations. His preference being to stick to what had already happened and to tell his students about it in long monologues while recounting war speeches from notable prime ministers and generals. One of the few exceptions was Lamorna's English teacher during the exam years. Mr. Pool was incapable of monologuing, he wanted his students to contribute. He seemed only to ask pointed questions, rarely giving his own opinion; preferring to invite others to give theirs, providing they could give evidence from the set text or somewhere else. She realised that this was pure discussion and that this was now the time to learn how to do it. Lamorna made notes during class on the books they were reading in one notebook and in her journal she kept a running log of how Mr. Pool involved and encouraged others to talk.

Once at university she utilised her observations and found that this made her a favourite of some of the lecturers and tutors. Not all of them though, as she quickly learnt. Being told to keep her mouth shut at school, in front of twenty-five classmates was one thing, being dressed down in a lecture hall by a doctor of robotics with two hundred and fifty students in attendance was quite another. This however did not get her down too much, this was why she was there, to learn, to find her way and develop her skill-set. Her degree was in advanced architecture. She had played with building blocks a lot as a child, with civilisation-building games as a teenager and figured it was as good a choice as any. She loved speculating about future societies, dystopian totalitarian tendencies of large states and the integration of new technologies in cultures. How buildings affected people and influenced their lives was utterly fascinating to Lamorna.

One particular university, Trinity University, stood out to her while she was still at school. While website perusing she stumbled across an advert for virtual reality living and just had to click. She was taken to a website for a small IT company called *'Optix'* which was manufacturing prototype glasses which could augment reality and change the colour of walls, the names of logos on t-shirts, numbers on buses and the level of lighting. Aside from the moral issues she had with revising and editing reality, she was enraptured by the possibilities for good in the technology: by increasing the level of light using chromatic filters the risk of car accidents could be reduced. Colours affect people's moods, so it just be great to redecorate a flat completely befitting your desires without having to lift a finger.

Lamorna read further into the company, none of the prototypes were in fact full-functioning, but the lead researcher had graduated from the Trinity University's advanced architecture degree course and she made it her mission to follow in his footsteps. He had advanced with first degree honours just two years previously and now led a four person team in developing the prototypes for the company. His name was Jason Chamberlain and he had foregone completing his doctorate in order to concentrate on Optix's research.

Even in the short video on the website the pure excitement and speed of developments was clear to see. Alongside product mock-ups and 3D renderings they displayed some of the production meetings and concept drafting. Invariably there was fervent discussion and lots of hand waving, not a lot of waiting in turn to speak. There seemed to be no one in charge of the meetings, just a free-for-all, she wanted to get her foot in there as soon as she could. She bookmarked Optix's website and downloaded the application forms for Trinity University.

After waiting a year to finish school, passing her exams with acceptable results, she moved to the big city and commenced her advanced architecture degree. The large lectures of the first year, with mass-production sorting of wheat from chaff, gave way to smaller seminars with less theory in the second year, where there was also much more practice involved. The computer programming aspects were new to her, having only previously created a very simple website using templates and some expenditure spreadsheets. Lamorna took the programming in her stride however, seeing it as a necessary step towards her future goals. She found the ethical discussions which arose during the group projects much more interesting. Some of the other students had evidently not enjoyed such a good English teacher at school as Mr. Pool and were not as used to having to form their own opinions and they therefore lacked the desired languid salubriousness of argument. It was during these discussions that Lamorna found an ally in Felix Harper. He was a non-aggressive sort, his head invariably stuffed in a book of Karl Popper's or Mary Beard's. They formed a sort of double act in the seminars they shared, he would play good cop to her bad cop.

It was also with Felix that she found someone at university who shared her preference for dark grotty pubs and Thin Lizzy. They often met up at the weekend in The Hatchet and discussed futures of mankind, be they fictional or theoretical. Here Felix taught her mind palace building: The ability to create a safe-space in the brain where you can be at absolute peace and in control. The palace would start empty, could be a country house, crystal castle, a cave or a hot-air balloon, but it would be only for you and should not be a real place. In it you could also store all manner of important memories and pieces of information. Lamorna had little idea of how hers could look at the time, but she grasped the idea quickly enough and stored it in her own memory banks.

One thing Felix and Lamorna didn't expect was that come graduation that they would end up working for the same company, working under the maverick scientist Lamorna had seen on the website years before. Optix had grown to become the market leader in augmented reality and was really the only organisation doing a convincing enough job of it.

***

Now, back in her hospital bed Lamorna thought back on all that she had experienced up to this point in her life, she felt like she had been missing something up to now. Some kind of focus, direction or guide. She thought back to her first evening with Master Su. Then she remembered the round object Su had placed in her hand, then telling her *'I am small as a grain of sand'*. Where was that little thing now?, she wondered. Had somebody taken it? Where are my clothes? My bag? As her head hummed she tried to focus on where she had left it. When she had left Su's it was in her jacket pocket, she had removed it and put it away in her drawer. *'I am as small as a grain of sand'*. Such a short sentence, what could it mean? The ball was about six centimetres in diameter, much bigger than a grain of sand. She took a different approach, tried some word association, which had worked well in the past for her. But she lacked the ability to concentrate and ended up going in circles. She often struggled in such situations at work and would normally push on through and fight to solve the problems and meet her deadlines. Since Felix had told her about the mind palace principle all those years ago she had never really tried implementing it again. She ruminated on her safe-space, beginning construction on her mind palace. The first thing she would need to do would be to choose a site, somewhere by the water definitely. She thought about the Antarctic, about the North Sea and also Hawaii. She settled on the beach of her youth and childhood however, the Cornish west coast. There nestled in the bay she could, if she concentrated hard enough, in her mind's eye, she could see over the entire Atlantic Ocean and view the North American east coast. The bay was over a mile wide, each side, dark sheer cliffs nestling the waters between. She could see blue-grey swells approaching from miles away. The horizon was a crisp line even though the sky above didn't lack for clouds; she loved the rain and appreciated their work. She wanted to be protected from the elements in her mind palace however and imagined how it should be constructed. She rejected building directly on the sand, she knew the tale of the three little pigs and the hungry wolf. She didn't want to be up on the top of the cliff, heights weren't her thing. She settled on being built directly into the rock, tucked in and protected on three sides, like that of a villain's lair in an international spy film. The front window looking out over the ocean would be one twenty metre wide pane of glass about three metres tall. When stood in the centre of the window it would be as if she was floating in front of the ocean and that would be all she could see. The flooring would be dark stone to reflect the rocks around her, one metre squared tiles on the floor. The walls a soft white, not too harsh and not too clinical.

She remembered the next part of Felix's instructions: the mind palace is normally there to help you store and recall information; one can compartmentalise knowledge in different rooms on different floors and retrieve it when necessary, just by entering your mind palace and going to the right place; you could even create a floor plan with different topics, like in a department store. For now, Lamorna had simply the desire for peace and contemplation and would use the mind palace for this purpose. To future proof her retreat she created two great sliding doors on each side wall which would provide access to the lower floors. Otherwise she had nothing in the main room itself other than the flooring; the window over the ocean was all she needed and she was able to begin.

As the weeks of her recovery passed Lamorna was better able to focus on her castle of stone. She would imagine herself standing in the middle of the room and look out over the ocean, watching the rolling waves. She found it very difficult at first, the construction of the place itself had been a fun challenge, but now using it for its purpose and following through was very difficult. Other thoughts kept her captive and refused to let her focus at first: Her colleagues in the office, her boss, the doctors and nurses, their fussing and the organised chaos of the hospital. She found a use for the doors on each side of the room, just as Felix had said they could be used to gain access to storage. However, Lamorna found another use for them: she could simply shut people out, refusing them access to her and her brain. The great sliding doors, until now made of clear glass, she decided to exchange for a frosted, opaque tone. If anyone entered her thoughts she could merely shut the door on them. Lamorna did not want to completely deny the thoughts at all, because she felt she would become anxious at the thought of not knowing what was behind the door. Better the devil you know, she told herself.

In the tranquil peace of her mind palace Lamorna fell asleep most nights in the hospital. Standing centred on solid stone she looked out and tried to hypnotise herself with the waves. Thoughts would come into her head and disturb her concentration, but she let them go and they could, if necessary take their place behind the sliding doors. She kept the main room pristine so as not to allow distractions. She needed a calm environment to sort out her head. In the beginning she could only concentrate for moments at a time, but as she practised she was able to envisage being there for a number of seconds and then minutes at a time.

As she grew more secure Lamorna would often venture out onto the sands. The time spent at the ocean was just as important as the physical healing. She would try to imagine being back there, standing on the soft sands, looking at out the swelling waters. Lamorna's tired eyes closed in her bed and she disappeared into this other place, feeling her feet slowly seeping, pressing deeper into the cold, wet ground beneath her.

Her toes were digging in, but not in a playful way, but more like gripping on to something she couldn't bear to lose. *'I am here'*, she said to herself, now totally consumed by the winds blowing in her face, the fizz and crash of the waves and the cawing of the seabirds around her. And then the clouds came, the dark ominous foreboding enveloped her. Cracks of thunder pealed from the sky, the sands shifted beneath her feet. And she fell to the ground; helpless and cold she began to shiver. Her calls for help barely left her mouth, such was the force of the wind. As she clawed her way back toward her cave hideout, she felt her body sinking into the wet sand, she gasped and panicked, tried to kick herself free, but to no avail. Then it was that it dawned on her that her legs were once more gone. She was alone on the beach without a soul to help her and then with a shriek she awoke, bathed in a cold sweat she found herself once more in the bright hospital ward. The raw power of her dream was matched only by that of the cold ocean she ruminated. Lamorna still felt that pang of loss in her gut however, for the home she left behind, for her missing legs and that deep-seated fact that she was totally alone. As the weeks passed she could feel how important it was to think about home, about the ocean. She had not often returned there since she was a teenager, yet still called it home and felt a longing to return. She had always just put it off. That would have to change she told herself, this time intending on following through. No, it had to be more than an intention, or a promise.

***

While in hospital she attended therapy with Doctor Shoot; Lamorna loved the name and looked forward to the sessions. The first session was not the fight she assumed it would be. She wanted to get better, she had turned a mental corner. She did not like the feeling of being seen as a poor victim and wanted to changed this as soon as she could. The good doctor welcomed her in, shaking her hand and guided her to her seat, opposite the doctor's desk. Doctor Shoot was a pale blonde haired woman in her late forties, tall and athletic. Dressed in a long dark blue wooden roll-neck pullover going down to her mid-thigh, under which she wore black jeans. She had a very calm manner and allowed Lamorna to say as much as she needed. Lamorna had her own assumptions about therapy: sitting on a chais-longe, talking about daddy issues while a bearded man stroked his beard and said *and how does that make you feel?*. Doctor Shoot sat more like a family doctor, a trusted authority figure, sat opposite at their desk, a specialist there to help. You take your car to the garage immediately when you have a problem with your engine she thought, why don't we call these people as soon when we need them? She wondered.

As she unpacked her work issues and subsequent accident she laid out lots of facts for Doctor Shoot. In fact it was so much information that Lamorna lost all sense of time and indeed after about two hours the good doctor had to send her out. The time flew by and Lamorna felt energised and looked forward to their next meeting, scheduled for the next day. She had some homework to do: to write a bullet-point chronology of her life thus far - a classic, at least one assumption turned out to be correct. She went back to her room and got started; she had work to do.

And so the rest of Lamorna's time in hospital passed. Combined with her time with the book club and trying out new things, the ability to walk again meant that she had a responsibility, a duty. Indeed, she planned on changing the world.

10 - THE DEEP GREEN SEA

On the day Lamorna was discharged she thanked the nursing staff, collected her papers and made her way out of the front door. Some of the guys from the book club had said goodbye; kind hearted people she knew she would instantly lose contact with, but that was okay. They wished each other well and she was sure not to make any false promises of reunion. She climbed in the taxi and made her way home. The long hour ride from the forest-set hospital took her along the river, over mountains and through moor land. She hadn't realised that she was so far away from everything else and made it her aim to come back before too long.

She hadn't missed the greying city, her implants remained off for now, the smell was what also hit her; more a blanket of smog and waste than a neon playground. After paying the driver she fumbled for her keys upon reaching the front door and made her way in. Other than the stream of dusty light cutting the living room in two nothing had really changed. Nobody had been inside, she surmised. Her washing-up was green and mouldy, her fridge was bare at the best of times thankfully, and her bedroom was a mess. She felt safe; this place had been her nest for long enough and some things don't change. Moving around the place would take some getting used to with her new legs. At first she bumped into the furniture and kitchen counter, needing practice to feel comfortable with the prosthetics. The doctors had told her it might need a few weeks.

Lamorna was looking ahead to the outside world, she had plans. She wanted to do something about Chamberlain. Exactly what, she wasn't entirely sure. Optix's eighth version was in development and they were promising something ground-breaking; Chamberlain had his best people working on the features for the next steps. As one of those key people Lamorna had, until recently, been quite closely knitted with that team, providing important support. But with the accident she had been out of the loop for a long time, it felt like years beyond memory. She needed to rest at home longer than she felt was necessary or even advisable. If she returned too soon, she would be sucked back into that dark hole they called Optix. And besides, Chamberlain had most likely removed her clearance on the day of the accident. She was hesitant to find out; if she tried logging in, Chamberlain would notice. So she left her computer on the shelf, put on some music and began tidying up. She started with her bedroom, that was the easiest; just the most basic furniture and a medium-sized bed with drawers integrated underneath. She removed the bedclothes and put them in the washing machine along with the contents of her over-filled clothes basket and her bag from the hospital. Once that was done she cleared the floor, threw away a lot of old paperwork and collected junk in a box to dispose of later.

Lamorna's living room and kitchen were not such an easy job: There were colours in the pots and pans which she didn't know existed, disgusting odours she thought only possible to create in a lab. Even Optix couldn't yet capture the rotten fumes which nature could muster, given enough time to fester. Lamorna's desire to vomit was severely tested: mould growing on mould, supplemented by expired vegetables and ex-pizza crust. She simply threw a lot of dishes into the bin; others she put in the bath and turned on the water. They would need a good while to soak and already looked like a horrific art installation: 'A Life Unlived' she could call it. Her living room was full of crap that she didn't need: Keepsakes from her parents' holidays abroad, terrible photographs she had taken on her limited walks outside, small clay sculptures she had made on a whim. As well as magazines on a myriad of topics: electronics, music production, cooking and adult education. She cleared a whole lot out, desiring an uncluttered and well curated living space. While in the hospital she had kept her bed organised, having only a little table and a small shelf above her bed. On the table she kept her current book and on the shelf she had a bottle of water. That was the kind of orderliness she wanted to integrate into her flat. Too long she had kept things that may one day be of use, or had reflected some desirable aspect of her self, her nerdiness, her supposed uniqueness. She had spent too much time projecting the outward image of somebody at once in control and also needing to fit it and be accepted. Maintaining that facade is what had helped keep others at a distance; she needn't wonder why she was there alone.

Lamorna took all of the cookbooks, an array of differing cuisines without any specific focus, and put in them in a box. They were soon followed by a variety of knick-knacks and equipment she would never need again: egg slicer, ice-cream maker, egg poacher, other eggs things, a skipping rope, art prints, some books she had read and wanted to pass on, photo frames and some other sport items. These objects held some weight in her mind, she told herself that it was important to let them go. She never used them, she no longer wanted them and these things would only drag her down. 'I am as small as a grain of sand', she repeated to herself.

Looking at the walls she then proceeded to remove

pictures by Klimt, Matisse, Picasso and Dalí. She had at one point put them up thinking that they reflected her aspired taste, somehow trying to elevate herself via artistic osmosis. That the pictures perfumed the air around her, improving her culturally, spiritually and cognitively. In the end the pictures were much better served in a charity shop, they would make nice little gifts for first year students looking to appear elite. She had at one point painted a few larger canvases in the style of Mark Rothko; probably her favourite artist. Although she never went for the massive canvases he used and her colours were never as intense. So in the end her work appeared more like that of a primary school kid drawing coloured boxes with simple acrylics. Without being too downhearted she put the canvases back into her bedroom and promised herself she would reuse them when a good idea came to her, and not before.

Slowly, her living room cleared up. The room was still not empty and Lamorna considered tipping the entire room on its side and just letting gravity do the rest. As the rug, sofa, tables and chairs, speakers, ornaments, books and candles went flying she could rest assured knowing that it was all behind her. Unfortunately, until physics or architecture caught up with her imagination, this would be best left for another day. The sofa and other furniture could stay, for now. Maybe all she needed was some cushions and a short table, maybe she should just move out. She also left this decision for another day. It was enough to peel back at the layers she had applied to herself. They now felt foreign and old, like dead skin sloughing off her body. These old masks had served their purpose and were now obsolete. The cultured artist mask had never really worn right: She had to keen peeling back the layers.

By surrounding herself with such renowned artists Lamorna had wanted to give the impression of taste. Her guests could admire this characteristic, be impressed by her knowledge of twentieth century modernist art, but there were no guests. Whether the observer ever truly connected with the pieces and saw something within themselves was never a priority and until then not something she even considered. The art was there to impress, nothing more.

The myriad books on her bookshelf served a similar purpose, her curiosity for the sciences was born from her inhaling encyclopaedia as bedtime-reading as soon as she could read. The falling asleep part had not worked so well. The books rarely bored her and she would continue to read long past her parents themselves had gone to bed. She knew how to utilise stimulation, to provoke herself into staying up into the hour of the wolf. Her early behaviours sowed the seeds for her later sleep deprivation, legitimised by her *'just wanting to find out about this'*.

This was all compounded by living alone, without a steady partner she had no one to call her out on this. Bull-headed and focussed, Lamorna didn't merely fall down a rabbit-hole of information, she would burrow and meander through that cave of knowledge, gleaming anything she could from its surface, filling all her pouches as she went. Wading through puddles of darkness, feeling her way through tunnels where any manner of fantastic beasts lurked. She returned to the cave system every night, allowing the details to seep in. Lamorna was a difficult student. A know-it-all, no particular teacher of hers was able to really challenge her. Of course, she wasn't always writing straight A's in tests, no particular subject would captivate her for long enough. A true generalist, Lamorna was most at home by establishing a broad overview of knowledge for herself. Forever finding blind spots which required a light being shone upon them. She was forever equipping her own space telescope to discover the wider reaches of her galaxy. As the light from distant stars reached her she would incorporate that energy and it would push her on to find out ever more, until satisfied and she moved on to new plains. This aspect of self was innate, so much time and energy had been dedicated to it, too intensive her thirst for more. Yet hers was no Faustian pursuit, no bartering with a devil. She needed no final resolution, no transcendental experience. She was inanely, innately curious. So her books were allowed to stay. 80% non-fiction, 18% novels, 2% empty notebooks, waiting for words.

Lamorna's collection of musical memorabilia and equipment was also vast; forever justified by a desire to improve her set-up. She played a number of instruments to a middling degree; she could be a one-woman mediocre rock band. One corner of her living room was dedicated to her guitars. She had often flipped guitars, changing out one for a slightly better one. Again, her thirst for more coming to the fore. The same with amplifiers, cables, signal processing units, microphones, recording software and user interfaces. She knew how to develop this particular hobby. It probably being the one she most stuck with. There wasn't much to be disposed of here, she really would use it all at some point. It all needed some streamlining and reorganisation, certainly. You can have too many guitars, especially if you don't play them often enough. Also, if you are not writing music, why retain so much recording equipment? And what was the point of having enough guitars to outfit a whole band if you didn't want to play in one? She put a lot of the equipment into boxes and made classified ads to sell them. Her favourite guitar, an old Canadian acoustic, she would retain and sell the others. It was the creating that was important, not the objects themselves.

Lamorna had cleansed herself of the weight of her own things and could move on with the next stage of the plan.

11 - MEGALITH

A few days later Lamorna received a call from Su, who had been quiet the whole of the time she was in the hospital. Lamorna reasoned that Su wanted to leave her in peace during her recovery, even if she found that a little odd. She was only slightly resentful about it, but believed that Master Su would be able to explain in due course.

"Good morning Lamorna, how is life back home?", Su asked, her voice uncharacteristically bright and breezy.

"Hi Su, good of you to call. How long has it been, two months?", Lamorna's voice was in quiet contrast to Su's; maudlin, monotone.

"Did you learn anything in the hospital?", Su prodded. Lamorna looked at her phone's display, seeing Su's name. She felt ignored and let down by her. Lamorna didn't react to the question.

"Lamorna? What insights did you gain? And are you really okay?", Master Su was losing patience and she wondered why her apprentice was not being any more forthcoming.

"Su, I lost my legs. I was locked up for 8 weeks. I didn't know anybody there. And I missed you. Where were you?"

"I can see that it was an intensive time for you, dear Lamorna. I can imagine that you were thoroughly tested for what comes ahead". Su's voice was flat, her volume low.

"As if I haven't been through enough already, Su. I felt like I was in a kind of purgatory, an in-between place where I was only a lich, a ghost. The pain was horrific, I was bored out of my mind. My roommates were partially crazy and at the beginning I couldn't get out or see anything or meet anyone. I was imprisoned, scared and alone."

Su's voice now grew in excitement, "and how did you move past that?"

Lamorna, now growing agitated, "I couldn't move past anything Su! I was unable to move at all. How would you feel if you lost your sight? Your voice? Your mind? Never have I ever felt more alone, Su".

"That's because you were, utterly alone and without escape. That was necessary for you, to be left with the only person who can get you out of this. Each day being the same as the last, every cursed minute feeling like an age. Each moment in your hospital bed, reliant on the doctors and nurses for information. No distractions, only suffering. It is exactly such experiences that form you Lamorna. You will look back on that time as a critical period, not as a terror, not as a hell, but as your making. All of those people you met will have given you something. Just as each person will have gleaned something from you. And I am sure it will not always have been positive. You were not able to be anything but authentic in that environment. Completely destroyed and vulnerable, you had no armour anymore, it had all been broken down over the past few years as you lived further and further away from your true self; the accident was just the crowning glory. You have been ignoring it for too long, dear Lamorna. You have been too easy on yourself in some important ways, ignoring too much. You always tolerated your lack of focus, your excuses for not doing what was necessary for yourself. Not taking true risks, and not showing yourself for who you are."

Su took some breaths and waited for Lamorna's reaction, which was not yet forthcoming. "And as no one was able to attack you, Lamorna. That is the thing. That hospital was a microcosm of the outside world, no one really cares about you, you don't let anybody in to get to know you. Hell, you don't know you, don't you get it? That hospital was full of people involved with their own crises, in their own private Hell, prison cells shared, but the lives are divergent. Only that time together was a convergent point in space-time, an eye of the needle if you will. But as you know, it is harder to find the needle itself sometimes, than for a camel to pass through its eye. And you never looked for it, you didn't even realise that this was necessary. You spent all of your time running away from yourself. Only focussing, if one can really use that word here, on externalities, on outside influences. Believing that you were somehow growing and feeding your mind. Every book on philosophy, biology, all of the *'-ogies'*, each podcast listened to, each renowned artist looked at, every symphony listened to, all of them took you outside of yourself. They were either an escape from your little life, or you were merely trying to impress others with all that you knew."

"Hold on a pretty second", Lamorna interjected. "Are you trying to tell me that I should have spent my life staring into a mirror and keeping myself ignorant all this time? I can't tell if you're just being mean or actually trying to gaslight me. That is ridiculous. What nonsense!"

"Lamorna, please don't consider this a personal attack, that is not my intention. My point is that you have lacked all balance. Always looking to the greats, be they scientists, musicians, writers or philosophers, has taken you further and further away from the core within you. That unique element which can make you great, which sets you apart. Curiosity and potential are not enough; at some point potential disappears and we turn old. Potential is there to be turned into something, not to die a death left unfulfilled. The old man in his armchair, sat newspaper in hand, complaining about world affairs and how these politicians don't have a clue how to run the country. This man, he once had a chance to do something about it. He could have informed himself about town policy, he should have got involved in local politics and run for office himself in some capacity. Instead, he remained an observer, safe in the knowledge that he had made no mistakes. And because he took no action, no one was able to crucify him for his deeds, no public shaming, no corruption scandals, no bribes, no illicit affairs. His hands remained clean, his conscience also."

"I suppose, yes, I see what you mean". Lamorna, readied herself for more; for she knew it was coming.

"Yet, all of his criticism of those politicians was merely a projection of his regrets, his impotence and his inability to take control of his own life. His poor partner most likely gets slapped for leaving his brown slippers in the wrong place. They probably receive no word of thanks for the warm meals they place in front of him every day. There is no joy, no danger and no life in such a person. All of the *'could haves'* act as nails driven into his wrists and ankles. A meticulous crucifixion. If one maintains that behaviour for long enough, one is unable to move. Every criticism is a small dagger. When aimed correctly and timely it can be freeing. The aspect of violent potential is of paramount importance, dear Lamorna. Think of the violence necessary to rescue a small child from a potential kidnapper; you must be able and willing to be brutal and dangerous in order to be good. The child, held tight by the kidnapper, requires it of you. Meekness has its place, yet it is not here. The dagger, correctly wielded, buys that child its freedom. And delivers justice to the kidnapper. Now let us contrast that with the daggers thrown by our old man with the brown slippers. He has no noble quest, no higher goal. He looks at the world and complains. The only risks he took in life are probably linked to his high equity pension fund. His partner is full of daggers, any small movement will cause them pain. His aim is good, an experienced torturer. But accuracy alone is not enough. He set himself the wrong goals, and the wrong target. His inadequacies he also projects onto his partner, thus causing them further pain and darkness. That is a life in shadow. This is a hell."

"The slow crucifixion, you call it. Is there any way to undo it?", Lamorna enquired.

"I think you misunderstand the point", Master Su retorted. "At first the man was throwing daggers wildly out at anyone and everyone, full of caprice and bitterness. But over time, the daggers turn around in the air and return to him, Over time, they pin him to his own cross. Over time, all his life's blood will seep out of him. He will be confined to his chair, his mind unable to free himself anymore. These will be the actions that define and eventually defy him." Lamorna nodded. "It is living outside of our heads that is necessary. We are more than brain, more than thoughts. Our fleeting ideas are the boundless potential within us. Nevertheless they require focus, practice, time and energy. It is simply that which we do that defines us. No more and no less." Exhausted, Lamorna looked at her hands. "And what have you done, Lamorna?"

"Not enough", Lamorna, now looking around her flat, could see that this was her opportunity. "I want to bring down Chamberlain before he corrupts the very world we live in."

"Now we are talking, get to it. Make a plan", and with that Su hung up.

12 - EGGS AND CHICKENS

Lamorna set about by making breakfast, she was hungry, thirsty and had neglected to shower, but that could wait. She made some toast with peanut butter and jam and a pot of tea and made her way back to her dining table. She started with the words *'End of Optix'* on the back of an old poster. She continued with the words *'Jason Chamberlain'*, *'the program'*, *'Alpha team'*, *'servers'*, *'architects'*, *'users'*, *'media'*, *'unforeseen things'*. She imagined that her attempt would require inside help, as well as persuading the users to abandon the technology.

Some of her ideas were somewhat fanciful and ridiculous, others could be fleshed out. No ideas were however wrong. Each idea could contain the key to bringing it all down, revealing the lies and exposing the people to the truth. She looked for news online, read of plans for offshore servers built by shady construction firms. There was to be a new texture sensitivity roll-out, rumours that Optix was to move into another realm where touch, tactile response, was integrated. She wondered how that could be possible with the current hardware. Otherwise, there were just rumours of clandestine meetings between Chamberlain and lobby groups, as well as Chamberlain and some politicians.

She could get into the building and shoot Chamberlain, that would end it. She would go to prison for the rest of her life and become famous. That was a bit dramatic, best left for others. She could try to hack into the system and corrupt the data. Going anonymously to a media outlet would be another option, telling tales and creating an absolute shitstorm about how Chamberlain caused her accident, habitually drives others out of the company and is trying to corrupt the world. That was her current preference, being the lowest personal risk to her, it not being criminal and there being the potential to cause some damage to the company. Whether any business practices would really change after the initial revelations would be another issue however. These things tend to blow over after the news cycle has chewed everything to ribbons and the unfortunate whistleblower's character has been well and truly assassinated. Without a public source, also well known, which she was not, it was likely to fade out of the public eye as fast as it came. The whistleblower idea wasn't without some merit however and Lamorna decided to keep it as a plan B and develop the idea further at a later time.

Perhaps the best form of revenge would be for to start a rival company and show Chamberlain that it was possible to run an ethical tech company which didn't abuse its workers and still offered life-altering services. She could start at home, programming and trialing some ideas out, getting funding from here and there. Working from the ground up. She could picture it already: in her press conferences she wouldn't mention Optix or Chamberlain, she would speak only of her own company, deny their entire existence. She would only accept private investors to ensure that Optix wouldn't buy her out, keep safeguards in place to ensure complete independence and run the company from the perspective of an entry-level worker. Like at Optix, promotion would be based on merit, but without the battle royale style fight to the top. That would really show Chamberlain how it could be. If Lamorna didn't care what he thought, this would probably be the best idea.

However, that was all that Lamorna could think about. Bringing him to the ground, getting revenge. She wanted him to feel it, to feel his legs pulled out from underneath him.

13 - THE BRIDGE

Alone in the forest at dusk, Lamorna was looking for something. Whatever it was, she couldn't find it. Above her in the sky the bright full moon came into view. As the night drew in it became colder and her searching became more frantic. Tearing up the forest floor like a wild boar, she was scrambling greedily for sustenance. She grew more and more frustrated at her search. Her hands were black and her hair ragged. Lamorna began to run, past rows and rows of trees; each more regimented than the last. Each tree a perfect two metre distance from the next, a geometric grid. The paths ran at right angles to each other, there were no curves to be seen. All randomness had been eradicated, everything was preprogrammed. The cold and calculated night was her prison. The faster she ran, the darker it became in the forest. She must have passed hundreds of rows of trees before she arrived in a great clearing. Looking up to the sky, now freed from the tree cover, she once more saw the great moon, its light bathing all before her. The tree trunks, all lined up, stretched out in rows for miles and the treetops were also equidistant; who placed them there like that?

Ahead of her she saw a black pool of water. Moving closer, she dipped her toes into it, its chill slowly, inevitably, crept up her legs, through her spine to her brain. Sinking and sinking deeper Lamorna tried to clutch at anything that would prevent her head going under, but it was to no avail. She couldn't scream out for help. All air was already pulled out of her lungs, replaced by heavy helplessness.

She fell beneath the surface, her hair felt as if tied around her face, like tentacles of algae. She was blinded and struggled at her face so that she could see again, freeing herself of the black mask wrapped upon her. Lamorna then realised that lengths of algae were wrapped around her ankles and she was sinking deeper into the pool, which had now opened up into doomed depths of open sea. Her eyes, although free, struggled to see ahead of her, for now the moon's light fought to reach so many fathoms below the surface. It was then that she felt solid ground under feet and the oily arms of algae let her go.

There in the murky depths Lamorna could faintly see some dark forms at rest. As she swam closer she came upon an underwater collection of black cubes, all resting on the sea floor, hewn out of smooth obsidian. Each exactly the same as the next. The cubes began to vibrate, she could see the movement of water around them. And as they increased in frequency they moved to form a stone circle as wide as a large house. The low grinding sound of the stones moving was all that Lamorna could focus on, the agonising minutes of their movement froze Lamorna in place as if suspended in time. The sound was as though bones were being ground into meal. There she stood as if caught in a bear trap, but looking upon the stone circle she wondered if she could touch them, try to look closer at their surface or to swim to the surface.

As the circle was complete the water pressure around Lamorna suddenly increased. Lamorna began to panic now and found breathing underwater difficult. Up until now she wasn't even aware that she wasn't holding her breath at all; part of her felt at home in these depths. The great stone circle suddenly pulled apart, like a ravenous python dislocates its jaws to better ingest its prey. Then it was that the twin halves of the circle rose up as jaws to meet her. Getting ever closer, Lamorna screaming silently, the teeth made to devour her.

And that was when she awoke from her dream bathed in a cold sweat, her sheets soaked, her head thumping and her heart racing. She felt shell shocked and tongue tied. She tried to shake off her dream, but it hung over for a long time. Lamorna would need to ask Su about it, providing they had enough time. She would surely have something to say about the lined-up trees and their regimented nature, the dark pool and its black jaws ready to consume her. Beyond the obvious lawful obedience that she had previously shown at Optix and then the black abyss which she had fallen into while trying to prove her worth, there must be other insights into the dream. *'What were the black stones? Did I want it to consume me?'*

All being equal she would have preferred to stay in bed, check her Platform feed, put on some music and ignore the world. But this was not the day for that. For this was the day of. And she had to focus on the task at hand. There would be time enough to discuss her dream at a later point in time. She had a shower and dressed in black, head to toe. It was a cloudy day, so she put on her jacket, locked her flat and entered the lift. The ding of arrival made her head ring, every little sound caused her to shudder. The headache was right in the middle of her forehead. Going through the main door she saw that Renn was parked outside. She hadn't seen it since she met Master Su the first time. She began to make her way through the side streets to get to her rendezvous with Su. The road surface was slimy and full of potholes, in stark contrast to that which she saw through her implants. The alleyways and side streets were immaculately painted and finished, not a spot of graffiti or urban decay in sight, such subtly brilliant mummery.

Su had suggested the war memorial as the meeting place. It was in the upper west side of the city, close to where Optix were due to make an announcement at the guildhall.

From a distance Lamorna could spot Su stood next to the black obelisk. In the damp air it had a wet sheen to it and appeared to be made of the same obsidian as the underwater city in her nightmare. A shimmer of names was engraved in its four sides, looking more like heat ripples. Renn guided Lamorna to the foot of the monument and she greeted Su. Su was today also wearing a long black robe, in place of her usual royal blue, "greetings Lamorna, here we are. At a place commemorating the mighty fallen. Are we ready?".

"As much as ever, Su. I saw this in my dream, but it was different, deeper and darker", Lamorna divulged.

"Our dreams prepare us for what is to come. It is our job to interpret them properly. Tell me, did you wake from your dream refreshed, yearning for more? Or did it shock and appal you?"

"I dreamt I was pulled below into murky depths, held by great black tentacles, guided to an underwater prison. Su, I was completely frozen and faced with a great stony sea-city, which then made to consume me. What does it mean?"

"The darkness is coming. This feeling of helplessness is not foreign to you. It is a shadow for you to overcome. You could bathe in this lack of agency for years to come, or you can swim against it. It is up to you, but you must be the one to do it. You alone. When you swim, no one can hold your hand, you need both of them yourself". Master Su let go of Lamorna's hand, turned around to pick up a pair of motorcycle helmets, handing her one. "This way Lamorna, come with me." The pair climbed aboard a matt black dirt bike which Su had procured for their mission. Bikes were quick and could get you out of all kinds of tight spots. It would be good to have one around. Who knew what might happen if everything went to plan? Or indeed, if it didn't.

The deceptively short trip to the guildhall needed only a few minutes and they turned the bike's engine off a couple of streets away, so as not to raise any suspicion. Whilst rolling the dirt bike into its getaway position the pair talked through their plan. The Optix announcement was to be made before the close of the day's business. Upon reaching the getaway position behind the guildhall Su and Lamorna exchanged final glances and then Master Su assured Lamorna that regardless of how their plan panned out, Lamorna would get her revenge.

Su and Lamorna took their positions. There was a reasonable crowd gathered before the old guildhall. It was built as a mock Greek temple, when seen without Optix implants it was a dark beige, covered in elaborate graffiti, seemingly a well-beloved haunt for artists. There was a conglomeration of press photographers and journalists at the front, all of whom had their phones out ready to record any and everything. An army of security guards was also in attendance, arms folded, also dressed in black, like at the front of a metal concert. Any moment now the doors of the guildhall would open and Jason Chamberlain would walk out. Lamorna could hardly wait. She still had her hood up and didn't want any colleagues or members of the press recognising her. The large square in front of the exchange was filled with at least five hundred people, Lamorna surmised. Each and every one eager to hear in great detail of Optix's wondrous success and its bold next steps. At that moment Lamorna regretted not bringing an automatic rifle with her. The moment the door opened she wanted to bury a magazine full of bullets into Chamberlain's chest. She wanted him to see down the length of her sights and see the white of her eyes before she pulled the trigger. Knowing that she was behind his downfall. Better yet, she wanted to plunge a knife into his belly and feel the last breaths be drawn out of his lungs as his heart gave up. She wanted to hear the bubbling deep in his torso as the blood filled his airway, her hand on the hilt until it left an imprint on his dead skin, long after he had perished.

Instead, she was frozen in place when the large wooden double doors of the guildhall slowly creaked open. The flashes and noise which engulfed the square jolted her awake and out of her fantasy. There was a deafening clamouring for Chamberlain's attention, to *'look this way'* and to *'smile for the cameras'*. She despised the love and adoration that was forever thrust in his direction, at his pristine veneer of a reasonable human being, the worship that his loving public provided him.

As he slowly walked down the steps, waving and giving peace signs as he did, Chamberlain smiled at the welcoming congregation. The long steps made the guildhall look more like a court of law, while Chamberlain was a defendant happy to announce that all charges against him had been dropped. Lamorna knew, however, that they very much had not been. She would make sure of that.

"Good evening dear fellow citizens, esteemed media and glorious humans. We at Optix are proud to be able to make a hugely significant announcement. In the last weeks and months we have been working on a deal to bring together the realms of technology and sociology, finance and government. It has taken a lot of dedication and patience from my team, and a good deal of grace from our partners around the world. Our work in the public realm has never been more important and with the constant threats of criminality, as well as moral corruption. This latest deal will help secure international prosperity as well as individual freedoms. Our newest friendly acquisition will enable us to continue to be your dedicated provider of aesthetic prosperity. Think of it like this: Change is a difficult thing for everyone. But does the caterpillar ask itself if it wants to metamorphose into a beautiful butterfly? Does the chick question its existence before it finally pushes its way out of the egg? Of course not, such thinking is a folly! They both accept that it is their nature to follow the given laws of existence. They push forward in beautiful anticipation of what lies ahead for them. The chick and the butterfly, these wonderful creatures with so much potential ahead of them. We admire them, cherish them and appreciate their value to our world. And so it is with our Optix users worldwide. Change is afoot, dear users. We will break out of both egg and chrysalis and move forward into a new plain of existence. Choices are coming for us and we need a strong system which keeps you alert and awake to any possible dangers facing us in these troubled times. At this point I would like to thank the partner governments and fellow lawmakers, for all of their hard work behind the scenes. And so with no further ado, as we eagerly await what is to break through the shell, I can announce that Optix….".

Just as Chamberlain was about to unveil the crowning glory of the day's proceedings a low boom rang out across the square and simultaneously an array of five bright spotlights lit up the facade of the guildhall. In that moment Master Su also activated her wrist-mounted Optix blocker and rendered the localised use of the Optix implants useless, all of the attendants were now only reliant on their very own eyes. A peel of shocked screams and surprised *'aahs'* rippled through the crowd as they could see the city's decay in all its glory. Master Su and Lamorna wanted to open everyone's eyes to the fraud going on right in front of them. Governments ignoring the necessary work and instead of making deals with Optix in order to keep the wool over the public's eyes. Their plan in full effect, Su and Lamorna were elated to see their message spelled out in front of the crowd: The graffiti emblazoned on the front of the guildhall read: *'Optix and Chamberlain want your souls and your minds. Turn off your Optix and open your eyes'*. Photos were taken, videos posted to Platform and the chaos in the audience was palpable.

Frantically, Chamberlain turned quickly to the side of the makeshift stage and entered firefighting mode. *'Where was it coming from? Who was projecting these words onto the side of the building? Why would they do this? Do they not see all of the good he was doing for the world?'* He hadn't even gotten to the good part! The Alpha team was huddled around Chamberlain as he animatedly gesticulated and bellowed at them. Lamorna could only make out how Felix was trying to reassure Jason Chamberlain about something, pointing at his own eyes. It was at that moment that Lamorna realised that they had understood what had happened and that this was not a projection, but reality itself. The building had the words painted on them, the implants had been somehow deactivated and all of the spectators could see for themselves.

"Someone has blocked the signal", Chamberlain screamed in the one breath, while commanding with the next, "We need to change channels. Reroute to another frequency, localised users only". And thus the ever efficient Alpha team and Chamberlain had already solved the problem, in a much shorter time frame than Master Su and Lamorna had predicted. Nevertheless, the damage had surely been done. The world's media will have seen that Optix was vulnerable and read their message, the cracks would begin to appear, surely?

Once Chamberlain had been able to locate where the blocking signal was coming from it was time to get out while they could. Lamorna cast a glance to her right and saw security guard make a line straight for Master Su. She called out to her, but the commotion and noise from the crowd was too great. Lamorna had to make for the rendezvous point. She fought her way out of the throng, checking over her shoulder again and again to see if anyone was following her too. She couldn't see if they were, but made haste regardless. Lamorna had to hope that Su would get out too. Most of the crowd were still blinded by the truth they had been exposed to, their mouths agape and eyes wide. Getting out was no problem in the end for Lamorna. She followed the road around to the back of the guildhall, but the bike was already gone. *'Had it been stolen? Had Master Su moved it? Had she left without her?'* Surely Su wouldn't leave her all alone to deal with the fallout from their stunt.

Standing in the middle of the road, Lamorna thought of alternatives, but there were no taxis around, no parked cars. This part of the city had been closed off. Panicking she wracked her brains for alternatives. And then as she looked down the road she saw the black outline of Renn approach out of the murky cityscape, Lamorna hadn't turned her implants on again yet and retained the ability to witness the dismal cityscape. The black bicycle had come to collect her. She then gathered that Master Su must have gotten to the dirt bike first and had been tracked. She needed to leave immediately and leave Lamorna behind, thus saving her from further incrimination.

Lamorna mounted Renn and they made down the road toward downtown. The streets were increasingly wet from the light rain now coming down. Lamorna had to hold on tight and not lose her grip. Renn took corners at speed, Lamorna lowered her leading leg, leaning into the corners, wasting no time. They approached the flyover leading to the industrial district. The bicycle struggled to maintain speed as they started climbing the ramp up to the bridge, which spanned the long drop down to the river. Lamorna's chest was ready to burst as they climbed the ramp, she was also anxious that there might be a roadblock out of sight at the crest. But she didn't have time to fill in that particular nightmare, as another waited to greet her there at the apex of the bridge. As she approached the crest of the bridge her heart almost pressed its way through her chest; awaiting her at the top side of the ride, next to the metal barriers were a pair of motorbikes, including Su's black dirt bike. The skid marks, together with the plastic and metal residue showed that there had been a coming together near the middle of the ascent and the bikes had then careened off to the right at great speed. Lamorna left Renn and ran to the motorbikes. It was definitely Su's bike, but whose was the others? One of Chamberlain's cronies? She ran back and forth looking for a sign of Master Su, but she was not to be seen. The vast cityscape gave no clues, despite Lamorna being able to see almost everything from that vantage point. Then, in the chill of the night she heard arguing voices over the railing. Tentatively, her legs as if cased in concrete, she made towards the side of the bridge. Every step was torture, she guessed what she would find there.

"I did it for her, you cost me everything!", Lamorna heard a man's voice shouting, "you only ever were out for yourself Su, you use us all like pawns in your phoney war!".

"Just accept it's over, Xerxo. Let it go, this will do you no good. Just learn to accept how things went, we can't change them now, only our outlook." Master Su's reply was unmistakable. Even now, hanging onto the side of a bridge, Su was unable to prevent her sophisms.

"You destroyed us. You never just let it lie, and neither will I", Xerxo responded with bitterness and grief in his venomous voice. "You deserve this for your trickery, lies and manipulation Su. We should have left you in your cave alone and despairing, but no, you were never happy. Always sapping the energy from others until they were used up, discarded and the hunt for the next saviour was all that concerned you. So, I made sure you could never let me go, made myself valuable to you. That red rope tied us together, but Chamberlain came calling to me once I realised you never needed me on the end of it. And now your value to me is so much higher, Su. The only way I can repay you is in death."

Finally, Su's past had caught up with her. The poor wizard had come alive, Xerxo had wrought his revenged and turned his coat. Lamorna bent over the railing, trying to reach Su's arms, straining her body as long as she could to take a firm grip. Seeing the problem at hand, with Xerxo clamped around Su's legs, Lamorna's hands gripped around Su's wrists, careful as to not loosen Su's grip on the bottom of the railing. "What is this devilry? Su, I need you to hold on a little longer. Shit! You never prepared me for this, Su. I'm going to get you back up here!"

Below Su, Xerxo held on as long as he could, determined to pull his former ally down with him. "I told you I would never forgive you, sweetness. This is what happens at the end. When there is no rope to save you, no net to catch you, we lose everything. You should never have kept me around!" Xerxo's voice was filled with nothing but hate. How much longer Xerxo held on until his grip eventually weakened was later unclear to Lamorna, was it mere seconds? A minute? She did not know. Or care. But the time she had left with Master Su was running out, deep down she knew this.

His mind long made up to exact this revenge. And as he finally let go he smiled, knowing that Su could not hold on for much longer either. "You deserve everything you are getting, Su, your interfering games are over. See you in the next life". Xerxo lost his grip on Su's legs, raking her calves with his fingernails as he tried to cling on to life and he plummeted down in a kind of slow-motion before crashing against the surface of the water and being carried away to his doom.

Lamorna held Su as tight as she could. But without a miracle, she could not lift her up. Not even her leg prosthetics could help her, no special rescue function, rocket pack or grapple hook. Lamorna scrambled for an idea: a magic rope, a harness, a floating platform, hot air balloon, a helicopter, a sentient flying robot. None of those things either existed or were available within an arm's reach. Lamorna struggled to maintain her grip as her strength waned. She felt her heart almost explode at the effort; pulling people up from bridges was so much easier in the films. The adrenaline in her body was keeping Su alive. Lamorna couldn't let go. She denied herself that option. She couldn't accept that she would fail Su at the sternest of tests. Lamorna cursed herself for not being stronger or better prepared, for not seeing this eventuality, not seeing through Xerxo, not knowing more about Master Su's dealings in the past. She prayed that maybe she could hold for five more minutes and somebody would come and help, maybe even the police, even if they were then locked up for years. And then the sadness hit her, she wept, her tears landing on Su as she hung on below, "I can't, Su".

"I know, Lamorna. And that is okay. You're not one for giving up, so don't. You won't give up, I know it. It's okay. Those we love never truly leave us".

Finally, Lamorna's grip on Su's hand loosened and in those tantalising last few moments Lamorna felt an electricity pass through her body, a transmission. Of what she did not know. Su looked into Lamorna's eyes, in each of them she could see her own face clear in Lamorna's black pupil. Lamorna could only sob the words, "I'm sorry. I love you", and yet Su looked up with a calm kindness, "In your weeping you will part oceans". And so Su fell. Her view remaining directed skyward for as long as she could, her calmness unchanged. The cold air filled her lungs which she could no longer exhale; she no longer feared the fall and no longer the landing. Lamorna's tear-blotched face appeared smaller and smaller as the distance between them increased. Su's body slowly turned and twisted improbably gracefully, her black robes flapping in the wind and her arms outstretched. She sailed in a corkscrew flight. Lamorna almost managed a smile at the realisation of it. In Lamorna's eyes Su was flying, not falling.

Su felt a great weight on her chest as she flew through the air. Breathing was impossible and she felt a panic as she attempted to spread out her arms to catch herself. The flapping, caused by panic, prompted a grin from Su herself as she felt the air fly by. Her wish to take flight finally, at life's end, fulfilled. As the river's surface rushed up to meet her Su closed her eyes and was at peace, knowing she had sent Lamorna on her way, it was now her duty to write the next chapter.

14 - FOOTPRINTS

Su was gone. Her body lay somewhere in the abyss and Lamorna would never see her again. Lamorna wished she had fallen into the depths. That it had been she who would not go on. That she had been condemned to nothing. That would make it easier to go on with Su, who had become everything to her. She couldn't exactly define it, having never really known a person that way before. The categorisation wasn't necessary in the end.

She felt once more amputated. Once more confined to a bed, riddled with anguish. Once more alone. The next days and week were a struggle for Lamorna. Su had been her only friend and she grieved her loss. Most nights she couldn't fall asleep until the early hours and on others her night was interrupted at 4 a.m. with panic attacks; being taken back to the bridge. Throughout her days she could feel the same tightness in her chest which struck Su as she fell to her death and the constant reminder left her sometimes simply standing in her flat not knowing what to do. There were worse ways to pass the time. She tried sleeping during the day to catch up on her rest, but there she only met sorrow. In her head she ruminated on the different places they had met. The last of which, the bridge, was a particularly haunting place for her. Perhaps she should visit it again and throw herself from it this time.

She tried to get back in contact with the people on Platform, but the majority of them had been hurt by Lamorna abruptly cutting them off. She had re-isolated herself, Su was such an intense contact for that entire period and now she was alone again. Lamorna knew what Su had told her, not to give up. But that was not easy. She doubted everything. Lamorna read the letters that Master Su had sent her; looking for insights into what to do next, but the pain was too much. She thought about burning them, wishing them to disappear. Lamorna needed a change of scenery; she had spent too much time inside weeping. She could do that outside too if she wished. She got on her bike and went to the forest to clear her head; having shut herself in for the past six days not knowing how to proceed, she figured she needed to take baby-steps. She got her bike out of the cellar, lugging it up the steep steps and left her building. It was a crisp morning, about eight degrees, Lamorna slipped on her helmet, and pedalled along the road. The traffic wasn't too bad and the cars seemed to be in a good mood today, none brushed up too close. She almost felt invisible, suiting her fine, not wanting to be seen either. She only pined for contact with Su, felt tears well up in her eyes, put it down to the onrush of wind from cycling, and pushed on.

As she approached the forest she noticed two of her former colleagues on the side of the road. Lamorna didn't want to be recognised so she pulled her scarf up over her nose and looked in the other general direction. Her disguise failed terribly, they recognised the bike and muttered something to each other, but Lamorna was none the wiser and was mildly satisfied with herself. She got to the car park, locked up her bike and helmet. The forest's lakes offered a good number of different ways to walk and every one felt different, especially if you were used to being there in the nights where only the moon lit your way. She took a route which hugged the largest lake in the forest, the Darwin lake. The path took you close to the edge the entire way around it and the light glimmered on its still surface. The wind was calm and the ducks on it were able to feed and swim in peace.

Here, where she and Su had shared so much time together, Lamorna found it at first hard to relax; so many familiar sights and evenings spent philosophising and contemplating possible futures. The path was not too muddy which meant the going was good, Lamorna felt fit, thanks to the years of hamster-wheel training, but her head needed to be cleared. She knew that she had to let go of Su, but simply didn't know how. The guilt hit her in waves and stopped her in her tracks where she stood. She had let Su fall, she couldn't save her. If only she hadn't gone to the cafe, met Xerxo, been more suspicious of him. Why didn't she just plain refuse to go the Bluebird hotel? And as for the plan, what plan? Writing graffiti on the guildhall was not a plan. Of course there would be recourse, Chamberlain wasn't born yesterday and the dirt bike was an accident waiting to happen. Lamorna and Master Su were an accident waiting to happen.

She realised that she had never asked Su enough questions about herself. Did she have her own family or friends? How much of the fairy tale had been true? Had Su used her purely for her own gain? What was Su's plan for the future? Su had appeared to be a calm, calculated and composed person. What Lamorna lacked in information in Su, she made up for in feeling. She sat by the lake, the blue reflexion of the cold sky split the light, paying no mind to the damp ground beneath her. She stayed here for hours, it was the perfect hideaway; no others came by, no questions, just Lamorna alone with her guilt. She lost herself in music or books which she took with her to the forest and sometimes just stood in the shallows and inhaled them.The main issue was finding suitable music to listen to. So many songs about magic, forests, bridges and water were basically taboo. They reminded her of Su and caused her to well up again. Instrumental tracks, minimalist strings or beats served her well. She was able to imagine her own lyrics to them; they were like painting by numbers.

On other days Lamorna had spent a lot of time in bed. She would generally get up early enough, feeling drunk with her lack of sleep, but she would make a pot of coffee and some toast. However, during the breakfast, normally after a slice and a half, she would lose herself in a downward spiral of regret, guilt and grief. She sat at the table and simply wept for Su. *'Why hadn't she done more to save her? How much more could they have accomplished together? How much of this was Lamorna's fault?'* After spending some time with her forehead pressed against her dining table Lamorna would pull herself up, a squelchy peeling of skin being felt, and trundle toward her bedroom, shouting into her pillow: "I'm so sorry, Su! I didn't mean to hurt you! I should have been the one to fall! You didn't deserve this! Why didn't you see this coming?!". These fights with herself would take up most mornings. It was exhausting and Lamorna didn't know to whom she could turn. The isolation stung like a knife lodged between her shoulder blades. Unable to remove it herself, she simply leant back on it, convinced that she needed the pain to be felt. In fact, it reminded her of her duty, her purpose. Without that pain she probably would have given up there and then. Then there really would have been nothing left. So, the cold knife could remain there. It reminded Lamorna that this was all real. Despite the pain she felt, she still wondered whether it had all been a dream? Was Su a figment of her imagination? Was Su really dead and gone from her life? It went as far as Lamorna doubting she had the accident, losing her legs. Even the Optix technology seemed improbable to her. How far could someone fall without crash-landing?

Despite her doubts, the stunt at the guildhall had shaken Chamberlain. The entire week he had been metaphorically lynched in the media; widespread calls for his resignation had been made, the share price had crashed and rival companies had been pushing their own agendas. The media lapped it all up, the other companies too. They finally had some airtime. But Optix wasn't going to fail, not because of a little graffiti, Lamorna knew that. But everyone saw now that they were not infallible; they were vulnerable. Finally, Chamberlain was exposed and the company were on the back foot. Lamorna had made some change, however transient. This fact buoyed her somewhat. Thankfully, there was no mention of any suspects. Xerxo took their identities to his watery grave.

The past months, all a blur, she had faded in and out of the shadows. Only coming out at night, holed up in the hospital or under the cover of the forest trees, she was ready for the light again. Ready for more contact with others, ready for revenge. One morning Lamorna's phone lit up with a message from an almost forgotten colleague, she felt like she was being spied on again. It was Felix. Felix was possibly still an Alpha team programmer, who knows what kind of internal changes Chamberlain had made. He was of a similar age and had thick curly black hair and equally thick glasses hiding deep brown eyes. He was harmless enough, thought Lamorna, unlikely to still be in Jason Chamberlain's inner circle, but she couldn't be sure. *'How are you doing?'*, he had sent. Lamorna looked at the screen, second and third guessing his motives. She didn't want to assume innocence on his part. He had always been friendly enough in his awkward way, often too shy to say *'hi'* when entering the office late in the morning. He seemed the type to oversleep by a couple of hours and then roll into a t-shirt, jeans and trainers and just appear at the office door, he even smelled as such. Lamorna made some coffee and thought about how to answer. The standard *'OK thanks, u?'* didn't seem to cut it after all that she had gone through since leaving the Optix building that morning. She felt like she had lived an entire life since then. As she drank her black coffee, one hand on her forehead, elbow on the worktop, she thought through a number of strategies:

1. Send back a standard reply, non-committal
2. Tell him exactly how I feel
3. Suggest meeting for a coffee, in case anybody is snooping on the messages
4. Don't reply and block him
5. Write a full reply full of lies

Lamorna pondered the wisdom of each. She mused on what Su would advise her to do. In the end the important thing was to:

1. Not be fake
2. Do it because you want to do it, not because others expect it of you

The trick was to maintain their medium and long-term alignment. She dismissed ignoring Felix, not wanting to hurt his feelings, he was a good guy. She also thought it naïve to lay out everything in a text, divulging all possible thoughts and movements. She picked up the phone and gave him a call and suggested they meet after his working day in the greasy spoon. He was up for it and after Lamorna's day so far, she knew she needed to get out.

Donning her trusted high-tops she made her way down the road, this time going without her headphones. This was a novel thing for her, she wasn't used to being unaccompanied or being able to hear the hustle and bustle of the city. The sun was hidden behind the tall skyscrapers and was only to be occasionally glimpsed, seemingly jumping out from hiding places, these and other ghouls she kept seeing in the corner of her eye. When she arrived at the cafe it looked pretty empty and she took a seat in the far corner facing the door. The other patrons had their faces either stuck in a newspaper or in a sausage roll. Felix arrived on time, his shirt untucked and his hair a mess. "Some things never change", she chuckled to him as he approached the table. He was too awkward to give her a hug, so they tapped each other on the shoulder and he sat down opposite her.

"So, how have you been?", he opened.

"You gotta be kidding, right?", she angrily countered, thoroughly peeved at Felix's tactless question. He knew full well what had happened, surely?

"Sorry, I don't know what to say. You just disappeared that day and we never knew where you went."

"What do you mean? I was in hospital for weeks, months. Never heard a word from anyone, was left completely alone. Not even my family came to see me. And you come here and ask me how I am doing? Was there no email that went round at least to say that I had been in an accident?", Lamorna feverishly enquired.

"No, nothing. It was as if you had been abducted by aliens. I wanted to get in touch Lamorna, but I figured you just needed time to yourself. That's what Jason recommended to you, right? We all just thought it would be best to leave you alone. You have given so much to Optix, we wanted to show you that we could get by without you and not pester you into coming back sooner. You understand that right?", Felix was back-pedalling.

Lamorna was incensed. "I can't believe that nobody

knew I was in hospital? I lost my legs, Felix. Look!", Felix was shocked.

"Lamorna, I am so sorry. We just thought it was for the best", he defended himself.

"To be honest Felix, it would have made no difference. I get it. You all closed ranks after I left. No leaks. Nobody was to have any contact with me, be it officially or unofficially. You would have risked demotion or being ostracised if you had been found out. I've seen it before when others have fallen. At Optix we just believe out of some mysterious sense of solidarity that we can't be open about how things are. But it isn't born out of solidarity at all. It is fear. And you are all scared of raising your poor heads above the parapet, lest the mighty Chamberlain remove your head. He has you all under his control, doing his work and making you think that you are saving the world. You take his word as gospel and at the same time you are selling out your fellow humans. They are paying for all of this, it is through their eyes that he is getting all of the information he needs."

Felix agreed to an extent: "I suppose so, but we all have our careers to think of. I don't want to lose my job there and I know that we are improving things for everyone; I want to be a part of that. Besides, if you are talking about control, you would be the first person I would ask. Ever since we met I have wondered if I really knew you, Lamorna. You can be pretty unapproachable. It's small wonder nobody got in touch. You would probably ignore them or just lie and say everything was fine."

"What do you mean? I always said hi when you came into the office", Lamorna protested.

"And that's pretty much where it ended Lamorna, for everyone. I guess that is how Chamberlain likes it; everyone more focused on the task at hand, working on the latest version and new mock-ups. But the rest of us noticed something about you too, you know. You worked so hard for him and needed that satisfaction from him more than any of us. Chamberlain was your motivation and target of affection. He used you. He didn't care for you, as you probably realised yourself after you left. He hasn't changed in any way, other than making sure that someone takes your place in the Alpha team".

"You know what, Felix? I am not surprised. Nothing surprises me anymore. I am not that important, none of us are. All just cogs in a machine, inexorably turning and grinding more and more meat. Maybe I should try and make some changes, I doubt Jason knows who was really behind the graffiti attack".

"He doesn't. Not for want of trying to find out. He had us comb through everyone's Platform accounts, including yours, for signs of *'terrorist activity'*, as he called it. He was relentless. When he wasn't being taken apart in an online report or in front of a camera for the media, he was on our backs ensuring that we find the culprits. He called it an assassination attempt. He said that we were all the targets, that this was an attack on all of us and that we can't give in now. Not now that we are so close."

Lamorna was concerned that Felix had mentioned her Platform account being checked on by her coworkers. But she would have done the same. It would have been more suspect had Felix not brought it up. She believed she was in the clear, for now. Turning to Felix she said: "I need to go back, I can't stay away forever".

"Are you crazy? I mean, I would love to have you back in the office Lamorna, but that can't be good for you. That place is many things, but a healthy environment it is not. You told us all that directly. You spat that into Chamberlain's face and look at the thanks you got. Surely you need more time, more distance. Maybe even a completely new start. If you have learnt anything, surely it is that you can't put yourself in that position anymore. Where people take liberties with you, exploit you, where you're underappreciated. You won't be able to change things there, Lamorna. I just keep my head down and try to do a good job, but you are naturally more diligent and ambitious; you are just asking for trouble."

Lamorna looked unflinchingly at Felix and repeated: "I need to go back. I can't accept defeat, Felix. It might be pure ego, it might be hubris, or sheer idiocy, but it is an unfinished story for me. I need to show others, and more importantly, myself that I can come back from this and set things right. I know it is asking a lot of myself, but I know I can do it. Just you wait and see."

As Lamorna and Felix parted and made their respective ways home the blood red sky stood proudly over the cityscape. Lamorna was reminded of the saying; good weather was coming.

15 - CODES AND KEYS

Lamorna sat in her room staring at the walls of her flat as the sun shone on them. The warm light seemed to charge her living room with an ethereal energy, pouring sun radiation into her own private space. In that moment she was reminded of her mind palace, her ocean cave, her escape. Now in her flat she was no longer surrounded by reminders of her past life, of artworks for others to see, of instruments waiting to be played for an audience that did not exist. There was a new singular focus in Lamorna's thinking. As she had said to Felix: "I am not that important, none of us truly are". That included Jason Chamberlain, that included herself, that included Master Su. Any one person could be removed and most things would carry on. But when we connect together, we can bring down worlds. If she were to retreat again inside her shell and keep out all of the light, she could hide inside her flat and no-one would find her. Without any connection she would have saved herself the anguish of losing her legs, without taking the risk and speaking to Xerxo, she would have never met Su and never lost her. She could have carried on at Optix until she keeled over and been none the wiser. Could she have reached a save-point in her life and just always gone from there? Repeating her life, again and again, until reaching the most satisfactory outcome, for herself, for Xerxo and for Su. She wished that they could meet up another time, in another place, in another life.

Could there be an augmentation which allowed such things to happen, she wondered? Could a consciousness be transported and kept in storage? Could it be copied and split in two? Would it one day be possible for her to live two parallel lives, each jumping off from a particular point in time, yet never meeting again; completely separating.

These and other such follies spun around in her mind for a time without end. It was a fantasy. A way out from her current reality. If she could split herself, she could live without consequence, live without any need to choose a clear path. She would forever split those future consciences, cascading over years and decades, she would part her mind at every turn. Ending in thousands of realities, where she was present in every one, and none. Would Optix even exist in those realities? She was getting distracted and needed to focus on the task at hand.

It was time for Lamorna to get back to work. The thought of it scared her; it had been months, feeling like years, since she had been back to that place. She felt her shoulders tense up, her brow was furrowed and her breath grew shorter. She put off thoughts returning there, it would come soon enough. Putting on some electronic music Lamorna turned on her computer. As the beats played in the background Lamorna started on her workaround. She hadn't lost her knack for exploiting the software she programmed herself. "I can be such an idiot sometimes, lucky me", she muttered, munched on a ginger nut biscuit and got going. Within not much time at all she had created a localised reskin for herself, enabling her to change her appearance in the eyes of others. This was her plan. No bombs, no machine guns, no theft, just good old-fashioned espionage.

Her second modification was to activate an embedded line of code, not yet active. Some years before, Lamorna had worked on a project which never left the boardroom. The idea was Chamberlain's, and enabled users to spy on others. That would be an export technology, useful for espionage. All militarised nations would desire it, without the knowledge of the others of course. It never got past the idea stage, as far as anyone else knew, because so many of the architects, including Chamberlain's inner circle, were against it morally. What the exact ethical complaints were, were something the group was never really able to adequately articulate. It quickly escalated into a violently ideological shouting match between the more outspoken architects and Chamberlain. His inner circle knew to let him do his own fighting. Although the code in question was never any more than something Chamberlain and Lamorna discussed a few times after, she was sure that he had activated it for himself some time ago. He would keep something like that in his back pocket, for sure.

Lamorna wanted to ensure she was on a more level playing field than last time, she couldn't go charging in there with all guns blazing. A subtler approach was needed, even if she were to be disguised. The second modification could be adapted further, so she looked into coding a neural uplink. How it would work in practice, she had to see for herself. But at least she could save what she saw to a hard disk which would be found months or years later. It was time to go, she scanned the news reports and city traffic updates before leaving, Lamorna didn't want to risk any interruptions. This was finally it, back to Optix.

Moving outside of the apartment building she saw the dilapidation of the city. She kept her implants off, still no temptation to once more see the perfectly curated textures and tones she once held for reality. The broken down city, the naïve people ambling aimlessly, fumbling for a hold on their lives. They were well served by the lies; thinking was such arduous labour. Lamorna followed the road in the direction of the tram station; the rust on the metal doors, the peeling paint and erosion had their own charm. The city was showing its bones, its pocked and scarred skin tearing itself from the flesh. The decay was palpable now, the visuals no longer distracted her from the aged rot, the foul life going on here. The empty buildings stood out now like blackened, crumbling teeth in an otherwise pristine mouth. Some buildings remained well-maintained, often frequented by wealthy consumers, paying good money to keep the business grow. Restaurants were particular good at maintaining a good front, not only thanks to Optix. Appearances were everything, after all, at the table and the shop facade too, as a logical consequence. Out of curiosity Lamorna had the urge to activate her Optix implant just for a moment. She wanted to quickly see what stores the now hollow shells originally inhabited. Turning them on, the roads became an asphalt ideal, the skies turned a lighter hue and the decrepit store fronts were now vivaciously inviting emporiums. She took a glance down the road and out of the shadow of the dead street then stood thirty to forty pristine new shops. From fireplace and mattress shops to Eritrean, Korean, and Peruvian restaurants. Never places she would ordinarily enter and in the past she never noticed why these business were not so often frequented by others. They faded into the surroundings, like lounging figures in a renaissance painting. Su had once told her that such images were always merely a construct, a collage of influences and carefully removing any given figure would not necessarily adversely affect the completed image. Her words hung in Lamorna's head, a thudding echo, doomed to repeat in the long hall of her mind. No single individual was particularly important, none of them were. She turned off the Optix implant and continued down the road.

Lamorna approached the tram station, passing by ruins, bought a ticket and made for downtown. As she occupied a seat near the exit, she tuned into her thoughts, ignoring all else around her. She retreated to her mind palace, making the way there with the underground train, travelling hundreds of miles per second. Upon arrival leaving the lift and facing the panorama of the deep blue ocean. Ignoring all around her on the tram, Lamorna sunk deeper into thought, she was now able to concentrate her mind only on the crash of the waves and the pressure of the wind against the twenty metre wide glass walls. The rest of the vast room behind her was but a grey box in the back of her mind, lacking detail, left unused. That is not why she was there. Her need for the cold water, the clipping breeze and harshness of the rocks brought a calmness to her; a wall of white noise. A shield to stand behind, an acoustic guardian. Her heart rate lowered and the wind removed the sweat from her brow. And the rocks gave her feet a steadier footing, lest she slip and fall through the wide pane of glass ahead of her. With her view on the horizon and she saw where the sky met the water, where the world ended, where the ocean started. The coming swells turned to waves which crashed on the rocks below, inevitably falling to nothing, each different to the other, and each never to return. Yet on the horizon born anew and unyieldingly returning for another life, changed yet unfazed by previous attempts. Lamorna followed swell after swell from the far horizon to the black rocks. The hiss and deep thunder of elemental destruction. In an instant the wave submitted to the rocks. And over a lifetime the coast would slowly succumb to the ocean's erosion. In every wave lay a creative potential, and every face of rock had a destructive ability. Given enough time the waves and rocks would annihilate each other, their deaths imperceptible to all others except themselves. For their's was this momentary dance, forever ending.

Thanks to her meditation at the ocean Lamorna felt a lot more relaxed. A desire to turn back, escape from her mission, flee from the tram, cower and remain in her flat, had all entered into her mind. She had earned that right, she had endured enough already; one could forgive those invasive thoughts. Lamorna didn't feel any obligation to continue on this quest, this mission which she began with Master Su at her side; practically at Su's bequest. Master Su was no longer alive, she wouldn't know any different. Her watchful eyes would no doubt pass judgement given the chance, but her words couldn't enter Lamorna's ears anymore; enough of them had grown inside her mind and formed a new secondary consciousness. This Lamorna knew, she had almost accepted that. That new voice often appeared in her mind, a second-guessing taking hold, a new critic embedded within her mind. Such was Lamorna's programming experience, her talent with languages, that Su was now also embedded in her own code. Which parts she directly affected were still unclear; Lamorna would wait and see.

For so long she had done certain things out of ego, for too many years she had adopted masks in front of certain people and for certain situations. Now she saw this for what it was, something she had helped start, needed her help to bring it back to reality. A programmed falsehood needed to be reforged in truth. The self-victimising obligation had become a voluntary desire, an intrinsic need for action, a call to arms, of sorts. Lamorna heard Su's mutterings of approval and then the screech of the tram doors as they opened.

Lamorna proceeded with her headphones in place, the electronica now replaced by some good old Slayer, 'Seasons in the Abyss' was an appropriate song now. The rumbling bass matched the feeling in her gut as she turned the corner at gazed at the tower, at the road and the scene of her accident. Once more she wanted to postpone the meeting. Again the sweat collected on her forehead; her breathing was shallow and frequent. The adrenaline in her body was boiling her up, her flight response was urging her to turn back and board the tram. She put down her bag and she waited. Looking more closely at the road she felt less anxiety than when looking up at the tower. The accident was still fresh in her memory, yet it was the years of working in that building adjacent which dwelled on her psyche. Lamorna took another chance to collect herself. This time not fleeing to her mind palace, not sunk in dialogue with an imaginary friend, or grieving for a fallen comrade. Now she was harnessing all of the energy she had pent up in her desire to confront Chamberlain. So many times she had played out such arguments with him while in the shower, always having the perfect comeback. All too often she had spent the first or last moments of her day dwelling on things he had said to her, or others. So much toil and frustration, all packed into her. Misspoken words, unspoken complaints. Wool pulled over the world's eyes. Blinkered vision. This was the eye of the needle now. All of her energies had taken her to this place as she stood on the threshold.

16 - ARCHITECTS

Upon reaching the large double doors Lamorna activated her implant out of curiosity. As a standard the textures in the building were unalterable, no customisation possible. Jason Chamberlain had, in his own vain eyes, already chosen the optimal surfaces for all to see. He had commissioned the finest artisans, traditional architects and outfitters when designing the building; everything was carried out to his own exacting specifications. The finest white Siena stone floor, polished glass everywhere, exposed utilities, fabulous uplighting everywhere. It was built as a church, that Lamorna could see now. How apt that Chamberlain would save true analogue beauty for his own headquarters, while the rest of the world knelt at his digital alter. Jason was just another on the long list of leaders saving the best for himself.

So far, the building appeared unchanged, but Lamorna now knew enough not trust her old boss blindly. She couldn't rule out changes in the last few months or things she had missed previously. She was not so easily fooled anymore, this was her trusted long-term superpower: a fully-charged and meticulously calibrated bullshit detector. She had pulled out an old ID card, made her way to the lifts and got in. "Stage one complete", she muttered to herself. Then reminding herself of all of the previous steps which had led to this: very much not a first stage. Up until the third floor she was alone in the lift, thankfully not made of glass, that would have been too much. Lamorna looked in the mirror. Her face was now altered, the visual reprogramming had given her a pointier nose, a black bob and a beauty spot on her left cheek. Her eyes were now brown, her cheeks somewhat rounder and her ears eyebrows thicker. Dressed in a simple black top and blue jeans she looked like a modern professional, nothing special. An untypical spy costume, she thought to herself. *'Didn't they normally arrive by sports car and don tuxedos?'*. It was at that point that she was then joined in the lift by a colleague, from the marketing department: a vaguely professional looking creative, no doubt well-schooled in all manners of sales speak and money-parting jargon. She was quite snappily dressed and wore what looked like fake glasses, probably to attempt to appear more intelligent. They stood together in silence; most younger colleagues weren't that keen on making conversation, neither was Lamorna to be honest, who was happy to enjoy the peace and quiet for a few precious seconds before reaching her destination. The woman quickly pulled out her phone and checked her socials, frowning accordingly. Relieved, Lamorna waited until the seventh floor. Her pulse and internal temperature were rising again, she wished she had a fan built into her prosthetic legs: "A strange time to think about upgrade, Morna", she said to herself.

"Eh?", her colleague answered.

"Oh, don't worry. Just talking to myself", Lamorna replied.

"Ah", gave the remarkably eloquent marketing robot as a form of answer.

"Ta-ra", Lamorna said as she heard the ding and made to leave the lift.

"Oh, no, I'm Rachel", the colleague replied.

Lamorna looked back at the woman and shook her head. Not expecting such a moment of levity in her day today. "Sorry. See you Rachel", she answered. They parted, the marketing robot looking more than confused, while her more experienced counterpart stifled a giggle.

Back on her old floor, with Chamberlain's office located at the very end of a long corridor, she saw some commotion. Among her former colleagues were some other guests, dressed in exquisitely tailored suits, accompanied by assistants, wearing significantly less expensive suits. Lamorna turned a corner, out of sight, to the right of the lift. To the left would have been the break area: not a good idea. She wasn't worried about being recognised as she knew that her reprogramming would hold up. The bob still sat right, her nose was still pointy. She felt an ache in her legs, however. If she still possessed knees, you could say they were wobbly. Lamorna was nervous. She could feel the sweat on her lower back, her heartbeat thumped, her breathing shortened. She reassured herself that the cameras in the foyer would have flagged her up by now if she had been compromised.

All being well, she would find Felix in his office quite quickly. She made her way along the wide corridor and passed some other offices, with nameplates on them of people she didn't recall. At that moment her heart sank, Felix's office used to be the fifth one. No sign of him. She followed the corridor further, none of them were his. She had little choice but to turn back and go past the break area. Other than being recognised, halted or arrested, she was more scared of being stuck in a conversation with someone. Her time away had provided her with plenty of necessary distance from this place, as well as these people. Before she arrived at the lifts she considered leaving again, this would be her chance to get out again. She parked herself there for a minute, whipped out her phone and checked her socials. No messages, no calls, no changes. The only thing happening today was this, here, today. No one person was going to prevent it. Lamorna resolved to go past the break area and only keep her eyes pointing forward. She took a deep breath, moved ahead and then she saw Felix walking toward the lift from the other direction. He called it and stood waiting, whilst devouring a frosted doughnut. She hesitated before moving toward the lift. Once more, she felt some resistance from her legs. It was as if they had their own agenda. Pressing on, Lamorna got in the lift and was joined by Felix. He pressed the ground floor button, she thanked him and they both went down in absolute silence.

"After you", Felix offered, as the doors parted. After thanking him she made her way slowly towards the exit. As she suspected, he was also on his way outside, probably to get five minutes of Optix-free air. A former smoker, he maintained his work-life balance by checking out of the building every two hours and strolling up and down the street outside. Once they were out of sight of the entrance Lamorna caught up to him and approached him.

"Got a light?", she enquired. Felix spun around in surprise, removing his sunglasses. Her disguise was good, but there was no mistaking her voice.

"Morna?", his eyes were bloodshot, his eye sockets blackened as if by soot, "Lamorna, that can't be you. What are you doing here? What happened to your face, what did you do?". His breathing was frantic, his eyebrows were pointing to the stars.

Lamorna smiled at Felix, his expression softened somewhat. "How could you tell, Felix? Was it my dry wit?"

"What are doing here dressed like that?", he replied.

"I couldn't just walk in as myself", Lamorna confessed. "I need to get a feel for the place again first, you know? It isn't easy. And it isn't the legs, the accident or Chamberlain. I can get by. I am tired of looking for excuses, Felix. Look at the way we are talking now. Could this have happened before all of this? Of course not! The accident was not the best thing that ever happened in my life, I'm not stupid enough to believe in that kind of warped sentimentality; a cuddling of a trauma, a heavy blanket to wrap around my insecurities. No, it was a heinous act, Chamberlain caused the accident. He manipulated what I could see. He put a park in front of me, where the road was. I was too stupid, too angry to see the wood for the trees. But that is just one example; he has manipulated everyone, everything has been corrupted. We cannot trust our very eyes and we are not babies who see by sticking things into our mouths. Although, who knows what the next patch will bring. I wouldn't put it past him".

"Lamorna, don't you think you are getting a bit ahead of yourself? You worked on all of these things with him, you know how he ticks, his motivations, his ways. He just wants to develop ideas to their full potential. To give people what they desire, before they are aware of it. Like any visionary." Felix adopted a defensive stance, Lamorna could see that his whole posture changed and he adopted a less harmless tone to his voice.

"And in doing so he is removing anyone else's ability to see clearly. He isn't this benevolent genius you all think he is. We both know what kind of boss he is. He could argue his way out of a boxing match . He knows what to say to get people to do things for him. And that's why I came here today; this needs to stop. Somebody needs to finally push back and I can't rely on anyone else to be that person. This is the change I need to see in the world, Felix. Otherwise I won't be able to live with myself. I get where Jason is coming from, I really do. But that doesn't mean that he can do what he wants without consequence. He is getting you all to create something more.

He wants to push all human potential, regardless of what gets cast aside. He needs more and more, until you have nothing left to give and you are nothing more than a shell, a husk of a person."

"What do you want from me, Lamorna? By rights I should call Jason right now." Felix's demeanour had hardened again, he had been at the company almost as long as Lamorna and had always been loyal; on occasions competitors had pinched Optix employees, but Felix was happy where he was. We wasn't normally one to throw ship captains overboard. "You turn up out of the blue and just expect me to drop everything."

"Not at all, Felix. I don't expect anything of you. I am fine being alone. I shouldn't have followed you out of the building. I just wanted to say hi. A familiar face, you know?"

"No. I don't know", Felix replied. Looking at Lamorna's altered visage. "You keep up this facade and won't show your true face and I can't really believe that it's you. I have work to do, I'm sorry. I need a smoke now".

"See you around, Felix", Lamorna solemnly spoke. With that Felix turned, gave a sad wave and left, walking down the road past the Optix office building.

Lamorna collected herself. Admittedly, that didn't go as well as she had hoped; she had expected more acceptance from him, but it just wasn't in his nature to suddenly revolt and attempt insurrection. There in that no man's land of the inner city, between rotten buildings and high-price condos, one hundred metre high glass-fronted office buildings and boarded up off-licences, with scores of ignorant passers-by, she was reminded of her task. *'Nothing is going to change here until I go it alone. I've never been a big group person, I don't need a lobby or a shouting, screaming cheerleading squad behind me. Felix, Su and all the others helped me get to this point, now it is up to me to take it further, if that is what I really want'*, her logic unfolding in her mind as clear as mountain spring water.

She made her way back to the Optix building, its glass front shining a blue hue in the sun, which for her marked it as a target. She entered and made her way to the lift once more. Again, leaving at the seventh floor, she now took the left corridor, went past the break room and made her way to the larger open office space. There were many new faces, yet still a healthy smattering of old ones. "Good morning", she muttered to a couple of younger ones as she passed them on the way, they too were absorbed by their devices and just walked past.

Lamorna knew that she would not have a chance with direct confrontation once more. The inner circle would resist and deny everything, that much had been clear to her. Whether they would want to see the truth or not would be another thing. She would expect a big shouting match. Savia, one of Chamberlain's favourites, would probably attempt another, more sophisticated character assassination of Lamorna, or just have her escorted from the building as soon as she was made.

So Lamorna did what she deemed most logical. With her Optix implant still deactivated she looked for her old office. There was bound to be something there. There was a new name on the door, Albert Mink, still looking shiny. No sign of Chamberlain in the main office space, he was probably shut away in his own office like usual. Having noted her successor's name she walked towards a young guy sat at his cubicle.

"Hey, where's Albert gone?", Lamorna enquired.

"No idea. I guess he's out. He usually is. Just send him a message", replied the young man without looking up.

"Thank you kindly", Lamorna said, pleasantly and swiftly, smirking at the colleague who remained staring at his screen. "See you later", she added.

"Hmm", he merely provided as a response.

So she went back to his office and made her way in. Her desk was the same as before, same hardware too. There wasn't much lying around either, just a few old coffee cups, just like she used to have lying around. She always did keep herself heavily dosed, pulling herself through the days with the thick black oily liquid. She remembered all that time spent working on the textures for her premium customers, the tired, long discussions where Chamberlain just wanted a solitary minute of Lamorna's time. All the smokescreens and mummery. There was a time before the accident and now was the time after, Lamorna knew that, but finding herself back at the desk made her feel a certain way. She knew that she was good at her job, had a feeling for what the premium clients would want. She had put so many different ideas forward to the Alpha team, to Chamberlain. But it had lead to nowhere but deepening that hollow feeling inside which she needed to fill with the confirmation and praise from others.

Lamorna had rarely taken the time to just sit and reflect on her work there, there had always been a phone ringing or someone popping in. Now she was invisible, a veritable ghost. She sat there for a minute in complete silence and drank it in. This was a way of working that she could get used to: A closed door, just the low hum of the air conditioning for company and blank surfaces.

She recognised some inconsistencies with the walls from her time there before. She had almost always kept her implants activated, but the discolouring on the wall behind her desk had awakened her curiosity in the past. And now without her Optix active she inspected the surfaces once more, more closely. After a short search she noticed a subtle discolouring on an otherwise immaculate eggshell white wall, no bigger than a single postage stamp. At that moment she was quickly pulled out of her curiosity and heard deep voices outside her office. The most dominant one was unmistakeable. Lamorna felt herself panic. It was Chamberlain and he was heading that way with a larger group. She touched the discolouration and the wall collapsed backwards, a recessed door leading to a dark red-lit tunnel. Lamorna passed through the small opening and quickly looked how to close the door behind her, looking for a high-tech clue or voice activation.

But much to Lamorna's surprise there was Su's brass handle, screwed onto the back of the door to guide it back into place. Quite how it must have gotten there Lamorna did not even remotely know, only remembering it being an object Master Su had always carried around with her. But how had it appeared on the back of the secret door? Was it the same one at all? Lamorna put it all down to just seeing things, it was a dimly lit secret passage after all. A simple, unassuming handle, no fingerprint-scanning super sophisticated keypad, just a "perfect solution", which Lamorna whispered to herself and continued down the tunnel. The two metre wide tunnel remained level and after following a few corners she reached a larger brightly illuminated room, full of perspex cubicles, with yet more exposed utilities: This time there were thicker power cables, extra-wide air vents, extractor fans, girthy yellow pipes replete with hazard stickers and also industrial grade water sprinklers. Right in the middle of the large room stood three operating tables, a number of large gas canisters, overhead lights, a tangle of power cables and several metal gurneys. She turned to the first cubicle to find it empty. The next contained a singular chair with a young man strapped to it, his wrists bound and head strapped to the back of the chair itself. His eyes were covered with a medical blindfold.

Each of the other cubicles contained a chair and a young human. Each in various states of consciousness. Some were more alert, others utterly lifeless. Lamorna looked around for means of opening the cubicles and getting to them, to no avail. There were now no hidden buttons or secret levels, each transparent prison was sealed tight.

Lamorna then heard a sound. It was the charmingly persuasive voice of Jason Chamberlain. He was not alone however. He was in his presenting mode. He had guests, she knew it. She couldn't hide behind a cubicle, she would be too easily seen. She looked around for something to disguise herself with, but the canisters and equipment offered little in the way of help. The voices drew nearer, but they weren't coming from the same tunnel she had entered from. Now panicking, Lamorna remembered her plan. Remain calm, deep breaths, remember the ocean waves. And so she meditated on the idea of cold mountain water for a few precious seconds. Remembering one of its key properties: its ability to flow into any form. Which quickly led her to another thought. She was wearing a disguise already, why not adopt another, a way to hide in plain sight? She had not planned for this exact situation however, so this was a risk. But what better time than now to experiment? She was in a lab after all.

Lamorna swiftly accessed the self-texture mode within Optix and made herself completely transparent, she sat down in a wheelchair. She had simply disappeared, like clear water from a mountain spring. She parked herself to the side of the last operating table, out of the way of most paths through the large room and she waited.

"Here we have it!", Chamberlain exclaimed, "as I said before. We are so very honoured to welcome you to the very birthing centre of our next stage of development. Very few people have seen this and were are enormously privileged to show you what is happening here at Optix".

"What exactly are we looking at Mr. Chamberlain?", an older Asian man asked.

Chamberlain answered: "These are our pioneers. My inner circle. Our pathfinders to a new future. We have fought through all of human evolution to overcome the limits of nature, be it with the creation of simple tools to augment our hands, the development of vehicles to replace the need for horses, medicine to cure the diseases of the body, therapies to aid the psyche, weapons to fight our battles for us. With every development we evolve, find new levels to reach for and discover new rewards to reap. The human eye is not without imperfections, yet all that we see forms our perceptions. We created Optix to help us envision a better world and to behold the beauty already within our grasp. That world needs nourishment, care and prosperity. Too long have we let our wondrous world fall into disrepair and ruin. We need to protect what we have, give it the security and guardianship it so sorely needs. As you already know and expect of us, we have not been idly waiting and dreaming of a better future. We are bringing it to you. And so let me introduce to you the next level of Optix Defence. One of our bold pioneers". He whipped out his phone and pressed a short series of buttons. Then spoke a simple command, "Savia, arise".

Lamorna saw how one of the perspex doors of one of the cubicles opened and Savia rose to her feet and took steps outside and stood in front of the group. She looked emaciated and pale, her shoulders were sagging, her long dark hair was also greasy. Lamorna wondered how long she had been locked up, kept there in her cage.

Chamberlain continued: "For thousands of years we have developed the tools we need to survive, built houses in which to live, taken to the air to fly, visited the depths of the ocean, explored the galaxy. We have created new ways of living and enabled visions of a brighter future. We are magicians ever revealing new rabbits from the top hat. We are giants standing on the shoulders of mere men. With Optix we gave a people of seeing the world how they want it to be. And as we as a species strive for ever more and develop an even higher awareness and sophistication for aesthetics and beauty, we advance our minds, bodies and souls. We become something more. And that also deserves protection, lest it be place in harms way. Every eye has an eyelid. And so Optix Defence is born."

Chamberlain, observing his captive audience of officials, continued in his enthused tones, feeling for the mood amongst his audience: "We need guardians to protect us, we need angels to do our bidding, if we are to protect a heaven on Earth. You will look at your societies and see all manner of exploitation of your laws and norms. Deviants who would wish to take down all that you have created. Miscreant wrongdoers who deserve punishment for their crimes and misdeeds. The vile predator who is looking for a vulnerable child to abuse, the drunk driver, the sneaky thief and the serial adulterer. The clever rebel, cowardly terrorist and dangerous insurrectionist. The next generation of Optix is designed to make an even brighter future. The new implants offer an expanded range of features, enabling you to completely safeguard your populations and simultaneously weed out those undesirable miscreants, those filthy ne'er-do-wells and violent criminals. Overall happiness indexes will increase due to the feeling of security as crime rates drop, life expectancy will increase due to fewer violent crimes and public spending can be reduced thanks to the need for less active policing of city streets. Optix Defence will require only a minimal amount of hardware alteration; the standard implant will only need a five minute servicing at the local Optix store and then you will be all set to go."

Lamorna took in a series of deep breaths, she could feel her heart pounding, trying to push its way out. She had been looking at the audience and tried to make out anyone she recognised from the news or from Platform. She suddenly wished she had paid more attention to current affairs and watched the news more often. But she also had endured enough of blaming herself for things beyond her control. She then remembered that her implants were seeing all of this anyway, so it didn't matter if she didn't know who they were. For once she could accept not knowing something, there would be more than enough time afterwards to find out what was really happening before her very eyes. The world would know as well. Then the guests will be very much recognised, but for now she couldn't risk moving for being seen. Her phone would need to remain in her breast pocket while she sat and watched Chamberlain regale his guests with tales of a perfect world. "Your people will rejoice at your handling of domestic affairs, the economy will boom and your standing in the polls will be unbeatable. The years of political turbulence and upheaval will be forever over. No more worries of trying to please the voters, this will make them forever contented. Blissfully safe and secure in that knowledge that you are looking after them, yet they will be none the wiser. Should your proletariat dare to question the reason for all of the marvellous progress, they will see your wise heads and listen to your noble answers."

A member of the group, an elderly African gentlemen interjected, "but what about the more free-thinking people?

Will they not always find a way? In our country we have some groups who wish to bring down the old-guard".

Chamberlain continued, "there will of course be some dissenters, naysayers and then inevitably, disgusting rebellious acts. These will also be dealt with. Our Optix Defence system will be aware of illegal and immoral acts, allowing you to modify the parameters where appropriate".

The African gentleman seemed quite appeased and Chamberlain was able to further explain the consequences of crime under Optix Defence. He went on to reveal that during testing there were some issues where test subjects wished to reject the update. This was a particularly valuable insight and indeed led to the crime-fighting aspect of the Optix system. Up until then it was to be used to further increase engagement and integration with social media like Platform, making some phones redundant for content creation. Simple integration into Platform would further embed Optix into the lives of everyone on the planet. Yet with Optix Defence installed, by simply using their eyes as cameras they would all become integral parts of a worldwide surveillance system and be none the wiser. Each set of eyes protecting others from themselves and each other. A perfect network of defence.

"Imagine a world where we can be so honest with each other and to implicitly trust the actions of the other. We will be able to eliminate crime and dishonour. Upstanding citizens will walk around freely and confidently. Grandmothers, children, young attractive women will walk around without fear of being attacked, mugged or brutally murdered. Ever since my own mother died, mugged and stabbed by faceless cowards while shopping in the city, I have longed for a way to protect those less fortunate in our world: Those without enough water because others steal more than their fair share. Greedy farmers who grab land from their neighbours. Desperate drug addicts who take a life, when their own is of little worth. These disgusting individuals deserve the punishment that is coming to them and you can be the heroes to give it to them. And then when your society is cleansed of this evil, our world will be the better for it. Imagine if the great Mahatma Gandhi and Martin Luther King Jr. hadn't been gunned down in their prime. Imagine if Lennon and McCartney were still making music together. I believe in a world where these heroes can be free to make this world forever better. Which of you feel this too? Who wants to make a better world, for all of us?"

Chamberlain looked confidently at his small audience, the twelve dignitaries, accompanied by a couple of his assistants, were applauding him, all utterly besotted with the world-changing technology he was happy to provide them with, for no extra cost. Chamberlain eagerly accepted their exhaustive applause and then proceeded to provide them with a demonstration.

"Savia", Chamberlain commanded, "activate". Above the perspex cells seven monitors immediately turned on. And overlayed on the screen was a small HUD which showed the level of wear on the implant, signal strength and a traffic light system. Green implied no crime, red shone once a crime had been committed according to the letter of that nation's law, and the colour amber signalled a "grey zone". Here the nation's authorities would also be alerted of any deviant, risky or rebellious behaviour according to classical definitions, which could also be calibrated and then punished as appropriate. Savia's HUD was synced and the demonstration proceeded: "Strike me, Savia".

"Jason, of course, where exactly?", Savia responded, as if a complete automaton.

"Hit me in the stomach, right now, moderately hard", Chamberlain replied.

She proceeded to hit him in the gut, Chamberlain flinched slightly, the watching politicians gave a short gasp, and the red light on her HUD lit up bright red. The audience were visibly impressed, another peel of applause rang out, followed by some laughter. They liked what they saw. Lamorna, still hidden, was fighting back the urge to come out and reveal herself.

"What about rebellious, non-illegal acts?", asked a younger diplomat from Canada. "How can you judge if they are doing something wrong if it is not illegal?"

"That's no problem at all and thank you for the excellent question. There are certain actions which we would define as mildly malevolent, disobedient or rebellious. Let us consider Rosa Parks, climate protesters and the suffragettes. What they did was mostly non-violent, vaguely legal and what most people would determine to be generally peaceful. Yet what they brought about was a great degree of social upheaval and change, which has in turn enabled us to build on their great accomplishments. They, to their great credit, were able to identify certain remaining weaknesses in our societies, undiscovered by the governments of their times. These are the people to whom we owe many positive developments. However, their behaviours can be quite clearly quantified. The writing of political statements online, the organisation of protests, women's marches, sit-down protests, vandalism of public property, the defacing of great artworks. All of these acts have signifiers, require communication, dissemination of information. You will have the power to judge, thanks to the amber alert, which behaviours you wish to allow and which to condemn and eradicate. It is for such cases that you are, with some exceptions, publicly elected officials. Your esteemed place as guardian of the moral high-ground will be unaffected". Some members of the group nodded at and laughed with the British and Swedish princes, who were of course, not publicly elected. "Some behaviours are better left be. Rebels bring a lot of attention to themselves if they are incorrectly repressed or dissuaded. Some gain a larger backing because others get wind of state oppression. Prescience is a useful tool. Awareness of potential dangers to our precious democracy is of paramount importance. Please allow me to show you what I mean."

"Savia, I want you to strike the Prince of Wales."

"What the hell, Jason? You've got to be out of your mind. It's one thing hitting you when you ask me to, quite another to hit royalty without their permission."

Within half a second of Savia opening her mouth in protest the amber alert lit up on the monitor. Anyone in the room would have picked up on her absolute rejection of violence at her domineering boss's behest. And thus the attending dignitaries were immediately sold. They grasped the potential of this evolution of the Optix technology and lapped it up just as they did the first wave. The only difference back then was that they were approving its public use, now they would be clandestinely allowing surveillance technology to be installed worldwide. All rebellions could be stamped out at their first showing. The attendees congratulated Chamberlain and Savia on their outstanding demonstration, for availing fears of potential discord in the public sphere and inspiring hope in society for generations to come.

"I can't just sit here any longer!", Lamorna exclaimed as she addressed the celebrating group.

"What is this?", a shocked dignitary, bamboozled by the site of a speaking wheelchair exclaimed quizzically. The group all looked past the last perspex cell and saw the empty wheelchair.

Lamorna, now realising that she still appeared invisible, deactivated the self-texture function and returned back to her regular appearance. She could once more see her hands and legs; regaining a reassuring feeling once more of being truly present in the physical world. She then proceeded to stand up.

Chamberlain was fumbling his way out of the group, now facing Lamorna. "Lamorna? I…".

"I can't believe this Jason. I don't know what to say. You have taken this thing, this gift we presented to the world, and made it into a weapon of mass suppression. A disgusting corruption of the goodness and beauty we originally intended on bringing to the world. I can't believe it!", Lamorna had tears running from her eyes, landing on her pale cheeks.

"Lamorna. I really didn't expect you to be here, but it is no matter", Jason Chamberlain interrupted, as he attempted to rescue the situation and calmly reassume control. "My most honourable guests, esteemed dignitaries, Prime Ministers and Princes. Please allow me to introduce to you Lamorna Cruickshanks, a treasured part of the company and former member of our Alpha team. She previously aided us in the development of Optix's development and roll-out worldwide, as well as…", Chamberlain faltered.

"As well as having this damned idea in the first place. And you have taken it and made it into an atomic weapon, permanently aimed at the world's population. One false move, one wrong opinion and bye-bye! No, Jason Chamberlain, this is not my invention, this is not my gathering of corrupt men in grey suits, that is your doing. How dare you think they are adept enough at deciding what is right and wrong, or to believe that any one person could do that? What metrics are you using exactly? On what scale can you place the saving of a baby's life, by forcibly removing an abusive parent? Which political statements are dangerous? Perhaps you want a world without any political statements, where public debate is nothing more that a panel of grinning ignoramuses, where only harmless and pre-approved questions are asked, where no one is held publicly accountable anymore and all politicians enjoy unlimited terms and have carte blanche to do as they please! You list any number of technologies which have helped our evolution, yet leave out atomic bombs, machine guns, intensive farming, man-made viruses, concentration camps! I hate to think where you are ultimately going with this, Jason. These people have to see beyond your provision of this dangerous technology. Surely they cannot be so stupid as to believe that you would provide this without any strings attached, with no clauses, with no hidden conditions". Lamorna surprised herself. Normally she could only produce such convincing arguments well after the fact.

Jason Chamberlain fought to regain an element of control, but the tsunami named Lamorna Cruickshanks had well and truly arrived, "Lamorna! That's enough!", he tried.

"No it isn't, Jason! It never was enough, was it? You will always want more until everything is all tied up, your whole world in a pretty little box. Every thought a series of 0s and 1s. Every potential problem a massive fire which needs to be extinguished forever. What way is that to live, Jason? And not just for you. They already have the wool pulled over their eyes because of Optix, faking their way through the world. Now you want them to compromise themselves, censor themselves or utterly deny themselves any independent action! It is never enough, because you will never be happy until every single thought is preprogrammed and categorised. Every aspect of life kept in its own special drawer, then hermetically sealed in its own packaging. Only ever opened with express permission and after satisfying five layers of safety protocol. But that isn't life Jason, that's a simulation. Or at best, a replay of past life."

Chamberlain, now addressing the foreign and domestic dignitaries, attempted some damage limitation, "my guests, you are listening to the rantings of a rantingly misinformed and delirious former employee and cripple. Nothing more than lies, a horrifically twisted, unfounded attack on me personally and ungrounded in the inner workings of our fine new innovation. I kindly ask you to gather back in the conference room while I discuss the matter with my employee privately".

"That's just typical of you Jason. It isn't that you still try to treat me as your lap dog. It isn't that you think that I haven't already thought of a back-up plan. It is that you assume that they are too stupid to make their own informed judgements".

Chamberlain's face contorted in sour obstinance, akin to a greedy child being pressured into sharing a new toy: "That's enough Lamorna, I can accept you attacking me, but not my fine guests. Savia, reprimand Lamorna! Keep her here for questioning."

Savia moved towards Lamorna, all signs on the monitor were still green. Savia's demeanour didn't fully align with that which she said. She appeared amiable, even friendly, "I am sorry Lamorna. I can't let this happen. Your actions have caused a great disruption to Optix." Everything green; the lights on the screen showed full compliance on Savia's part. "We all have our own dreams of the future, Lamorna, and not everybody's look the same. Jason's is one of order, control, without rebellion. I do not know what your view of the future is Lamorna, but I will not allow you to continue with this disruption; this must end".

The dignitaries were able to breathe a sigh of relief as they witnessed Savia move swiftly to apprehend Lamorna, who appeared as if frozen in stone, resigned, she knew there was little she could physically do to stop her. Besides, she needed to see what else Savia had been reprogrammed to do. Jason Chamberlain, stood smirking, in a wide stance, with arms folded. Savia was now stood beside Lamorna with a hand on her shoulder. Lamorna once more felt some irritation in her legs; the prosthetics were giving her a mild shock. Savia gave Lamorna an uncharacteristically tend squeeze on her shoulder, then looked at Lamorna as if to say it was all going to be okay.

In a flash, Savia's HUD turned from green to amber and she turned from Lamorna to Jason Chamberlain, "What really shocks me is that I never did anything about it earlier. I cannot help you anymore, Jason". Savia smiled back at the group. "You have twisted everything we made together, for whatever end. And I will not have any more part of it".

"You infernal idiot, Savia! What do you think you are doing!? You always lacked perspective!" Chamberlain's smirk turned from greedy satisfaction, through an ashen grief, into a wolf's rage. "You wouldn't think that I would let you do this, would you? I have worked too hard on this to have the pair of you get between me and this great advancement, something I owe to the world. It is true that a certain price must be paid for this next step in our evolution as a society. And Savia, I am sorry to say that you will be making the first contribution. Yours will be the first offering". As he spoke Chamberlain subtly lifted the cuff on his left sleeve and pressed a button on his watch, activating an important failsafe which detonated the

Optix Defence implant in Savia's head. Her eyes were instantly burnt out, her brain imploded and she fell dead to the ground beside Lamorna. The heavy slump of her body landing gave the dignitaries the cue to scream in horror. They saw her hollow black eye sockets, brain matter slowly oozing from them. The shouts and screams echoed there in the room for a moment before the surprise subsided and the captive fear set in.

Frozen for a moment, Lamorna then slowly turned to see Savia's body. At once the first dignitaries made for the doors, which were locked. They shook the doorhandles and pounded on the doors, to no avail. Lamorna didn't think Chamberlain would stop here; he was in danger of losing everything now. This was the start of the great collapse of everything he had built. In a sharp moment his fortunes had been completely turned. The Japanese politician's assistants guarded him, putting their bodies between him and Chamberlain. They were unarmed, but more than capable of dealing with their captor. Lamorna observed the situation and monitored her breathing once more.

A stand-off. She needed to keep her cool in order for everyone else to get out of here alive. She heard the swirl of the waves in her ears, their crashing on the rocks, one after the other. The white noise helped her tune out the shouting and crying from the group. She looked at the faces of the guests, all turning a particular shade of scared. The man in the first cubicle, another test subject, had also slumped to the floor. It seems the failsafe was daisy-chained to destroy all of the experiments at once.

"Nobody do anything rash! Lamorna, stay where you are! Do not worry dear friends. Savia's implant must have had a major malfunction. I am terribly sorry to say that such unforeseen catastrophes can happen during beta testing. She was a dependable member of the team and I am sure that the implant affected her judgment too, come the end. This is, of course, something we will remedy posthaste. Never fear, come the roll-out all implants will have been extensively field tested and safety approved". Up until this point Jason Chamberlain was not entirely sure who had noticed him setting off the detonation in Savia's head, so he tried to play it neutral, even if his mention of an *'offering'* had been a poor one.

"That isn't going to happen, Jason. This has gone on long enough and we can't let anyone else get hurt. Savia didn't deserve this, she gave you everything, have you no shame? She was in Alpha team, Jason and you used her for human testing. You killed her. And only because she didn't do what you commanded her to do. This is not a war, she is not a deserter, she deserved more. She didn't deserve this, Jason. Savia was thrown to the wolves, how can you deny killing her?". Lamorna's gesticulations were getting wilder, she had to be careful here; she didn't know if anyone else was armed.

"I have had enough of your insolence, Lamorna. Be careful of what you say next. It will not be advantageous to speak in such terms amongst our guests here. They saw what you did, what destruction you have caused here.

"It's always your lies, Jason. It was ever thus. Sharing the wealth of the company, with all workers. Grooming us to lead Optix with you. You tell us you want help people lead a better, happier life, free of the visual decay surrounding us. You would help build a better, more moral society. And in doing so you are happy to sell your ethics to the highest bidder, fool world leaders into becoming totalitarian tyrants and kill your most loyal colleagues. Your lies are no longer your dirty little secrets, Jason. Nor are they merely confined to this single room. This beautiful invention of yours was indeed capable of exposing shameful revolt and misanthropy; it has the darkly beautiful potential to tame and bind us all. And thankfully one of its first victims is you, Jason. You have been so kind today in sharing your vision of the future with all of us here on Platform. You have a worldwide audience, wave for the camera! I don't know exactly how many people; I've been pretty tied up here, stuck in the moment, without being plugged into my precious device. But I am very sure that these implants of mine have seen enough use for a lifetime. I'll be sure to send them to you when I am done with them. But I don't know when we will see each other in the flesh again. I for one will not mourn you when you are gone, this world has endured enough mummery for now. We need a new start with a fresh pair of eyes."

"What are you talking about? You can't mean…?", panic set into Jason's voice. He spun around looking at the dignitaries, Savia's body and Lamorna.

"It was my idea. Of course I would use it. I always let you get the credit for what we developed here. Now it is time for me to get mine. My implants have been broadcasting since I set foot here in the building. They have seen everything, they, the people have heard everything", Lamorna said emphatically, as a broad grin appeared on her face.

"Lamorna, please. You can't be serious. I know that you are lying. I know you well enough for me to see through this elaborate bluff. You don't fool me, you never could. Always too honest, too happy to help, to serve me. I don't know what it is exactly about you, but you need me, Lamorna. You need that person to tell you *'well done!'*. So, congratulations! You have done a great job of embarrassing me here in front of my guests. Your little stunt here and at the guildhall, as I assume that was you too, have set us back. You have cleared your conscience of all your demons and can well and truly get going. I don't ever want to see you here again. Consider yourself blacklisted in this industry; you'll never get another chance like this one."

"Jason, I don't need to fool anyone. The truth speaks for itself. I am glad I came back here today and placed my head back into the mouth of the dragon. I had to see past the veneer, below the surface, Jason. I knew there was more to Optix than just making the world appear more beautiful. I knew that you hungered for more power, more domination. But the truth is nobody needs you, Jason. Not for too long anyway. Some people teach you a lesson and then you move on from them. We don't need your lies anymore!". Lamorna's last statement hung like a leaden cloud in the room for a moment, before a muffled knocking sound could be heard from the other side of the large doors. Chamberlain, Lamorna and the distinguished guests turned to look at where the noise was coming from. All of the cubicles were still closed, Savia still lay dead, no one was moving. The air was thick with mystery, our protagonist had achieved a sense of absolution and then the sound quickly became a crash; a flash of light, shouting male voices and six special forces operatives came through the door. Each wielding a submachine gun with a laser sight pointed right at Chamberlain's chest. "Jason Chamberlain, get down on your knees, hands on your head!", the lead operative commanded.

"Please! You have the wrong person, I swear. I didn't do anything. That's the one you want; here next to my poor Savia!", pointing at Lamorna, Chamberlain was fighting his last fight.

"On your knees, hands behind your head!", the soldier repeated, now in a louder tone.

"I can't do this, I can't." Chamberlain, looking at Lamorna mouthed the words, "you won, congratulations" and then gave a last verbal command. "Sayonara", he said to himself and, just as Savia met her end, Jason Chamberlain's implants exploded and he collapsed in a heap of his own bones. Lamorna screamed, "No!". She witnessed his eyes burn out, each one appeared to instantly turn into a deep black-red hole. Just as Chamberlain fell to the ground, her prosthetics couldn't hold her up any longer and so Lamorna also tumbled to the ground.

The operatives swarmed Jason Chamberlain's body and confirmed this death. The dignitaries had long since fled the room. Lamorna was left now alone with the six special forces agents and the two dead bodies.

"We need to get you out of here Ms Cruickshanks", said one of the operatives.

"I need a minute here, can you give that to me?", she requested.

"Yes, we can give you that. But please end your broadcast now. They have seen enough", Lamorna looked at the agent and nodded in compliance.

"We all have", Lamorna added in a sombre tone. "All too much".

The agents moved to the perimeter of the room while Lamorna took stock of what had happened. Kneeling down next to Jason she wept. She wept for all she had done and also all she had hopefully prevented. She had wanted to expose Chamberlain, not lead him to suicide. She had wanted to limit Optix's power and reach, not bring it all down. Had Optix Defence gone online, there would be no freedom left at all, that was clear to her then, yet she wept as she felt overcome with guilt for her actions. She had seen two longtime colleagues and collaborators die because of her actions; Lamorna didn't want this for neither Savia nor Jason.

She thought for a moment of what Master Su would think of all that she had accomplished today. Would Su have quoted the utilitarians; were their deaths a lesser evil? Would she have weighed up the utility of paying for the freedom of the world's population with Savia and Jason Chamberlain's lives? Was this the best case scenario? Was it the most desirable of outcomes? It certainly didn't feel like it; Lamorna felt too much judgement being passed on her to contemplate this annihilation and utter destruction. She had so many unvoiced misgivings with his way of working with people, his vision for the company and his manipulation of the truth. There was still much that she wanted to settle with him, as she had wanted to with Su too. So much unfinished business. She wept further until she could no more. *'Here at the end of all things'*, she thought to herself. She then remembered that she was still broadcasting, despite what the agent had said to her. Finally, Lamorna deactivated her implants and made her way towards the special forces agents for debriefing.

17 - V

Lamorna, holed up in the Optix boardroom, had been interrogated by the police detectives for six hours after the incident at Optix, only getting home at midnight. She was utterly drained from their incessant questioning and probing. Surely they had seen everything there was to see and heard all they needed. The entire world, first of all on Platform, then on the news, had seen it all, heard everything about Optix Defence, seen Chamberlain divulge everything about his plans, observed how those political leaders had supported him and waited, drooling in anticipation at his next revelation. As she sat there in the Optix boardroom she could only coldly repeat what her original intentions had been, to expose Optix as a fraudulent enterprise, fooling us all with its oppressive lies. They probed with other difficult questions pertaining to revolutionary groups and terrorist organisations; asking whether Lamorna had intended on killing key figures within Optix, whether she was operating alone, whether any foreign governments were secretly backing her, whether competitors had secretly financed and coordinated her efforts. For most of the interview Lamorna sat and shook her head, she could manage little more. Her attention would fade back to the destruction she had born witness to, the explosions, the death and those deep black burning eyes. Her mind trying to rationalise her experience, she saw a hooded figure in the doorway watching closely, taking notes, passing judgement. She felt completely at the cold mercy of the interviewers, taking turns coming to interview her. Always the same set of questions, always asked in the same way. They were, of course, testing the veracity of Lamorna's answers, recording any slips, alterations or inconsistencies. Again and again her mind would drift to Jason's limp body and Savia's touch on her shoulder. She recalled his last words to her and the horrible sound of the explosion; a wet thud. Their lives disappearing in a puff of smoke.

Lamorna observed the hooded figure, watching it out of the corner of her eye. Never really disappearing, but drifting away once Lamorna tried to focus on it. Assuming the figure was just the interviewers' superior, she tried to calm herself and remain in the room, mentally as well as physically.

The specialists had fully reviewed the footage from Lamorna's upload and found no tampering. So robust were Lamorna's statements that she was able to finally leave. The dark hooded figure had also long since departed.

Lamorna was accompanied by the special forces agents as she made her way via lift down to the foyer; swift was their march and foreboding their demeanour. When she arrived at Optix she had been alone, unassuming and determined to incriminate Jason Chamberlain and further damage Optix's reputation. Lamorna felt as if her legs wanted to give way yet again and was thankful for the escort to the front door. She swore to herself that she would never visit the place again; Optix was history for her, if not yet for everyone else. She took a taxi home and spent most of the ride with her head in her lap, only occasionally looking out of the window; the beautiful sunrise she missed completely. Upon her arrival at home she made directly for the freezer and poured herself a generous tumbler of vodka. Only once most of the bottle had been emptied did she finally pass out.

Some hours later, her mouth feeling as if mothballed, Lamorna lay in bed. It was a chilly morning: the windows were full of condensation, her arms were cold to the touch and she craved a hot drink. She had slept badly, waking up regularly throughout the day. Lamorna looked for a further bottle of alcohol in vain, then eventually took some sleeping pills and slept through until the middle of the following night. Although her body was at rest, Lamorna's mind was trying to process all that she had seen at Optix the previous day. She had dreams of Chamberlain again. And of Savia, indeed all of the test subjects, her colleagues, in the meandering Optix hallways. Of elite troopers hunting her down, pinning her in the underground car park and bombarding her with suppressing fire. The ringing of the bullets in that confined space stayed with her. She wished that an entire swarm of bullets would bury themselves into her body. That the terror would end. That she would be absolved of guilt. She screamed for mercy in those dreams. And they repeated themselves, night for night. A closely constant companion.

Standing guiding those elite forces would be a black cloaked figure with arms folded forebodingly. Whether arriving in the underground car park, making her way up to the foyer, in the lift, past the canteen, in the boardroom and in the secret lab. The cloaked figure was always there. On other nights the action took place on the city bridge, outside the guildhall, at the Bluebird hotel. The elite forces were always there, on her tail. Wherever she went they would follow her around. And a black-cloaked Master Su was there to lead them. She was seeing Su continually, wherever she turned in the Optix corridors, simultaneously leading her through the building and chasing her, haunting her. Every exit led back to the same place, the room where their bodies lay, the room where the politicians applauded Chamberlain's monstrosity, the place where her ghost caught up with her. She dreamt of Chamberlain as an utterly desiccated and horrifically mummified ghoul, with dark pits for eyes. Jason's body crawled on the floor toward her, as she cowered on the floor, having fallen out of the wheelchair. There as she lay helpless he would begin to scream at her, but his words no longer made sense, the only clear thing being his wails of agony from the burning, piercing the echoing of gunfire, his cries reverberating off all four walls. Masked in black the special forces were all stood in a straight line, firing in cold unison. Only their blackened eyes remained eerily visible. Lamorna was struggling to escape Chamberlain, most nights he would claw at her eyes until only a black emptiness was left. Occasionally, she was able to get away from him, before being shot by the firing squad and flying through the glass window, then awaking just before she struck the ground.

Every night there was one operative in the firing squad; an impossibly elusive figure wearing a long black robe, it was Master Su. Her eyes had turned a hateful black too. In addition, the operatives all became to howl and scream while shooting incessantly. Nothing hit Chamberlain, despite the storm of rounds coursing through the room. The damage had already been done. Whether by his own hand, or due to Lamorna's interference, Jason Chamberlain was dead and gone and she had to deal with the consequences.

Hollow pangs in her gut pierced her with jabs of hunger; she hadn't eaten in days, being unable to face anything before she left to go to Optix on that fateful day. She took a quick look in the cupboard, soon rejecting the idea of cooking and made herself some toast. Forcing it down with some strong coffee Lamorna was again reminded of the burning smell from her dreams and rushed to the sink and vomited, she needed to be emptied of this. She took a shower to clean herself off, sitting there for the best part of an hour, just letting the force of the water strike her head. Each droplet of water a bullet from a gun. The water coating her in blood.

Even the dark blue towel hanging on the back of the door looked just like Master Su; Lamorna, no matter how she tried, couldn't get away from her. Flashbacks from the special forces, from the meeting at the Bluebird hotel, from their lakeside talks, from her fall; they all came to her in a cinematic menagerie of melancholy. What if she had never met Su? Had never been driven to question her time at Optix? Things would have been so much easier, much clearer. Less complex, less challenging. She could have worked a couple of more years at Optix, then jumped ship and founded her own company or worked for a competitor. Or written a book and become a high-profile whistleblower, exposing the sinister inner workings of the company as well as its evil and tyrannical leader. Alternatively, she could have threatened him and demanded hush money, then moved to the Bahamas and enjoyed coconut cocktails for the rest of her days. Until he sent hitmen after her, that is. Another option would have been to stay, worked for her master and devoted her life to the Optix cause, eventually withering away into sad mediocrity, the shame of a life unlived and utter moral death.

Master Su had complicated things and at the same time guided her to find some kind of purpose. But this didn't resolve the agonising guilt Lamorna felt. The question was, what would? She couldn't bring them back, Savia, Jason and Su were gone and it was her fault. She remained in the shower for a while longer and turned up the heat of the water. The steam collected in the small bathroom as if she were inside a great locomotive; her feelings of shame collecting, driving the pressure ever higher in her mind. Singing in the shower helped a bit; sometimes the music made her feel worse. Besides finding it hard to find a suitable tune, eventually Lamorna ran out of hot water. After wrapping herself up in large towels Lamorna sat on her sofa and checked her phone; she tried to avoid any news about what happened at Optix and just checked her Platform account. No messages, not a zip. After some swift doom-scrolling Lamorna eventually summoned some energy from the depths and made herself some coffee. While waiting for the kettle to boil she kept flicking through her phone; there was the typical collection of short videos on cooking, film gaffs and music news, but nothing that could hold her attention for more than five seconds. Then the hiss of the kettle distracted her and its screams took her back to the secret lab at Optix. The squealing reminded her of her own shrieks as Chamberlain killed himself, as well as managing to pull her back into her own dreams.

Lamorna sat down once more and began drinking her fiercely hot coffee. As she did she picked up her phone once more. Dare she risk opening up a news app, or her message service? *'I need to go to a land of make-believe'*, Lamorna told herself, *'or bury my head in the sand'*. That's when Lamorna was reminded of the gift Master Su gave her, Su's wooden box with the ball of sand. She went to her bedside drawer and retrieved it. The beautifully ornate olive wood was as expertly crafted as anything she had seen; the dovetailing was exquisite. Inside she found the sand ball once more and held it carefully in her hand. *'If only this thing could grant wishes, I would probably want to see Su just one last time'*, she thought to herself. The ball however remained inanimate, with no sign of a goateed genie appearing from within. *'I would beg her to stop haunting me'*, Lamorna thought further. She placed the ball back inside the olive box, which made an unusually loud *'clunk'*. Lamorna sat with her head in her hands and wept for a while. The day turned to night and then inevitably back to day. Time passed and Lamorna remained locked inside.

After an uncertain amount of time Lamorna awoke on her sofa and saw that her coffee cup, the wooden box and her towels were lying on the floor. At some point she had grabbed a throw to cover herself and not freeze. Lamorna slowly surmised that she needed to do normal things, like a normal human and get out again, occupy herself with a distraction, a respite from blame and responsibility. Lamorna looked online at what was going on that day in the city. There weren't any films which took her fancy and she needed something now to take her mind off everything. Concerts would be only come the evening and she couldn't wait that long; she needed to get out now as the ceiling was in danger of crushing her where she sat, once more alone on her sofa. The youth theatre was putting on a performance of a fantasy story she had seen a good review of and bought a ticket. She quickly got ready and made her way out. Lamorna hastily locked her flat, rushed down the road and just managed to catch the tram. Once more her prosthetic legs were playing up. It was as if they had a will of their own sometimes; they weren't entirely hers.

By the time Lamorna had finally left her flat, after all that had happened at Optix, the news cycle had moved past the initial shocking information about *'a suspected terrorist attack, human testing and mind control, suspect in custody, Jason Chamberlain and Savia Mbuemo dead, special forces operation, foreign dignitaries, Prince of Wales safe'*, and onto the deeper dealings of Optix and Jason Chamberlain. By now Felix had been installed as acting CEO and was in the middle of an intense media firefight. Lamorna watched the news screens on the tram and could see how nervous Felix was during an emergency press conference outside the Optix building, pretty much exactly where she had her accident. "That's a coincidence", Lamorna spoke under breath.

"Sorry dear?", an elderly lady opposite Lamorna asked. "What was that?", she repeated.

Lamorna, removing her headphones said, "I just meant that it's interesting to see the press conference. Do they know what happened?"

"They sure do. It's come out that Optix was trying to do some kind of mind control on people and it was stopped because there was a spy in there. And then some soldiers came and killed the owner. So, now there's a new sheriff in town, this guy here on the telly", the lady explained.

"Oh right, that's quite something, I suppose. Did they find out much about the spy?", Lamorna sat stiff as a board, anxious that more agents would come to arrest here once more.

"Not really, just some disgruntled employee apparently. They used a spy camera they says, all very exciting deary. But they got him telling everything and what not. Not a very smart chap it seems, that Chamberlain fella. But thank god he got his comeuppance. He was going to use these eye things to spy on people in foreign countries and when the dictators don't like what they see, they could blow up the people or something. A load of old tripe if you ask me. What do people need those eye things for anyways? Never needed 'em when I was a young lass and I can still see just dandy. All this highfalutin nonsense really does my head in. Funnily enough. I did theirs in too, I heard. Haha!", the old lady continued to be amused with herself. Lamorna thanked her quickly, bid her a good day and then stuck her earphones firmly back in. That last quip had been just too much for her. She didn't need to hear anymore about heads being done in.

The tram passed giant LED billboards as it made it's way and Lamorna could read the headlines, *'Optix planned to enslave humanity'*, *'Chamberlain dead: what next for Optix?'*, *'Prince of Wales forced to quit public life!'*. Then followed advertising from a life insurance company, complete with a hooded woman, a widow. *'Must move on'*, Lamorna thought.

Rattling down past the finance district and over towards the theatre, Lamorna took another look out of the tram window. The shimmer of the mighty river had caught her eye and she felt compelled to get out. At the next stop, at the middle of the bridge, Lamorna made to stand up, but her legs didn't react. It was as if they had entered a kind of sleep mode, or perhaps they had become sentient and were trying to prevent her from looking down into the river again. She tried standing again and this time they cooperated. Lamorna nodded to the little old lady to say goodbye, the tram doors slid open and Lamorna was hit by the glassy, reflective surface of the river. It appeared still, calm. She full well knew that its current was fiercely strong and unforgiving. Her gaze was fixated on the water. The cold blue sky, with rarely a cloud in view, filled her eyes and the white glow of the sun was the projector. To Lamorna's eye it appeared that the speckled sunlight was dancing on the water's surface. As Lamorna stood there transfixed she observed the shimmering fairies and their parade, prancing and dancing in carousels of light.

Once the tram had disappeared Lamorna was struck by the quiet, *'the mighty river makes no sound'*, came to mind, and she further recalled that *'the empty can rattles the most'*. As she stood dead centre of the river she took in the sheer width of its reach; twin sides of the city were brought together by the the embracing flow of these minute molecules of hydrogen and oxygen, never touching each other, yet sliding over and under each other, forming water, giving life, embodying progress and transition. Once they had broken the river's enchanting surface, neither Su nor Xerxo had stood a chance in its murky depths, possibly being swept out to sea after being dragged along for many miles beforehand. Maybe the prancing fairies were the souls of Xerxo and Su, entwined in the dance forever, never coming to rest.

Water brought people together, one of life's necessities. As a child she had been surrounded by it and she had moved further and further away from it. During her moonlit meetings at the lake Su had had helped her rediscover its energy. The water was telling her something now. Lamorna stretched up on her tip-toes to look at the water directly below her as the wind began to pick up. Each individual water molecule had come together separately. Somewhere in the south, streams formed rivers, converging with others to form this, the mightiest of great rivers. An endless cycle, a perfection, the water ascended to the sky eventually, before returning to the mountains as rain. This chance meeting was never to be repeated. She could never see the same water again. Yet it would continue to flow, regardless of which queen or king sat on the throne, regardless of energy crises and technocratic dictatorships. The water would pass this point regardless of whether the bridge fell, the city burnt or the human race had disappeared, or become enslaved by a hive mind. Only once an ice age comes, or Earth's final demise, when the Sun will become a red giant and the planet is consumed by fire, will the river be no more.

Thoughts of an end captivated Lamorna, a final silencing; once more she gazed at the skittish light dancing on the cold surface, enraptured by their fleeting beauty, their spontaneous uniqueness. She was forever reminded of Su, the smallest and biggest things brought her back. The sparkles appeared as dust from a magic wand, as stars in a night sky, as sugar spilt on a table top. Each time she looked at them they were formed anew and would never be the same. She made a mental photograph and resolved to remove herself from the barrier, over which she was by then heavily leaning.

The bright city lights were so much brighter on the east side, the number of buildings also much larger. Tall buildings, more riverside restaurants, the main train station, more cars headed in that direction too. But her way was leading to the quieter west side, where the theatre was to be found. She made her way back to the tram stop and then continued eastbound towards the theatre. The rackety tram made a right turn after the bridge into a cosmopolitan area of the city, with small boutique shops offering leather wares, vintage jewellery, bicycles, cafes with outdoor seating and a few good looking charity shops. Lamorna told herself that she would take some time to stop in a cafe after the show. She had spent years not going out and avoiding live music and theatre; now was the time to change all that.

The theatre, located on the main street had large red letters forming *'live youth theatre'* on its sign. The security guards reminded her of the special forces, wearing thick black protective vests; she swiftly walked past them, careful to avoid eye contact and showed her ticket to the usher. The show, about young skin-changers, titled *'Wargs and Witches'*, was due to start, just in time; Lamorna had spent long enough on the bridge. She made her way into the theatre and was guided by to her row. Most of the other seats were already occupied and to get to her place she had to do the apologetic shuffle past the other seated audience members, her prosthetics knocking into some of the other guests in the process. Thankfully this was no cinema and there little danger of spilling people's ridiculously overfilled and overpriced popcorn. Most of the other guests were families; Lamorna felt, not for the first time, out of place. She took her seat, put her satchel on the floor beside her and took a quick sip of water from her bottle while it was still cold. Lamorna could see how old the theatre was; without her Optix activated she could she the red paint peeling from the walls, the wooden beams, painted a dark brown, had seen better days. *'This place must be at least a hundred years old'*, she told herself, making it a survivor of the last great war. Lamorna observed some light scaffolding towards the back of the theatre, there was indeed maintenance work to be done. Nothing remains as it was, she reminded herself. Decay, without repair, is inevitable. An inexorable atrophy; faded as memory.

The lights went down and the rumble of quiet conversation died, an automated voice advised that phones were to be turned off and Optix implants deactivated. This theatre was pretty old-school and Lamorna cracked a wry smile; *'Su would love this place; it's like her suite at the hotel'*, she mused. The heavy red curtains were bathed in a soft light, they appeared regal and required much pulling to reveal the simple stage decoration. The quite basic set design was charming and naïvely done. Any Optix interference would have only spoilt its charm. The story began in a forest, a young wild cat was separated from its family and forced to survive for itself, whereupon it made its way unbeknownst into the big city and was attacked by the local police. The cat ran and hid in a disused church and licked its wounds. Some of the younger audience members were sobbing and feeling sorry for the cat, named *'Shar'*, their stifled cries muffled by their parents. The plywood church construction reminded Lamorna of the children's TV shows she watched as a child and their flimsy sets. Lying with his back to the audience Shar the cat revealed his secret, as he slowly arose, removing his mask, he revealed himself to be a skin-changer and then appeared as a human teenager. There was the inevitable gasp of shock from some of the children, but Lamorna admired how his posture, voice, mouth movement and overall demeanour had changed; completely adapted to the new city surroundings. He was still a scared young animal, but now exuding a playful curiosity and energy which required adventure and knowledge.

When Lamorna had read the novel she was in her fantasy adventure phase, something she often buried her head in whenever things got too much elsewhere. The character transformations had thrilled her and she wondered how life would be as a wild cat, roaming the forests and mountains, living off the land. Scaling trees at ease, ripping flesh from bone. Some characters were only able to assume a single form: Of a stag, bear or wolf, as well as that of a human. Others could also become a flying insect or bird, soaring into the air with ease.

Lamorna most closely identified with the sea animals, who could plumb the depths of the ocean: octopi, seahorses and sharks. Octopi were particular fascinating, being able to camouflage themselves and become almost invisible. They were sensitive and solitary creatures who could use their considerable intelligence to outwit both potential prey and predator, hiding in sight and striking when the time was right. Alternatively they were able to flee from hungry hunters and fit into a space no wider than their own eyeball. Their pliable body able to contort and twist into any necessary space, should its needs require it. Also, it could grasp almost anything with its tentacles, being able to use them with great sensitivity and dexterity. Flying would also be great, but there is more peace to be found in the deep, Lamorna maintained. The octopus could slip into the cold dark depths, out of sight and have its peace.

The life of a wild cat had its appeal too though and Lamorna was able to feel poor Shar's helplessness and disorientation. She too often felt quite lost among her fellow humans, though thankfully she didn't have the problem of being directly hunted by them. Shar's story continued on the stage and during the intermission, snacks were available, but still no popcorn. In the audience Lamorna caught a fleeting glimpse of a blue cloak ahead of her. She shrugged it off and, once the bell rang, she immediately made her way back to her seat.

It being a children's story, Shar soon made friends with other skin-changers and was able work together with human children from a local school to convince the police not to attack the skin-changers, as they were not a serious threat to the humans. The skin-changers and the human children lived happily among each other and all was well come the inevitable happy end. Lamorna felt there was a good deal of nuance missing in this telling of the story, several subplots had been cut and the stage can only ever be a substandard replacement for one's own imagination. Truth be told Lamorna was distracted: she had noticed a raven-haired woman sat three rows ahead of her. The woman only ever stared right ahead at the stage and Lamorna was sure that she hadn't been there before the break. During the final moments of the play the woman stood up and left her seat, slowly gliding along the aisle and towards the exit as if made of air. It was at this moment that Lamorna's fears were confirmed, it was Master Su. The apparition had appeared during the intermission and had taken the empty seat in Lamorna's line of vision. Lamorna felt cold sweat on her forehead, her skin felt taut and ready to jump from her body.

Lamorna turned to see Su leave via the rear fire exit, her blue hood now appearing black in the darkness. She floated through the doors and they closed by themselves. Not for the first time, Lamorna felt torn between following Su and staying rooted to the spot. She had fought this battle so many times in the past. Rarely had Lamorna passed up one of Su's invitations since their first meeting in the hotel tower of the Bluebell Luxury Apartments. *'Whatever it was, she helped draw it out of me, yet she also demanded absolute commitment to the cause and I was a willing soldier, follower, apprentice'*. Lamorna, struggling with her own internal dialogue finally remained in her seat and saw out the end of the play. She owed it to herself; if it really were Su, she could wait. If only she had made her wait more often in the past.

As the audience clapped and the actors returned to the stage for applause, no fewer than five times, Lamorna gathered her satchel and unpacked her book. As the lights went up she waited until the majority of the audience had left and then slowly made her way out of the theatre. Most of the other guests were busy chatting in the foyer about the play, the kids were excited about the film adaptation coming next year and wanted to read the next book before it came out. Lamorna laughed a little and was happy for them, she knew that joy quite well and revelled in it. She made her way through into the foyer and spotted Su just outside the main entrance waiting for her; day had passed to night. Lamorna found the strength to maintain eye contact, without forcing a smile. Su's long blue robe completely covered her legs and feet. This had previously given Su the appearance of walking like a ghost, floating over the ground. As they faced each other they remained silent, for what felt for Lamorna like aeons; fearful for what was to come next. *'Was Su going to take her away? Consume her? Ask for help?'*

Master Su's face was quite sombre and somewhat more haggard than before, her skin was pocked. Her hair more matted, the corner of her mouth drawn down as if pulled down by fine strings and her brow now appeared thoroughly wrinkled. Stood before Lamorna she held her hands by her side steadily, as if very subtly balancing upon a tightrope. Master Su lowered her head and motioned to speak. Yet, before she could say a word, Lamorna cut in: "I know why you are here. It has been a long time since we saw each other, whether it is weeks or years it matters not. I know that you can hear me, so just listen. I don't know why you are here, whether it really is you or whether you really are just an apparition. But I know that I cannot deny that I haven't wished for another meeting. There have been dark days since you fell, since the night on the bridge. There are so many things I am unsure about, Su. Jason is gone, Optix is, I don't know what. I saw things I cannot describe to you, the horror just won't leave me. Their eyes, Su. They were completely gone. I faced them all and they are gone. Does that mean that I won? Is that what we wanted? Was it all your design, Su? Did you succeed? Is this what victory feels like? And now you want to get the old team back together, set the world to rights once more, look unflinchingly in the face of the darkest enemy and burn out their eyes? You shone a bright light on those darkest holes of my mind, Su, but what did we do with that power? Those days and nights were my enlightenment; in my moonlight nights you were my sun. And where did we point that light that it should burn them so harshly?", Lamorna stared right at Su, who was reticent to raise her face any further. "I cannot enter the forest anymore, Su, without being afraid of being consumed with the desire to lose myself in the depths of the lake. I try to drown out their cries with the water rushing over my head. When will this feeling end?, I ask myself. Then I remember, that this is what we both wanted somehow. That this was our design", Lamorna gestured to Master Su that they walk down the road to a cafe she had spotted earlier.

Lamorna and Su walked slowly side by side down the empty street. Now at night all cars had disappeared and the black night felt to Lamorna like a dark cloak covering them both. They moved in absolute silence. The careful footsteps were the only sounds to be heard all around. Lamorna pointed to the cafe she had spotted earlier, Master Su merely nodded and they entered.

Upon seating at a corner table they ordered some ginger tea with lemon and Lamorna continued where she had left off. "You came to me like a holy visitor, sent from another plane. But you couldn't stay. It was as if something forbade it. As if an expiry date was predetermined. I don't exactly know why you picked me out, Su. You don't even need to tell me, I wouldn't have seen things as clearly as I can now if we hadn't met. I can feel it in my blood and bones that we set out to do something together and it kind of worked. And now that time is over. You demanded so much of me, you believed in me. I would never have lost my legs were it not for you and I would never be able to see things as well as I can without you. Maybe had we never met, I wouldn't be here at all anymore. Had I just carried on blindly at Optix, I would have only run myself even further down into the ground. You challenged me to see the reality in my life and to fight for more; to fight for myself. In the process I was able to shed that tired skin and free myself of that dragon. You made a dragon slayer of me, Su. That is another thing I will learn to live with; the blood on my hands."

Master Su wiped her eye, but Lamorna continued,

"only now, can I fully see how it must be. And it must be this way because it is what I want. I no longer need old ghosts following me, dragons chasing me. Those fairy tales we told ourselves, they need an ending, like your witch in her prison. I won't be looking over my shoulder to see what is chasing me, or who is judging me. I have shaken off those shackles and leave them rattling on the ground, the red rope has freed me and the ogre is dead".

Su took a slurp of tea, her face grew more frustrated, yet Lamorna was still not finished: "More and more, I sense that I am haunted by you, no longer is it the kind of sweet pain of grief that colours my memories of you. Gone are those times where every bridge, river, mountain and forest reminded me of you. The feeling now is that of being chased, followed and spied on. A haunting spectre you are. I replay events in my head; seeking alternative outcomes, other paths and adjusted intentions. Every time I come back to the same fact: you are gone. You are a million miles away and the cold distance is calling. Our orbits are no longer in sync. There was a time when you could find that centre in me, a needle in the universe. It was hidden, you prised it out. We used that needle to tear at the very fabric of my sad existence, to pluck out Jason Chamberlain's eyes. We pulled back the curtain and saw things anew. We saw past the veneer, no longer behind a facade. I see the city anew; old splendours awaiting a rebuild and new paint. I now see the mountains and the forests hugging at their feet."

Lamorna looked at Su's pale face; her dark eyes sunken inside her soul, their power fading with each of Lamorna's words. "You, Su, need to let go of me, as I will also let go of you. We each need to move on. In this world and in the next. We keep moving forward, seeking the truth and banishing lies.

But I no longer need you to show me how."

Master Su, now more hunched than before, looked up and spoke calmly. "Lamorna, I have only ever wanted to help you. You were a floundering octopus in a wild ocean, stuck between your safe hole and the crushing currents. I called for you for a number of reasons; I confess not all of them were to your benefit. I wanted you to bring down Optix, I confess, but also for you to start on your own path. You needed to pass through the black of the abyss, to be reborn amid the pain and suffering. To live in that purgatory of the hospital and hear the stories of your bedfellows. You needed to lose me and to carry on with your plan, to see it through. To deal with the consequences of your actions on this, the bumpiest of roads. As a spectre I have haunted you in your dreams, it is true. I only ever wanted to guide you, protect you, help you see the light after the darkness of the abyss, sharpen your focus. You surely recall the story of the tortoise and the hare. You were a hare, Lamorna. But you never reached your goal, being too quick to find another one, and then another. It is also not in your nature to be a tortoise either. And lest you try it, life will pass you by. You need to gather yourself, listen to what is calling within. Dear old Marx taught us *'From each according to his ability, to each according to his needs'*, and your abilities are growing, but you still need me, Lamorna."

At that point Lamorna cut in, "my dear Su, there are many things I can't say, can't explain. I can feel you at the edge of my life, like a setting sun, a cool breeze and the shake of a leaf. You are untouchable to me. There are so many more things we could have accomplished together and you fell too soon. But I don't need you, don't fool yourself. And please don't take my words for arrogance. That is something I have to make very clear to you. I have learnt to put myself back together, all bones and sinew glued back into place. Your input and guidance were of vital importance. However, these next steps, wherever they take me, will be mine. I can't have you haunting me any longer, I want you to leave me".

Su's ashen face turned almost translucent, a glassy hue, as if made of a million tears. "Then I must depart", Su began. "You leave me little choice; it seems we are at an end. You will go on, you must do what is right."

"I must do nothing, but die", Lamorna retorted. "That is the most important lesson. I am free of such obligation, other than those rules of mortality. The *'must'* will die, never more countenanced".

"Indeed. Well said, my apprentice. Lamorna, I do not go happily into the night. But leave you I will, if not *'must'*. Look to the wind, should you need a spectre". As she spoke that last word Lamorna reached out to touch Su's hand. As she did, Master Su disappeared in a puff of smoke, leaving only a shaking tea cup behind.

18 - CAVERNS AND COVES

Some days later after the theatre visit and her last conversation with Master Su Lamorna sat once more in her flat. She couldn't remember how she had returned from the cafe, perhaps by flying broom or teleportation. In any case she had been brought crashing back down to Earth by reading of the latest Optix developments: The introduction of a full ethical audit, the shutdown of Optix Defence, a whole massive slew of political resignations worldwide. The cost paid seemed to be worth the reward, at least on the surface. The journalists didn't have to live with that reality, unlike Lamorna. If anyone could turn Optix into a nice, harmless company, it would be Felix. A safe pair of hands and all-round good guy.

Lamorna's head was spinning while thinking of a multitude of possible futures: Optix as a global oversight commission, anti-crime agency or devolving into just another virtual reality gaming company. Anything was possible. In any case, it wasn't her responsibility any longer. After the meeting with Su Lamorna had tended her resignation and also received a handsome pay-off, which Felix personally took care of. At least technically, she was free of any obligation to anything or anyone. Just as Lamorna began to feel restless at the idea her buzzer went. She jumped up off the sofa and skipped to the intercom, "Hi, I have a parcel for L. Cruickshanks".

"Sure thing. Come on up", Lamorna replied and opened the door to her flat. The nice delivery guy handed over a small cardboard box, "thanks", Lamorna said.

"You're welcome, Lamorna", answered the courier, who looked eerily like Xerxo. "You'll need to hurry up to catch your train", and with that he turned on a sixpence and left. Before she could even catch a breath he had vanished. '*I must be seeing things*', she told herself. Lamorna then made her way back to the sofa and took a seat. She opened the box, and slid out another, as large as a cigar box, again fashioned out of beautiful olive wood, this time decorated with an ornate octopus inlay on its lid. She traced her index finger over the inlay, along all eight tentacles of the majestic animal. Lamorna cracked open the lid and inside was a small folded piece of paper and a regular door key. On it was a short message:

Dear Lamorna,

The key is for your new home. Be bold, be courageous and be wise.

Yours, Su.

On the back of the paper a departure time was written, along with an address. In three days, at 3.10 p.m. there was a train down to the south coast, she was going home. Lamorna again felt as if faced with a deadline, being pushed and pulled in all manner of directions. She looked at the note and ripped it into pieces, but pocketed the key. Lamorna then remembered the other wooden box and pulled it out. In almost every detail it was the same, except for the inlayed octopus, which was inlaid in a darker wood. Lamorna held the round ball of sand in her palm and gazed at it for a while, meditating on its meaning once more.

Lamorna decided to settle her accounts here in the city, say her farewells to Felix, donate her belongings and pack light, only taking some clothes and important books with her, in a overnight suitcase, with both of the little wooden boxes, as well as her computer. She was done here and ready for her next step, ready to travel light. Once the three days had passed she made her way to the train station. The journey itself was quite uneventful. She had a place in first class and had spent the time reading and sleeping, with earphones in and sunglasses on. The light was sometimes too much for her, while the earphones gave her the peace she so dearly needed. Listening to some mellow beats while reading helped her concentrate on the story, one of a young Japanese man living in a parallel world to his childhood sweetheart. And the beats let her drift off into that fantasy world and then to sleep during the long five hour journey south. In her dreams she saw the same old images, of what happened at Optix, Su's hauntings, but this time there was more. A great flood came, a giant kraken swallowed her whole, and she sailed around inside it for days before being let out again, changed. After waking with a start, Lamorna once more buried her face in her book and plunged into a different parallel universe, one she could close the cover on.

Lamorna was happy she only took the one suitcase. On a full train, at the beginning of summer, there was no extra space. Hundreds of holidaymakers were also on their way down to enjoy the golden sands, good surf and the out of place palm trees. As the train slowly rolled into the station, more like it came to a stop at an empty platform in the middle of nowhere. She carefully disembarked, her legs were getting increasingly wobbly, from the train and stood and took it in. Home again. And yet she felt still a fraud. She hadn't lived here in so long, nobody down there knew her anymore. Perhaps she could change that.

There were more signs for holiday lets than anything

else, but Lamorna found a taxi and gave the driver her new address. The short drive took her along a winding coastline, through tight country lanes where only a single car could pass, if any. She loved being back and kept the passenger window open to let her hair fly. The short ride was more like being on a rollercoaster with its twists and turns; ascended crests gave way to breathtaking views which soon disappeared around the next tight right-hander. Eventually she reached the residential area and pulled in to her street, twin rows of palm trees lined the sides of the road and towards the end of the cul-de-sac the pink, blue and purple hydrangea were in full bloom; as if nothing had changed. The taxi stopped outside her childhood home, a small white bungalow with faded white picket fences, a driveway on the left hand side. Large front windows provided plenty of sunlight from the south. It was quiet, it was familiar and it was once more hers.

Lamorna removed the octopus box from her bag, held the old key in her hand, slid it into the lock and felt the satisfaction of it giving way, offering only just enough resistance. She was met by a heavy musk aggressively hitting her nostrils, almost strong enough to make Lamorna flee. She pushed past the initial wave of acrid foulness and made her way into the bungalow seeing all of the old furniture, laid out just as it had been, but covered in ancient dust. The old television, with its heavy wooden cabinet. The extendable dining table, never seating more than four at any given time. The dark brown three piece suite. The rooms were spacious enough and the narrow corridor to the bedrooms had seemed a lot longer in her memory. The kitchen, however, appeared unusually modern and well-fitted; newish paint and top-end appliances. How many years had it been since somebody had lived here? Five? Fifteen? Her footsteps in the ostensibly beige carpet left deep footprints.

She made her way towards the garden, through the narrow kitchen, opened the back door and waited at the top of the steps overlooking the old mud pit where she had played as a little one, now just acrid dust. The red swing had adopted a brown rust colour, with some peeling paint waiting to be plucked off. The old shed was still there, now with all windowpanes smashed. The clothesline still stood in the centre of the garden, the plastic housing of the line was now cracked and porous; exposed to the salt winds for too long. She would do some landscaping, that was for sure. She would have little need for most of those things going forward.

Lamorna went back inside and settled back in to her home. The following days were mostly spent sleeping. She was still haunted in her dreams by burning eyes, ghosts and ghouls. And her nightmares included scenes of torture, where she was in control of the testing of all kinds of subjects, human and otherwise. Eyes followed her every move, even the blackened ones, especially them. Lamorna began to take notes, looking to find a way to exorcise them.

In the weeks since Lamorna had moved into the house she replaced the majority of the old shaggy carpet with a simple oak floor and had the walls painted white. Lamorna commissioned a local artist to paint a mural of assorted sea life on one of the large white walls; local animals like the common octopus, choughs, pilchards and dolphins. All drawn in a technical, anatomical style. She also hung up some simple abstract pieces, which she had painted herself in her humble, naïve style; figuring she could simply paint over them whenever she got bored of them.

Lamorna had taken to meditating in the bright garden. But not before she simply took in the view with her own eyes.

From the house she could see over the hedge and down towards the bay, which was only a short walk away. There was nothing lacking in that view, no need for augmentation, implants, texture upgrades or manipulation. Everything was as it should be. Also, now that Lamorna lived by the coast it wasn't as often necessary to only dream of the sounds of the ocean; so often done before. Lamorna had found a quiet paradise in her garden, landscaping and replacing some of the older, worn-out features. Out of the mud pit she had built a seating area and removed the clothes line. Lamorna boarded over the windows to the shed and repainted it a deep blue shade.

After one particularly exhausting session one afternoon she walked gingerly into the kitchen, her legs once more causing her problems. That was a persistently niggling issue for Lamorna which sometimes curtailed her best efforts to get everything in the house and garden spick and span. Lamorna wobbled past the kitchen cupboards and then noticed a set of robes on a hook hanging on the back of the door, which brought a laugh from her. They looked like chef's whites. They had not been there before, she was sure she would have seen them. She picked them off the hook and found a note sticking out of the breast pocket. The handwritten letters were in the unmistakable handwriting of Master Su. While she asked herself how the note could have got into her pocket, she read the words:

1984

Pull back the looking glass

Game for a laugh, Lamorna donned the white robes and made her way to the full-length mirror which was in the hallway. It was dusty and dirty with small handprints all over it. She looked to the side for a keypad, to no avail. There was no way to remove it from the wall either, which made sense if it really were a secret door. She examined the frame, nothing. Looking closer at the surface of the mirror she spied an area in the bottom right corner which was much cleaner. She gently ran her fingers over its surface and in that moment a silver touchpad appeared. She entered the '1984' code and waited, hoping that this particularly secret entrance wasn't as sinister as that at Optix. As the door slid open she took in the cold salty emanating from within. The wide doorway, dimly lit at first, faded into the darkness. At first there was no way of knowing how long the tunnel was. Then there was the sound of an electrical generator activating.

The steps were then softly lit by floor-height strips of light and Lamorna took her first tentative steps. As the steps wound down the curves of the soft gradient she took in the soft sound of water droplets, the faint blowing of a distant wind. As Lamorna went further down into the rock she passed alcoves, cavern dwellings, revealing small rooms for secret meetings, then larger expanses for gatherings of twenty people or more. Ever inquisitive, Lamorna took a left and made her way down the path towards the one of the larger meeting rooms. *Who was all of this for and why was it here? Who turned on the lights? Where does the tunnel lead to?'*, she justifiably asked herself. But there was no turning back. She was alone for now, she was sure of that.

Carved out of the dark rock there were doorways which opened up into cavernous expanses with tiered seating, like a lecture hall. The low-level lighting gave the room an occult feel. The steps leading to the back of the space were quite steep and she held firmly onto the guardrail to make her way up to the top. The stone seating was also hewn directly out of the rock and she asked herself how this had been constructed and by whom? You would need heavy machinery to hew this out of rock. She stood there for a moment at the back of the room and took in the expanse buried beneath the ground. *'When had the last person been down here?'*, she thought to herself. It was then that Lamorna spied a minimalist console recessed into the wall at the back. The button *'screen'* took her interest and she pressed it, which set a number of things in motion ending with Lamorna being greeted on a huge screen which descended from the ceiling at the front of the room.

There on the huge, cinema-like screen Lamorna was greeted by a recorded message from her very old friend Jinny: "Glad you finally made it my deary! Goodness, that was quite a journey, wasn't it?! I know what you're like and you'll have lots of questions, to be sure and I assure you, way back I felt the same! You can't imagine what it was like back when we got all this up and running though; we had to write actual words on actual paper to hand over things to each other, we actually kept a ledger! I suppose it's all for the best though, this computer malarkey." Lamorna was taken aback and at the same time she was absolutely delighted to see her old childhood neighbour Jinny on the big screen. She did not seem much older than when she had last seen her. With that Lamorna cracked another crooked smile and listened intently to her old friend.

"Well now, since you were last here we have made a few changes to the place, upstairs is a bit run-down, no doubt you'll want to change that. After your parents left I moved in with my cats you see, that way I could keep a better eye on this place too. By the time you find this place you have probably already done all the painting and cleaning and what not, knowing you!", Jinny was beaming a huge smile, showing each and every one of her rotten yellow and brown teeth. Lamorna could practically smell the cat food through the screen.

Jinny continued, "come the end I was near blind and couldn't smell or taste a thing. Meaning it probably reeks to high heaven up there; be sure to empty the litter trays often, otherwise you'll not be having many guests round too often my dear!", again Lamorna flashed her mind back to when she was small; that place really stank.

"Well, like I was saying, down here it is all a bit different like, the caves down here are ancient, they have been here many a year, the glass is new though, we had a kerfuffle way back and only had the new panes put in about ten years ago. So, the caves themselves are here to be used as you see fit. You can let people in from above, in from the house, or from down at the bay. Lots of apprentices tend to come by sea, it's traditional, see." At this Lamorna was taken aback, *'did Jinny say apprentices? Did this mean more people were coming here, to learn? From whom?'*, Lamorna looked around in vain for other instructors, master wizards or headmasters.

Jinny continued while Lamorna was speaking to herself, "there tends to be a yearly intake of about five new'uns from abroad, up north or sometimes from way yonder". She really meant it, Lamorna started to feel a mild anxiety and then she quickly realised that this was her job now; this was what she was good at. She had been the one who had brought down the mighty Jason Chamberlain and Optix, had pulled the wool from everybody's eyes and exposed a great political conspiracy. She could help others to see past what the eye receives. She would need to be patient with herself though, she won't always be able to achieve such quick results.

"They're normally about your age, sometimes a bit older, or a bit younger, but thirty to forty-five is normally about right." Jinny's recording continued, "they will come for many different reasons and need some midwifery deary. There was this one fella who had jumped ship in the middle of the ocean, not having any kind of life preserver, quite how he got here I'll never understand. He landed on the beach down yonder, was nothing but a runty thing. But he became the most magnificent addition and a very able paladin. Another time there were this artist who got caught up in all kinds of trouble, she couldn't get up in the mornings no more, needed a whole new change. I worked with her for a while, then she came here. She works in the caves now helping the new recruits unlock their artistic potential; you'll meet her soon, no doubt she'll be concocting something in one of the break rooms. There's quite the artistic community in town too, you'll see." Lamorna paused the recording for the moment and took a look around the other rooms in the caves, she left the computer console on however, intent on returning soon.

The caves stretched out deeper, fractal expansion extending with ever stretching fingers into each and every outcrop of the bay. Lamorna had to be careful not to lose track of where she was, thankfully there were numbers carved into the rock every now and again. The other rooms which led off from the main stairway were a mix of libraries, informal spaces, kitchens, meeting rooms, sports facilities, sleeping quarters, courtyards with skylights so that plants and vegetables could be grown. All rooms were hewn out of dark rock with great recesses in the walls for different facilities like sinks and cupboard space. There were training rooms, a cinema, theatre, dining hall, a great hall, and an indoor running track. It was like an underground fortified university and all of it was to be under her control. Lamorna suddenly felt a great pang of responsibility and wondered about the great cost of keeping the place running. How large was the staff? How were they paid? When are people coming? She decided on returning to Jinny's message and made her way back up to lecture hall. She hit the play button.

"Now Lamorna, you'll no doubt be wondering what goes on down here and what are all these different levels and rooms for. Aside from the obvious ones, like the theatre and dining room, it is in the name after all, the most important rooms are the sleeping quarters and the time rooms. This is where the real work is done. As you have learnt over the past months the most important thing at the beginning and end of the day is to ensure that you've good a good amount of shut-eye, isn't it lovey?". The warmth of her homey accent felt like a hug from a long lost relative. "Listen up Morna, the beds are adaptable to the guests and the lighting is also fully adjustable so that everyone gets their forty winks. And then the meeting rooms are designed so that people can get their ideas out and discuss the best way to go forward. Don't forget: No idea is a bad idea! There are all sorts of gadgets and whatchamacallits embedded in the consoles in the rooms. Also, you can adapt the size of the time rooms with the sliding glass panels; you can get between three to thirty people in the rooms with a touch of a button, they just slide around according to what you tell them to do. Easy! Anything more than thirty is pretty fruitless in our experience and you are better off just giving a lecture yourself in one of them big halls. You don't want fifty people all putting their noses in your business when all you want to do is inform them of what needs to be done. Why have a meeting, when it could have been an email, right?" This drew a belly laugh from Lamorna. So much wasted time sat around in meetings until long in the night. No longer!

"Right, these rooms are great for training up the apprentices and letting them develop their own skills, as well as making their own mistakes. Here you can impart all of your newly learnt meditation and time deceleration techniques and school them up. You'll find that most of the best ideas will come from the apprentices anyway, so just go with the flow".

Lamorna was getting the hang of this, it was basically a cavernous training complex with dorms. Her own adult boarding school, with a crazy person living upstairs with a complicated backstory. Pretty cool all being told; it certainly beat being stuck in the city and the fish and chips were better down here anyway.

"You can see the quartermaster for more information on the inventory and what you need to keep the place running, he is a merry old soul who also knows a few good shanties for keeping up moral". *'This was getting better and better'*, thought Lamorna, *'my own personal pirate for all my swashbuckling needs. I bet he has a black beard and a ponytail too'*. Jinny continued, "He knows his way around this place pretty sound. Been here longer than me. The time rooms have a number of surprising functions, which I would like to leave up to you to find out. The way they behave is pretty yunikew to be honest". Lamorna puzzled the word together, *yunikew? Yu-nee-q? Unique? right!*

"Don't let the surprises scare you though, they're mostly harmless and quite practical. I don't really have much else to say deary, just keep your chin up, see with your real eyes, overthrow tyrannical mega-corporations, just like you have been and don't lose sight of what is important to you. Cheerio Lamorna, my dear, so long and thanks for looking after the place!" Lamorna laughed a gleeful chuckle and bid farewell to her old friend.

***

'It must have been such tremendous work to hew these rooms from the rock', Lamorna felt the weight of history on her shoulders and allowed it to rest there for a while. She sat for a time in the room where Jinny had spoken to her and just took in the damp, cool chill of the underground air. *'This was it. My new home, my new life and a massive chance to build something'*, Lamorna told herself. It was her old home, but now she had to do something new with it.   After a time Lamorna slowly stood up, cursing her prosthetic legs as she then made her way through the black doorway and back into the cool air, looking further down the stairway. A dark hole. The low-level lighting showed the path to lead down into absolute darkness. How long it was she simply could not tell; the naked eye could only perceive so much. So Lamorna resolved to simply walk down until she reached the end, once more passing some of the rooms she had already seen and then an ever unfolding multitude of new ones. Deeper and further down she delved until the darkness reached its end point. That was when she reached the cleanest of black basalt surfaces. It shone even in the low light; indeed it reflected the little available light like a mirror. *'Could this be where I need to turn back?'*, Lamorna thought for a moment. *'Or is this yet another gateway?'*. She felt around for a button or a lever, electronic, wooden or metallic; she did not care. As she looked more closely, as in the house, she could see in the bottom right corner there was another keypad. She entered the code *'1984'* once more and a low, booming rumble made itself heard. A bone-crunching, creaking sound was seemingly causing her organs to vibrate at a low and slow resonant frequency. Lamorna observed the black basalt rock wall slide to her left. Then a crack of light gave way to a

wondrous blue expanse of ocean and Lamorna let out a sigh. She felt the rush of sea air invade her lungs and stepped through the door and onto the wet golden sand, the high tide having not long subsided. It was a mild summer day and there was a light sea drizzle in the air with some swollen clouds hanging low in the sky. The beach was a vast expanse and the ocean occupied almost her entire field of vision.

Lamorna felt memories of playing her as a child rush back over her as she made her way along the sands, although the feeling of the rough wet sand on her toes was not one of them of course, but it was something more elemental and less simply sensuous which struck her. The overall atmosphere of the place just sat right, she knew that she was finally home and no longer visiting, no longer somewhere, but now *'here'*. This was where she had learnt to swim, had played so often and been happy. Here, Lamorna knew, she could most ably be just herself; away from the city and the fakery.

Lamorna looked out over the ocean and saw the individual waves coming to greet her. Each one *'yunikew'*, as Jinny would say. She looked back over her adventure, with Su, with Chamberlain, Xerxo even. For they had all shown her something missing in her life at the time. Jason had taught her the importance of trust and how it can be abused. He had not always been evil in his intentions and even now it could be possible for the Optix technology to be used for good. The wielder was key, not the tool itself. He taught her how to say no, even if she had paid a hefty price for it. She would need time to work out whether it was worth paying. The people at Optix wanted to make a better world, for everyone to see more beauty in it. The method was deeply flawed and consciousness remained only on a superficial level; yet there was potential there. Something to build on.

Looking back over that time with Jason, she realised that she had been a different person during that time; too focused on the task in hand, too willing to let all else fall by the wayside and too guilty of coercing others to do the same. The feelings of guilt suddenly coming back to her, *'how many others had fallen sick due to her own manipulation of them and her hard task-mastery? Merely passing on the pressure to the next person'*. As she looked up to the Sun and asked what she had to do to change this mindset, to alleviate those feelings of shame and blame, she remembered Su's teachings and listened to the waves. Each wave, one by one, will approach you and each one will fizzle out. And so it is with every one of life's moments. They may stick in your memory, but you must take the lessons from them, not the negative aspects, lest they burden you anew. She had to let go of the guilt and forgive herself. She looked up to the Sun again and asked "How can I let go of this?", letting the words hang in the air, pausing and taking some deep breaths of the ocean air as a salty bead slowly crept from her left eye. Lamorna muffled a response, anticipating what the Sun might say to her: "Let yourself feel it each time, but this will pass".

"But surely I must be able to let it go?"

"Yes, you need to forgive your past self. She did not know what you know now. As you spiral ever upward you will return to this point again and again, but that feeling of guilt will pass."

Her bedfellows in the hospital had taught her the value of perspective. Each one of them had lived through their own crisis with Lamorna; they had each gone through the eye of the needle alone. It was possible for each of them, regardless of temperament or circumstance. Also, it wasn't necessary for her to save them, or be best friends; knowing that their time in her life would also pass.

She wasn't the same Lamorna anymore, having shed that particular skin. Less passive and naïve, no longer able to trick herself, less people-pleasing. The veil had fallen; Master Su had seen to that. Su had helped Lamorna see, that was the most important lesson. As well as the importance of asking herself the right questions and then having the courage to act on the correct solutions. By listening to herself she could find the core of the matter and then use her imagination to develop a good solution. This was the true sight. Seeing past the surface and scratching for more depth. There was work to be done; Lamorna saw that she had only just begun to chip away at what she had started. The mirror was starting to clear.

As the waves lapped at the sands Lamorna listened intently to the sound of each wave crashing and fizzling out. She was back where she had begun and then it came to her and she remembered Jinny's words: *'This is where you are from, this is where you are, this is where you will be'*. Lamorna sat down there on the sand and felt the urge to remove her prosthetics. Once they were detached she let out a sigh and finally enjoyed the feeling of the wet sand on her own skin once more. The rough, coarse sand rubbed on her scar tissue. "This is my price for all of this. But I am here and this is where I want to be", Lamorna told herself resolutely.

Her hands played with the malleable sand and she formed a mound. Upon that mound she patiently formed yet more sand into the very rough shape of a castle, with four towers. She dug out a moat and saw the sea water rise up through the sand. The castle was a part of the beach now. That was the moment when Lamorna got the olive wood box out. The sand ball, had now taken on a darker hue that matched the colour of the beach. She took it carefully in her hand and then placed the golden ball upon the castle's top. Its purpose and significance finally came to her. What felt like years ago, Master Su had made her promise to look after it, to keep it secret and safe. And thus, ever dutiful, she followed Su's command. As far as she could tell it had never been about the ball of sand itself, the ball was merely the cherry on top of a longer, bigger story. The castle she was building was only getting started. She was the architect, she was the builder and the inhabitant. The protective walls may have murder holes, but the courtyard and marketplace were the melting pot of human interaction. She would no longer be locked up in her tower, cowering in fear, nor locked in a dungeon. She was to become the queen of her kingdom, guiding others to find their own. The ball of sand was anything she wanted it to be, it was a spark of imagination and inspiration. It was a beginning and an ending. It was of this place.

Lamorna smiled and closed her eyes. Sat at the ocean with the wet sand beneath her, she was home once more. The sensations she had only dreamt of before were finally real; the salty air and crashing waves surrounded her. When she eventually opened her eyes once more she took in a fire red, orange and yellow sunset, as if broad wings were stretched out across the Atlantic sky.

ABOUT THE AUTHOR

Kevin is an educator, currently teaching English at a private school in Germany, where he lives with his family. When not writing he enjoys making music, cycling, and consuming copious amounts of chocolate.

Optix is Kevin James Richards' first novel.

Also by the Author:

Fiction
Castle of Stone (novella), The 4 Walls, The Core of the Matter, The Master and the Apprentice (short stories)

Poetry
Subjects and Objects, Autumn Songs, Resolution, Elements, Clinical, Ghosts, Winter Songs, Eden Fall

FSC
www.fsc.org

MIX

Papier aus ver-
antwortungsvollen
Quellen
Paper from
responsible sources

FSC® C105338